D0345065

Psych Major Syndrome: A common affliction wherein a psychology major, overwhelmed by conditions, effects, and disorders, begins to overanalyze her own life

Psych Major Syndrome

Alicia Thompson

Disney • Hyperion Books
New York

For making this book sparkle, I'd like to thank: Laura Langlie, Christian Trimmer, Alessandra Balzer, Sara Liebling, Nisha Panchal, Michael Yuen, Tooraj Kavoussi, and everyone at Disney • Hyperion Books.

For keeping me sane: Mom, Dad, and my siblings, TJ, Brittany, and Kyle; my friends/readers/partners-in-crime Charis, Jackie, Kristin, Mary, and Marina; my always hilarious housemates, Shane, Jon, and Jeremy; and, of course, the folks at Dunkin' Donuts.

For everything: Ryan, my new husband and my best friend.

First Edition
1 3 5 7 9 10 8 6 4 2
Printed in the United States of America
This book is set in 12.5-point Centaur.
Library of Congress Cataloging-in-Publication Data on file.
ISBN 978-1-4231-1457-4

Reinforced binding
Visit www.hyperionteens.com

For Grandpa Don

ROTTER INCOMPLETE SENTENCES BLANK

1. I like to read incredibly unrealistic and badly written romance novels.

2. The happiest time was . . . I can't remember.

3. Back home the house smells like incense all the time.

4. I regret buying Avril's first album on the basis of one song.

5. At bedtime I make up stories in my head.

6. I am very sensitive about the weirdest things.

7. What annoys me is when people confuse "you're" with "your" or "its" with "it's."

8. People are stupid. (see above)

9. A mother can really embarrass you sometimes, especially when she insists on bringing her tarot cards to all parent-teacher conferences.

10. I feel a low level of dread on a regular basis.

11. My greatest fear is of being stranded in the desert or buried alive. Or never finding happiness.

12. When I was a child <u>I liked to play</u> <u>"pretend" a lot.</u>

13. I suffer <u>every time I have to drive</u> <u>my car.</u>

14. I failed <u>geometry . . . twice.</u>

15. Guys <u>are confusing, but nice to</u> <u>have around.</u>

16. I need <u>Dunkin' Donuts coffee to live.</u>

17. I hate <u>the way parking services hunts you</u> <u>down.</u>

18. This school <u>is a small liberal arts</u> <u>college in California.</u>

19. My father <u>wears an eye patch as an</u> <u>affectation.</u>

20. I wish <u>Rotter had never graduated with</u> <u>a psychology degree.</u>

COGNITIVE DISSONANCE: An inconsistency between what a person believes to be true and what a person knows to be true. In dissonance theory, this sets up an unpleasant state that people try to reduce by reinterpreting some part of their experiences to make them consistent with others.

"PSYCHOLOGY is a load of crap."

Considering I had been rehearsing this declaration ever since it first dawned on me about ten minutes ago, I was a little disappointed with my roommate's response. Ami didn't even look up from what she was doing, which appeared to involve painting sparkly nail polish on strips of bubble wrap. She's an art major who specializes in (of all things) installation art. I've totally given up on understanding it. I don't even throw away dirty paper plates she's left out anymore, in the off chance that they were meant to be some kind of statement on consumerism in this culture.

"Psychology," Ami corrected, "is your life." Lifting the

3

bubble wrap to her lips, she blew on it carefully, as if it were a thirty-dollar pedicure from that place in the mall that made my cuticles bleed. Luckily for America, I don't know any government secrets, because I would have told those women anything to get the pain to stop.

"Well then, my life is crap." I collapsed on my bed, flinging my arm across the row of *Jailhouse Rock* Elvises on my quilt. The quilt was a graduation present from my mother. She made it so that every time I lay down to sleep, I'd remember that she and my father were missing me. Seriously, her words. And it's not like going away to college was what made her get all Oxygen network on me, that's just how she is. If anyone can pull off saying really flowery, profound things, though, it's my mom. It's kind of how she makes her living, after all.

Of course, the quilt also reminded me that acoustic guitar Elvis was *way* better than fat, reflective-suit Elvis, and that you can find anything in the novelty fabrics section of Wal-Mart. But that was just a bonus.

Ami put the nail polish down and turned to look at me. "Your life is *not* crap, Leigh. Why would you even say that?"

Propping myself up on one elbow, I dug through my backpack and pulled out a crumpled sheet of paper with "Rotter Incomplete Sentences Blank" written across the top. I gave it one last disgusted look-over before thrusting it at Ami.

She scanned it, her gaze darting quickly around the page before settling again on me. "So?"

"*So?* Do you know what this is?" Ami didn't respond, and I

didn't wait for her to. "You know about free association, right?"

"Um . . . it doesn't cost anything?"

"Ha," I said with little real humor. "Knowing Freud, it probably cost you a vital organ every fifty-minute session. Free association is another of his little tricks to get at your subconscious desires or whatever. And that's basically the idea behind these sentences. You're given, like, no time to complete them, and what you say is supposedly revealing of your true thoughts and feelings."

Ami was giving me what I think of as her "psychology look"—nose wrinkled up, eyes squinted with doubt. "*That* sounds like crap," she agreed.

This is why Ami is the best random-selection roommate ever. At first, I hated her because she hogged the closet space. But it only took me a week to realize that she's totally awesome, and let's be honest—she needs the closet space *way* more than I do, since she has this funky-vintage-mod thing goin' on. She also always backs me up, and she totally humors my need to dissect everything. We've spent hours criticizing an issue of *Cosmopolitan* or an episode of *Gossip Girl*, down to the last detail. One time I commented to her (half jokingly) that we could verbally rip a glass of water to shreds if we wanted to. An hour later, we had covered water's lack of flavor and moved on to glass versus cup as a drinking receptacle.

I gestured now to the sheet of paper. "Like here," I said, "all I wrote was that I liked reading romance novels."

"Which you *do*," Ami affirmed, her eyes going to the rows of dime-store novels on my bookshelves. There are books of real literary merit mixed in there—mostly ones that I had to read in high school—but the majority of them have titles like *Sweet Sanctuary* or *The Scandalous Proposition* or, my personal favorite, *The Greek Playboy Tycoon's Virgin Mistress*.

"Which I do," I agreed ruefully. "And then later on I mentioned that I played 'pretend' a lot as a kid. Who didn't make up secret lands when they were five, with names like Monkey Land or Castle Land or whatever?"

"That's a lot of lands," Ami said, her mouth twitching. Note to self: Keep fantastical childhood worlds to myself from now on. My parents had promised me it wasn't that weird, but what do they know? My mom teaches shamanic dance at the local Y, and my dad takes a weeklong vow of silence every year. Their view of "normal" is a little skewed.

It's obvious why my mother is the way she is. Her dad was this superconservative military dude, and she ran away from home at a young age and joined the hippie movement. Clearly, *complete* reaction formation to her upbringing. But my dad? The jury was out on him. It's like the old nature versus nurture debate—was he *born* being a huge weirdo, or did my mom turn him into one with her fruitiness?

"Whatever. Somehow those two statements are supposed to represent an overall theme that I don't face things and that I prefer fiction to reality."

The line between Ami's brows deepened. "All that because you said you liked to read?"

"Also because I said I liked to make up stories in my

head," I was forced to admit. "And because, apparently, I show a preoccupation with details instead of the bigger picture, which supposedly hints at a desire not to *see* the bigger picture."

An expression flitted across Ami's face for a minute. I couldn't be sure, but it almost looked like agreement. "Where exactly did you hear about all this?" she asked. "I thought you were taking classes, not therapy."

"Yeah, but today in Intro Psych we did some of these subjective measures and then 'analyzed' each other." I snorted. "As if it's ethical to let people with fewer than two months of college analyze each other. We haven't even officially declared a major yet."

"Who analyzed you?" Ami asked. Trust Ami to get to the heart of the matter.

"Ellen." Ami sucked in her lips and nodded knowingly. Ellen actually carries around *The Dictionary of Psychology* with her wherever she goes. The worst part? She memorized it over the summer. Now she just carries it for show.

In gymnastics, Ellen would be that gymnast who knows she's not as talented as other girls and spends ten hours a day in the gym trying to make up for it. She also happens to be my biggest competition for pretty much everything, since I found out on the first day of Intro Psych that she wants to go into the exact same field as I do: body image and eating disorders research. She's convinced that she has the edge because she was bulimic for two months in high school. Meanwhile, I *know* that she has the edge because, when we filled out a first-day

7

assessment (for informational purposes only! We didn't even turn it in!), she kept muttering to herself, "You can do it, Ellen. Just focus. Focus." Yeah, 'cause *that's* not a little psycho.

Ami grabbed the paper from me again. "So where is Ellen getting the whole 'preoccupation with details' thing from?" she asked, her eyes searching the page as if the answer were hidden among the letters in a word search.

I didn't have to look. My responses were already burned in my brain. "The preoccupation with bad grammar. But it just bugs me! It's not 'How's things?,' it's 'How ARE things?' That's, like, English 101."

Of course, Ellen also maintained that there were another five sentences or so where I showed too much "concern over little things," not the least of which was the sentence about my father wearing an eye patch. Well, he does. And it's not like he has a bad eye—although he probably does now from never using the damned thing. He just thinks it's good for business.

My parents run a psychic boardinghouse in Sedona, Arizona. For only $129.95 a night, you get continental breakfast and a ten-minute psychic reading. My parents wholeheartedly believe in what they do, but they're not above a few marketable gimmicks. That's where my father's eye patch comes in. I think it may have broken their hearts when I chose psychology over psychic ability.

"You failed geometry twice?" Ami said, and snickered, looking up from the paper. "That sounds more like me. I thought you loved math."

"Statistics," I corrected, "I love statistics. Statistics actually mean something. Geometry is just a whole bunch of proofs and triangles. Why prove what you already know? If it looks like a triangle, I'm going to go ahead and call it a triangle without using that side-angle-side business."

"You just like statistics because they stretch the truth even more than you do sometimes," Ami pointed out—incorrectly, I might add.

I've always thought statistics were kind of like that saying you see on T-shirts. You know, "Guns don't kill people, people kill people"? Well, statistics don't lie. People lie. Sometimes statistics can make a lie sound better, but that's just good math.

That's not even why I like statistics, either. Mostly I like it because, with the exception of long division, it's the only math I've ever been good at. Fortunately, it's also the only math I will have to deal with as a psychology major.

When I tell people I'm planning on majoring in psychology, I usually get one of three responses: A) Oh! Are you analyzing me right now? B) Psychology . . . hardly an exact science, is it? or C) So what's wrong with *you*?

I know the answers to the first two. A) Probably, yes. B) No, it isn't, but that's why I like it. It's that last one that always gets me. People assume that psychology students have something wrong with them, something that they hope to learn about or maybe even fix. I'm not saying there's *nothing* wrong with me. I have plenty of problems—as Rotter's little busywork exemplifies—I just don't know if they're definable as any kind of disorder or condition.

I don't like strangers or strange situations. I am way too stubborn. I can be almost eerily calm and then get disproportionately upset about something stupid. I get some kind of sick pleasure out of waiting until the absolute last minute to do anything, as if I need the extra challenge in my life. I would prefer to have gum on my face than own up to the fact that I accidentally got gum on my face. And of course, one sentence out of every ten that comes from my mouth is probably not one hundred percent true.

(Okay, even that could be stretching the truth, but it sure does sound good when backed up by numbers, doesn't it?)

I'd always assumed that all my problems were personality defects, things that can't really be fixed any more than a natural pessimist can be taught to see the glass as half full. But the more I think about it, the more I see the main problem: I just don't like change. I'll spend countless hours every day wishing that I could undo something about myself, but when it comes down to it, I hug every last little foible of mine as though it were my security blanket.

It's like that classic joke—how many therapists does it take to change a lightbulb? One, if the lightbulb wants to change.

Ami, of course, continued without any regard for my introspective silence. "You don't really mention Andrew in here," she observed.

Oh, crap. "Andrew!" I leaped up from my bed in a flurry

of twin extralong sheets. "I totally forgot about our date tonight!"

There are times—like this—when I'm really glad Ami isn't a psych major. Freud—or even Ellen—would have a field day with the fact that I forgot a date with my boyfriend of over a year. Especially since I was the one who suggested the date in the first place.

Ami sprang up from her cross-legged position on the floor and followed me to the narrow hallway between the room and the bathroom that served as our closet space. I was rummaging through clothes like a madwoman, so I couldn't see her face, but I had a pretty good guess what it looked like. Ami's "Andrew" face—a mixture of frustration, distaste, and resignation—was even worse than her "psychology" look.

Ami's analytical abilities are not to be underestimated, either. You should've heard her break it down in our "glass of water" critique. "So what's up with that?" she pressed. "You managed to work in a plug for your favorite coffee and Avril Lavigne, even though I don't buy that you regret getting that CD when I find her playlist up on your iPod all the time. But you didn't even mention your high school sweetheart."

The way Ami said the word *sweetheart* made it sound like a disease, and I didn't respond. This was partly because I was busy trying to find an outfit that would look cute without seeming like I was trying too hard to look cute—*not* an easy task. But I also wasn't sure what to say, and, for once, I couldn't think of a way to spin it.

Right before graduation, when I had to have my wisdom teeth taken out and I couldn't eat anything that required chewing, Andrew surprised me with an entire case of chocolate pudding cups. And when I refused to take the prescribed painkillers because I was worried I'd get addicted and then, like Winona Ryder, start filching stuff from high-end stores, he stayed by my side and assured me that the pain would be over soon. It was the sweetest thing anyone had ever done for me. So why *didn't* I mention Andrew?

"Um . . . I wrote that guys are confusing but nice to have around," I said, grabbing a silky red camisole to wear over jeans. I surreptitiously peeked down my T-shirt at the white cotton bra underneath before swiping a lacy black one from my dresser. I knew it wasn't a crime, wanting to look nice for my boyfriend, but I still felt self-conscious being so obvious about it. I bundled the subversive bra in with my clothes and went into the bathroom to get ready, shutting the door behind me. I hoped that that would end the conversation.

Ami isn't deterred by much, and certainly not by a badly painted wooden door that won't even close all the way. "What's confusing about Andrew?" she sneered. "He's a pompous philosophy major who thinks he's God's gift to intellectualism."

I've never completely understood why Ami and Andrew get along so badly. I mean, yes, she's right. He can be a *little* overbearing when he gets started on one of his lectures about nihilism or what constitutes a soul. And he can be kind of arrogant to the point of sounding like a know-it-all. But that just means that he's passionate about his convictions . . . right?

That was actually the same thing that first attracted me to Andrew. He was the only guy in my high school who cared more about Plato than pigskin, and believed in soul mates instead of random hookups at parties. Ironically, we did meet at a party, but we didn't make out or anything. Instead, we talked for hours—I remember at one point he said something really profound about the human condition. Or it might have been about hair conditioner. It had been hard for me to concentrate with his brown hair flopping endearingly over one eye. No matter how many times he tossed his head, it always fell right back. It was the cutest thing I'd ever seen.

Obviously, Ami doesn't have the benefit of all these great memories, so she continues to think that he doesn't treat me as well as I deserve. Which, in a way, is totally loyal and cool of her—but completely unfounded. Well, mostly. If anything, his main problem is just that he's *too* smart. He has so much going on in his brain at any given moment that it's no wonder he's a little absentminded sometimes.

And yet tonight, *I* was the one who'd almost blown off our date. Because of this, I took extra effort with my appearance, even applying Ami's mascara to my eyelashes in the hope that a little definition would make my eyes appear more silver than gray. Andrew's always going on about my hair—which is the exact color of Dunkin' Donuts coffee the way I take it, with double cream and double sugar—and so I wore it the way he likes, falling in a straight curtain to the middle of my back.

My hair is the only thing about myself that I like. Not that I've got body image problems (well, aside from the normal ones). It's just that my nose is too sharp, my chin too angular, and I have this weird constellation of freckles on the side of my neck. And although I haven't had any problems being recognized as a girl since my second grade bowl-cut fiasco, let's just say that I always have to look in the "boyish" section when magazines are giving tips about what kind of swimsuits to wear (FYI, it's all about the halter tops).

It wasn't until I opened the door and saw Ami still standing there that I even remembered that she had been talking to me. Underneath her olive coloring her skin looked a little gray, her face twisted up with guilt.

"Leigh, you know I don't really mean that," she said. "You and Andrew have been together a long time—I lose my car keys every two months, so there's no way I could keep a boyfriend for a whole *year*. I guess he and I just didn't hit it off, but I don't have anything against him. Honestly."

Back in Sedona, there's a barbecue place by my house called Trust Me BBQ. We never eat there, based on the name alone. So the word *honestly* would've tipped me off even if it hadn't already been abundantly clear that Ami disliked Andrew from the minute I introduced them. Not that Andrew is Ami's biggest fan, either. He thinks she's an artistic flake (which she kind of is) and that she should live her life with a little more responsibility (which probably wouldn't hurt). He hates the outfits that she throws together out of old thrift-store finds, he hates that she stays up until four and sleeps until two, and he hates that she sometimes mutters things about him in fluent Spanish that I, who won the *sobresaliente* award for Spanish excellence in high school, don't even understand. He also thinks she's a terrible influence on me.

I don't know about that last part, but after spending the first couple months of my college career *trying* to get them to like each other, I've learned to accept the fact that they don't get along and probably never will. Ami is my roommate, and Andrew is my boyfriend. I just try to keep them separated and, failing that, hope they don't kill each other.

"So, how do I look?" I asked Ami, performing a small pirouette.

"Fabulous," she declared. "Except . . ."

"Except what?" I demanded, glancing down at myself. The shirt didn't show too much cleavage, did it? As if I had much to show. For shoes, I had elected to wear my "dressy" shoes, which basically meant flip-flops covered in this black satiny material with little butterflies printed on it. Two months in California, and I'm already totally out of the habit of wearing real shoes.

"It's just . . ." she trailed off, pursing her lips. "Maybe you could jazz it up just a little bit? I have some Bakelite bracelets that would look amazing, or these awesome pointy-toed stilettos that are genuine alligator skin. I got 'em for a *steal* in the Village."

I rolled my eyes. "Nice try, Ami, but no. When *you* dress like that you look like something out of a 1960s *Vogue*, whereas I just look like a seven-year-old who had a little too much fun going through her mother's wardrobe."

Ami chuckled before looking down at the paper still clutched in her hand, as though just remembering it. With one decisive motion, she crumpled it up and tossed it toward the garbage can, where it bounced off the wall and landed on the scuffed linoleum in a harmless ball.

"You don't need Ellen Chandler—or for that matter some guy named Rotter—to make you doubt your life," she said. "Just go enjoy yourself for once without overanalyzing it."

> **APPEASEMENT DISPLAY:** A gesture or
> pattern of behavior which signals defeat in a conflict

ANDREW lived on the other side of campus, in what everyone called the suites. Basically, these were the same as the regular dorms, only instead of one larger room, there were two separate rooms with a shared common area. They weren't as nice as the apartments or the singles (which were reserved for thesis students), but they were better than what Ami and I had. And they were *definitely* better than C-Dorm, which featured rooms the size of shoe boxes and a community bathroom. There seemed to be no rhyme or reason as to who lived in C-Dorm—freshmen, transfer students, or foreign exchange students. The only requirement seemed to be that you had to be a little eccentric and willing to put your desk in the closet.

Of course, by the time I pulled into the parking lot in front of the suites, my makeup was melted, my hair was flat, and the thin fabric of my shirt was sticking to my back. These were all side effects of driving what Ami refers to as "the green monster" or, as I like to call her, Gretchen.

Gretchen is my 1971 Gremlin, complete with stock bubble windows in the back that make her look like some kind of strange, ugly spaceship. She's my baby, but I wasn't kidding on the Incomplete Sentences when I said that I suffer to drive her. The seats are green vinyl, everything inside is unapologetically scalding metal, and the air doesn't work. Although apparently it used to, because there's a switch with the words COLD—COLDER—FOR DESERT USE ONLY above it, which is sometimes so cute I forgive the air for not working and other times such a tease that I want to break the little switch right off.

Andrew says that Gretchen is the most impractical car he's ever seen, considering that the gas gauge doesn't work and it takes a million tricks just to start her up. I call it my antitheft system, since it's nearly impossible to open the doors unless you know the right move (a hip motion somewhere between a bump and a twist) and any wannabe thief would run out of gas before Sacramento. These features are especially nice in light of the fact that the locks don't work, either. When I tell this to Andrew, though, he just points out that Gretchen's biggest safety feature is the fact that nobody would ever, *ever* want to steal her.

It's easy for Andrew to talk. He drives around in the

barely used BMW that his parents bought him as a graduation present. Yeah, I got an Elvis quilt, and he got a Beamer. Not that I'm complaining—Elvis is totally awesome. But Andrew's parents could've at least had the decency to get him a Kia or something.

Although I have to admit (not that I would ever say this to Gretchen's face), the BMW *is* pretty nice to ride in. It has air, a working gas gauge, and even the completely-frivolous-yet-completely-delightful option to heat your individual seat if you want to. But then, every time I ride in it I feel so guilty that I overcompensate by making Andrew ride in Gretchen, hoping that neither he nor Gretchen will sense my secret weakness for German manufacturing.

I peeled myself off the seat, bumping the door with my hip to close it behind me. There was a small slip of yellow paper underneath one of my semifunctional wiper blades, and I groaned as I slid it out. It had been flapping throughout the entire drive to Andrew's apartment, but I just ignored it, hoping it would blow away and I could forget all about it.

I don't know why I do this to myself. Most people take a very direct approach to parking at college—they buy a hangtag, put it on their rearview mirror, and then feel free to park wherever they want. It's a beautiful system, and I'm sure it works for some people, but it just isn't my style. I need more procrastination, more strategy, and apparently way more hassle in my parking life. It's already halfway through the semester and I *still* haven't purchased a permit, despite being reminded about twenty thousand times during orientation to get one.

I climbed the stairs to Andrew's dorm and knocked on the door. Andrew always tells me that I can walk right in, but somehow I'm just not comfortable doing that. Nobody answered at first, and I waited patiently for a few seconds before raising my hand to knock again.

My hand was still poised like that, suspended in a fist, when the door was flung open. It was Andrew's roommate, Nathan. I snatched my hand back, startled, and for a few minutes I stood there, like an idiot.

It wasn't just Nathan's timing that took me aback. He had answered the door wearing only a pair of low-slung jeans, his chest bare except for the acoustic guitar strapped across it. I'm loyal to Andrew and everything, but let me tell you—Nathan has a nice chest.

His gaze flickered down the length of me before he stepped aside to let me enter. "Andrew's in his room," he said curtly, leaving me to close the door as he strolled back to the couch, strumming his guitar.

"Thanks," I mumbled. I don't think Nathan likes me very much, even though I've never been anything but nice to him. Maybe there's something about roommates and relationships that just doesn't mix. Whatever it is, I always get this vague feeling of disapproval emanating from Nathan.

I stepped into Andrew's room, rapping lightly on the open door. "Hey, there," I said. "Ready for our date?"

Of course, I knew the answer before he gave it to me. He

was sitting at his desk, still wearing an old t-shirt and a pair of pajama pants, furiously typing on his keyboard. He whirled around in his desk chair to face me.

"Aw, Leigh, I'm sorry," he said, running a hand through his longish brown hair. "I totally forgot."

Never mind that I had done the exact same thing only an hour ago. "You *forgot?*" I repeated incredulously.

"I *said* I was sorry," he shot back. "It's just that I really have to finish this reading response by the end of the week."

"A reading response? Andrew, those are like three pages long. Double-spaced."

"Yeah, but I have to read six chapters of this book first." He gestured to a battered paperback with a French title that hopefully wasn't actually *written* in French. Although he thinks he's awesome at them, Andrew really sucks at languages. Once, he tried to speak French to this woman who owned the C'est La Vie bakery back home, and she gave him a cookie because she thought he was mentally challenged.

"Okay," I said. "But it's not like you have to read the whole thing. Just skim it for the good bits, come up with a discussion question or two, and crank out a few pages about how it made you feel."

"This isn't psychology, Leigh."

No, it was philosophy: the most useless major EVER. I mean, there's only so much that you can adopt of other people's ideas before it's just old-fashioned copycatting. And I know they say that imitation is the best form of flattery, but

21

I'm pretty sure that Kant would tell Andrew where to stuff it if he heard some of the far-fetched crap Andrew comes up with.

"I'm going to pretend you didn't say that," I said, nudging the door shut. No need for Nathan to hear *this* particular issue rehashed. "In psychology, just so you know, we'd call that *denial*. But, whatever. You're going to have to eat sometime— let's just grab a quick bite."

"Why don't we just walk down to the Hyatt and get something there?"

The Hyatt is what Stiles College calls the cafeteria. Well, not officially. But ten years ago or so, the same company that supplied the nearby Hyatt with their food also supplied ours, and so the name just kind of stuck. It couldn't be *more* of a misnomer, believe me.

"Come on," I said. "We've barely spent any time together since the summer. Let's just go out somewhere."

"Look," Andrew said, throwing his hands up in the air, "I'm sorry that you feel I don't want to spend time with you. But I don't know what I can do about that."

Whoa. That was *so* not called for. "How about not saying things like 'I'm sorry *you* feel' and just saying you're sorry?"

"And here we go with the pseudoscientific brainwashing," Andrew said. "I *did* say I was sorry. What more do you want?"

"For you to mean it."

In a perfect world, I would have delivered that last sentence with quiet dignity, leaving it to hang poignantly between us. Instead, it fell somewhere closer to pathetic. I could feel tears burning at the back of my eyes and turned, not wanting Andrew to see the one that started slipping down my cheek.

"Just forget about it," I said.

I was hurt and I was angry and I was frustrated, but mostly I felt . . . stupid. I felt stupid standing there, wearing one of my best bras and as much makeup as I'd worn to my senior prom. I felt stupid for all the times I'd answered yes to the question, *Do you really think a high school relationship can last through college?*

Which, when you're the only one not looking to hook up with someone at orientation, you get asked a *lot*. Believe me.

"Wait," Andrew said, springing up from his chair and massaging my shoulders lightly. "I'm sorry, Leigh. I'm just under a lot of stress with this six-course load. Can we try this again?"

Even Andrew's academic adviser had called him "terminally insane" (not recognized by the *DSM-IV*, by the way) when Andrew said he planned on taking six full classes. But that's just who he is. "I guess," I agreed reluctantly.

He smiled—that same boyish grin that I had fallen in love with—and I felt my anger start to ebb away. "Great," he said. "Just give me a few minutes, and I'll be ready."

After Andrew closed the door, I lingered in the hallway, swiping my fingertips carefully under my eyes so as not to wreck my mascara. (Note to self: Do not borrow Ami's mascara if crying may be involved, as hers does not seem to be of the waterproof variety.)

Once I had myself back under control, I stepped into the common room, averting my face slightly as I crossed over to the couch. Nathan had put on a shirt, thankfully, but I was the one who felt really weird and exposed in my slightly too-revealing top and probably smeared mascara.

"Something to drink?" he asked.

My throat felt tight and itchy, and I could do little more than nod. I didn't mention what I wanted to drink, and Nathan didn't ask. Instead he grabbed each of us a Coke from the minifridge that served as an end table, setting mine in front of me before settling back on the couch.

I waited for him to break the silence, but he didn't, and instead we spent several awkward minutes watching TV. I didn't even register what we were watching until a car suddenly slammed into the guardrail in what the announcer said was "number twenty-seven on the top fifty most extreme car chases."

"That was pretty intense," I commented lamely.

"Yeah," Nathan agreed, his gaze never leaving the screen.

Like Ami and me, Nathan and Andrew were random-selection roommates. But while Ami and I have already made a pact—we'll room together for the next four years, no matter what, and we'll each be the maid of honor in the other's wedding—I can't tell if Nathan and Andrew are close or not. They seem to get along, but that doesn't mean that they don't secretly want to rip each other's throats out. Guys are weird like that.

I don't know a lot about Nathan. He wants to be a math major—I bet *he* never failed geometry once, much less twice—and he wakes up early every morning to run. Those two facts alone make me think that he must be uptight.

"So, um," I said, with no real idea what I was going to say next. Maybe something about how it seems like commercials are getting funnier and funnier, although it could be a self-reporting bias, since it's not like I remember every commercial that aired two years ago.

But then Nathan switched off the TV, stood up, and went into his room. Just like that. As if we hadn't been sitting on the couch, about to have a totally normal conversation about television commercials.

Every time I think that maybe Nathan doesn't *completely* hate me, I realize that the problem was never that he hated me. He just couldn't care less.

"Ready to go?" Andrew said, finally emerging from his room wearing a polo shirt and khakis. It was obvious he'd made an effort to look nice, and I smiled at him.

"Sure," I said. "Let me just dump out the rest of this Coke."

"Why'd you open one if you didn't want it?"

"I don't know," I said.

He gave me a strange look, but then his face lit up. "Oh!" he said. "I've got something for you. Hang on just a sec."

He disappeared back into his room, and came out holding a grocery bag. "What's in it?" I asked.

"A bunch of those sticky things to hang your posters up with," he said. "I grabbed a whole handful during orientation, and I've been meaning to give them to you. I know you love your posters."

I really do. I'd found this Web site that lets you order twenty posters for a hundred dollars—which is a ton of posters, but also a really, really good deal. So now I have enough to last me all four years, and that's even if I cycle out my decorating for the seasons like they're always showing on those design shows.

"Thank you," I said.

I tried not to let it all bother me as I followed Andrew to his BMW with the individually heated seats, but for some reason I couldn't shake it. Nathan is indifferent to me, Ami hates Andrew, and as for Andrew and me . . . well, who knows? He'll do something so thoughtful that I'm reminded of how perfect he is for me, but then we seem to bicker over the pettiest crap.

I'm starting to think that, for a future clinical psychologist, I'm really kind of clueless.

REALITY PRINCIPLE: In Freud's theory, the set of rules that govern the ego and dictate the way in which it tries to satisfy the id by gaining pleasure in accordance with the real world and its demands

WE opted to eat at a small Thai restaurant near campus. Or rather, Andrew opted. I'm probably the only person in the entire state of California who hates Thai food. But Andrew and I had Thai for our second date, and then it had seemed an awkward time to tell him that I spent half the night worrying that I was going to vomit peanut sauce all over his crisp white shirt. So unfortunately, once Andrew realized that there was a Thai restaurant every hundred yards in California, it was all we ever ate anymore.

Tonight I ordered the fried rice, just as I have every other time since the peanut sauce fiasco, and Andrew gave me a dry look over the top of the menu.

"You always order the same thing," he commented. "Live a little, Leigh."

Because out of all of them, fried rice tastes the most like Chinese food. I can close my eyes and pretend I'm eating at Shanghai Sun. "On our second date, I ordered the noodles with peanut sauce," I reminded him.

Andrew just shrugged, and I fiddled with the napkin in my lap while glancing idly around the restaurant. The obligatory mirrors hung on the walls, and there was one of those fountains with fake lily pads in the entryway. The restaurant was also lit like a mine shaft. I've never understood why dim lighting is supposed to be so romantic. Night vision belongs in a Paris Hilton sex tape—not in a restaurant that could potentially poison me with peanut sauce.

"Oh!" I couldn't believe I'd almost forgotten the linchpin of any good conversation—salacious gossip about people you used to go to school with. "Do you remember that kid from senior English, the one who called himself Pookie?"

"Yeah," Andrew said cautiously. "Why?"

"He's totally gay!" I said. "Apparently he even joined a homosexual fraternity. His parents have disowned him. Can you believe that?"

"Leigh, those are just high school rumors."

I gaped at him as if he'd said that *America's Next Top Model* was just some dumb reality show, instead of the greatest sociological experiment of our time. "Don't you get it?" I asked. "This means I'm three for three."

"Three for three?"

Holding up my hand, I counted them off on my fingers. "One, Danny. I always thought he was gay, despite whatever his girlfriend said. And then he came out, just like I predicted. Two, Melvin. Again, I called it, and again, everyone doubted me. But then he started dating that kid I had a huge crush on in sixth grade. Which brings us to three—Pookie. Seriously, I should have my own television show."

"You know what?" Andrew said, taking my hands in his. "If I'm going to miss a night of studying for this, let's at least talk about something important. And not just high school stuff."

"Fine," I said. Of course, all I wanted to do was swap stories about who from high school had become a raging alcoholic in the first two months of college. The statistics are disturbingly high. "Well, pick a subject, then."

"All right," Andrew said. "What about our theses?"

For a minute I thought he said *feces*. "What?"

"You've thought about it, haven't you?" Andrew asked. "What you're planning to write your senior thesis on? I'm considering an examination of Kant's musings on the pantheism dispute."

Oh, *theses*. I probably would've had more to say on the other subject. "Um . . ." I said, "I really haven't thought about it."

"Really, you haven't even *thought* about it?"

"It's not like I don't know what subject I want to study," I said. "And I have three more years to narrow it down into a thesis topic. It's not a big deal."

This is one of the drawbacks of Stiles College. It's a really small school, and they really bring the whole "take charge of your education" thing to a new level. This means that, while the rest of the country is worrying about pledge week, students at Stiles are freaking out about their entire academic future.

Andrew could be the poster child for this. "Next you'll be telling me you haven't thought about grad school yet."

Crickets. Seriously, you could hear crickets.

"You *haven't* thought about grad school?"

Andrew's habit of repeating things was starting to get annoying. "I mean, I've thought about it a little bit. Like, um, I wouldn't mind going to the University of North Carolina, or Berkeley. Or UCLA."

"Berkeley's a little liberal," Andrew said. "I'm sick of hearing about UCLA, though. Just because it's close by, everyone talks about it like it's the greatest school in the country. Name one worthwhile person who went to UCLA."

There have to be a thousand really important people who went to UCLA. Especially in the psychology field, since right now UCLA was actually ranked in the top three clinical psychology schools in the nation. I just couldn't think of any of them on the spot. "Jack Black," I offered.

Andrew snorted. "Let me guess. Communications?"

I actually didn't know. I don't think he graduated, though. But look at him—it's not like he needs the degree. He's a comic genius, for crying out loud.

"Well, what school do you think is better, then?" I challenged, already sick of the Jack Black example.

"Harvard," Andrew answered. "Or Yale."

Someone had been reading his *Generic Ivy League Weekly*. Don't get me wrong, I'd be thrilled if I got into a school with half the reputation of either Harvard or Yale. But surely there's more to it than just fancy names on a diploma . . . right?

Then, of course, there was the bigger issue. If I went to school in California and Andrew was in New England, three thousand miles away, where would that leave us?

Wait a second. Why were we stressing so much about this?

"Look," I said. "You don't want to talk about high school, and I think it's kind of pointless to talk about grad school when we haven't even finished a semester of college yet. So let's just talk about something else, okay?"

"Okay. You pick a topic."

I wanted to ask him if he thought we'd grown apart in the past few months, ever since it was no longer the same routine it had been back in Arizona of studying for the AP exams and making out in his bedroom. I wondered what *he* said to all those annoying people who asked if high school relationships could last through four years of college. I wanted to ask him if he was happy, or if he thought we were happy together.

I wanted to know why we had been going out for over a year and we still hadn't had sex.

"What's your greatest worry?" I blurted out.

Andrew looked genuinely surprised. "My what?"

"Your greatest worry," I repeated. "What's your biggest fear? What annoys you the most? What was the happiest time for you? Today in Intro Psych we filled out these question- naires, and I realized . . . we've never really talked about that kind of stuff."

"Christ, Leigh," he said. "I don't know."

"Just think about it."

"Okay . . . then I guess, clowns, clowns, and when I'm not around any clowns."

I slapped his arm playfully across the table. "Be serious."

"Oh, I am," he deadpanned. "Haven't you ever seen the movie *It*? And what about that one serial killer, the one who dressed up like a clown? That's enough to keep you up at night."

"John Wayne Gacy," I supplied. "The killer's name was John Wayne Gacy."

"Gee, thanks, putting a name to him really helps."

I rolled my eyes. "I put that my greatest fear was getting stranded in the desert. Or being buried alive, but really, I don't think that should count. It's like the default fear. *Nobody* wants to be buried alive."

"You're not afraid of getting stranded in the desert."

I gaped at him, affronted. "Yes, I am."

"No, you're not."

"Then why do I have so many water bottles in my car?"

Andrew opened his mouth but quickly closed it, shaking his head. "You're bizarre," he said. "Don't get me wrong—it's cool. But you're seriously deranged."

There was no use in arguing. There is at least a case and a half of water bottles that roll around my backseat, just in case I ever find myself stranded out in the middle of nowhere like this one girl I read about in a magazine. She was in a ditch by the side of the road for four whole days, and nobody even thought to look there. If she hadn't happened to have a jug of water in her trunk, she might have died. As it was, she still had to have her leg amputated because she cut it and it got infected. Or something like that—I was so freaked out by the threat of dehydration that I didn't pay a lot of attention to the gangrene part.

"So what's your happiest time, really?" I asked.

"Whenever I'm with you," Andrew said, smiling, "and you're being seen and not heard."

"Ha-ha." His evasion techniques were starting to frustrate me. "Come on, Andrew. Give me something real. Your biggest worry. What pains you. *Something.*"

Andrew rubbed his forehead. "Don't do this, Leigh."

"Don't do what?" I challenged.

"Don't analyze me," he shot back. His face was an unnatural, blotchy red, and the veins in his neck had started to throb. My heart was racing, and it should have scared me, the abruptness with which the mood shifted. But instead, I felt *alive.* It might have been an argument, but at least it wasn't the dueling monologues that Andrew and I had been trading lately.

Then, just as suddenly, the fire went out and a cold guilt settled in its place. Andrew really was a good boyfriend, no matter what Ami might think. And we were good together—no matter what *Nathan* might think. It really wasn't fair for me to demand so much right now, when we were both trying to get used to a new environment.

"I'm sorry," I said quickly, reaching out to take his hand the way he had taken mine earlier. Andrew was right. We probably wouldn't have any problems if I didn't go out of my way to create them.

"No, *I'm* sorry," he said, sighing. "Let's just enjoy the rest of dinner, okay?"

"Okay." I smiled at him, and for a brief instant it was as if we had recaptured everything that we had lost, caught up between us like butterflies in a net. I didn't even mind when the waiter brought me rice with peanut sauce by mistake.

Well, maybe I minded a little bit. I've always been grossed out by peanuts, and the smell of that peanut sauce was already starting to turn my stomach. But then I remembered what my Intro Psych professor said about couples therapy: they call it *working* at a relationship, because it's not always fun. Andrew and I weren't perfect. We never would be. But as long as we met each other halfway, we'd be fine.

When I came home from dinner, Ami was lying on her bed, bobbing her head along to music blaring from her iPod while straightening out hundreds of colored staples. It took her only a few seconds to notice me in the doorway, and she sat up, holding the earphones away from her ears.

"How was dinner?" she asked.

The question was simultaneously innocuous and meaningful. Dinner had been good for the few hours that I felt safe, secure in the knowledge that I wasn't alone. I didn't care what everyone else thought. I'm not the kind of girl who wanted to enjoy the freedom of being young or whatever. After all, there are people who *never* find someone to spend the rest of their lives with, so the fact that I got together with Andrew when I was only seventeen just means I'm luckier.

"It was nice," I said finally. Ami must have caught the weariness in my voice, because all she did was nod. A quiet moment passed between us.

"So . . . what are you making?" I asked politely.

"This?" Ami gestured to the staples as though I could be referring to anything else. "Eventually I'm going to glue these in abstract patterns on a mobile made from old coupons."

All of Ami's art is based heavily around rubber cement. "What's it supposed to mean?" I asked. I've given up trying to figure it out for myself.

Ami chuckled. "Honey, it's not supposed to *mean* anything. Sometimes art should just be pretty."

I stared at her, nonplussed. Then, the oddest thing happened. I just started laughing. I laughed so hard my stomach hurt. I laughed until tears were pouring down my cheeks. I laughed until I was crouching down on the floor, one hand braced against the dresser for support. And once I started, I just couldn't stop.

Apparently it was contagious, because in no time Ami threw her head back and started laughing, too—a full-bellied cackle that had me going all over again. "I don't even know what we're laughing about," she gasped.

"Neither do I," I admitted, wiping tears from my eyes. Ami's blunt statement had struck a chord with me. Sometimes art *is* aesthetically pleasing, with no other reason behind it. And I started to think . . . maybe other stuff was like that. Maybe it was okay if every little thing didn't have a rationale behind it or take on some scary kind of significance. Maybe I should just let it go.

> **PROSOCIAL BEHAVIOR:** Behavior that benefits other individuals or groups of people, also known as helping behavior. Prosocial behavior includes altruistic motivations, but also includes behaviors that may be motivated by egoism or selfishness.

THE campus coffeehouse and café was called, inexplicably, the Toad's Monocle. The toad wasn't our campus mascot—we were actually such a small school that we didn't even have any organized sports. In our bookstore, we sell these mini footballs with STILES COLLEGE: UNDEFEATED SINCE 1952 printed on them. Get it? Because we've never even played a game? It kills me every time.

The lack of sports was a *huge* reason I applied, in addition to the lack of any Greeks. Not Greeks as a people. I mean Greeks like fraternities, sororities, or their incestuous love children, the "frororities."

And yes, the Toad's Monocle does feature a very large

mural of a toad holding up a monocle. It's totally bizarre, but everyone pretty much just accepts it because the café also has the best smoothies *ever*.

I was ordering my favorite—a Bee's Knees, which is like heaven mixed with honey in a glass—when I heard the familiar voice of my academic adviser rasp behind me.

"Leigh Nolan," she said. "Just the psychologist I wanted to see."

I sincerely hoped that Dr. Harland *was* seeing a psychologist—and a real PhD, not some kid who still thought *Hell Date* was quality television. Dr. Harland is so old she could have attended one of Gatsby's famous parties, and so senile she probably thinks she did. That's why what she thinks is a funny joke—calling me a psychologist when I haven't even passed Intro Psych yet—seems a lot more sinister when it's not clear that she's joking. If she called me a cosmonaut, I would have to wonder if, deep down, she really believed that I was one.

"Dr. Harland, hi," I said, pinning an awkward smile to my face. "Just the professor *I* wanted to see."

"Come, Leigh." Dr. Harland is one of those people who use your name constantly. "Sit with me and we'll discuss your academic career."

After my evening with Andrew, the most gung ho college student ever to matriculate at Stiles, the last thing I wanted to do was discuss my future. But obviously I had no choice. There was no way that I could tell my academic adviser to buzz off and leave me to my Bee's Knees. Besides, she had the power to make some pretty crucial decisions in my "academic career," as she called it.

Stiles College operates on the contract system, which means that, each semester, you sign a contract for the number of pass/fail classes you plan to take and how many you need to pass. This inspires insane jealousy in my friends from high school who ended up going to Arizona State. My grandparents think I won't be able to do anything with the "novelty degree" I'm getting here, while my mom is disappointed that I didn't go to this goddess school she found in the mountains where you could major in Reiki or holistic thinking.

Let's just say that this past summer was an exhausting whirlwind of "Yeah, not having a GPA is totally awesome" and "I promise it's accredited."

"So," Dr. Harland said, taking time to adjust her long skirts over her runny panty hose. Her panty hose always had runs in them. I wondered whether she didn't notice or just really didn't care. "Psychology. It's a fascinating subject."

"Sure is."

"Have you given any thought to what area of psychology you want to study? I know it's early, but you might even start to consider what your thesis topic will be."

I was seriously beginning to worry that there was some hidden thesis deadline (like, THIS SEMESTER) that I didn't know about. What was with everyone? "Actually, I have thought about it a little," I lied.

"Oh, that's right—adjective usage on Internet personals sites."

Not even close. "Close," I said. "Body image disturbance in adolescent girls."

She nodded sagely. "Right, right," she said, taking a sip of some extremely aromatic tea.

For some reason, I felt the need to explain. "See, I just think that it's hard being a girl nowadays. Like, if you pick up any teen magazine, there are conflicting messages. Some articles tell you to be yourself, but then there are celebrity features and advertisements and advice columns that tell girls that they're not good enough as they are. You need to be thinner, cuter, flirtier, and more fashionable."

There was an awkward silence as Dr. Harland just stared at me.

"Well, not *you*," I said.

"Let's hope not," Dr. Harland said pleasantly.

I took a deep breath. "Anyway, so I'll probably conduct a survey or something on body image in adolescent girls."

I had a whole other speech prepared, something about the way that magazines exploited low self-esteem in an effort to sell more beauty products and acne medication, but Dr. Harland just waved her bony hand. "How are you going to obtain this sample?" she asked.

I couldn't believe I hadn't thought this far ahead. Oh, wait, that's right. I had SIX whole semesters before I even had to declare a thesis topic, much less conduct the study. "Um . . . the mall?"

It was as though I had just announced that I was going to inject newborn babies with arsenic. "The *mall?*" she repeated incredulously.

My Bee's Knees was starting to coalesce at the top of the glass, leaving a watery mixture of honey and nutmeg at the bottom. "Of course not the mall," I quickly backtracked. "That would clearly violate standards of random selection and a representative sample."

Dr. Harland looked partially mollified. "Not to mention ethics," she said. "Don't forget, Leigh—to study minors you have to go through their parents and possibly their school-teachers as well. It's not an easy process."

Internet personals were starting to sound pretty good. Nobody tries to protect middle-aged perverts pretending to be Brad Pitt. "Well, I'll make sure to prepare myself. You know, for my senior year. When all of this will be important."

"Actually," Dr. Harland began, finally looking some-what pleased, "I just heard through a colleague of mine about this mentoring program at a local middle school. Not only would it be an excellent experience, but it would also give you the opportunity to work closely with your population of interest."

Mentoring? I wasn't so sure I was "mentoring" material. "I mean . . ." I started to say.

"Excellent," she beamed at me. "Then I'll give Linda over at Simms Middle your e-mail address. I'm sure I don't need to tell you, Leigh, how important it would be to get your foot in the door of a school—both literally and figuratively—if you want to work with any school-age population."

"No," I admitted, although I desperately wanted to add the word *ma'am* to the end of that.

"You're a smart girl, Leigh," Dr. Harland said suddenly, as though it had just occurred to her. "It's good to see you thinking about your academic future here at Stiles, and giving back to the community, as well."

My smile was as weak as the Bee's Knees, forgotten in my glass. "Yeah," I said. "Well, it's never too soon to start."

Simms Middle School didn't look anything like the middle school I had gone to. My middle school was very flat, a sprawling tan stucco building with marmalade-colored tin over all the walkways. It was, in a word, hideous. Okay, maybe two words—it was *absolutely* hideous.

But Simms was tall—three stories!—and painted beige with apple green trim. It had two enormous wings that were connected on the second and third floor by covered walkways that stretched across the space between them. While my mascot had been an annoying but hardly intimidating hornet, Simms was home to the proud mountain lions. The cafeteria even had a patio area with little round tables and umbrellas, just like the ones outside Taco Bell. I was so jealous.

I looked down at the paper in my hand. School got out at 3:30, and the mentoring program began at 3:40, which meant I had only a few minutes to find it. ROOM 134A, the paper read. How would I ever find a room with a letter attached to the end of it?

"'Scuse me," a little girl said beside me. Although I guess I shouldn't say *little*. She was only an inch or so shorter than I am and had to be at least thirty pounds heavier, although most of that was in her chest. She had the hugest breasts I had ever seen. I couldn't tear my gaze away, even though I knew I shouldn't stare. This girl was *thirteen*?

She flicked her coarse black braids over her shoulder. "You go here?" she asked rudely.

Perfect. This thirteen-year-old candidate for breast reduction surgery was asking *me*, eighteen years old and still excited to fit into a B cup, whether I went to her middle school. "No," I said, a little rudely myself.

The girl made some kind of smacking sound with her teeth and her lips. For a million years I could try to replicate that sound without ever approximating the utter disdain she conveyed in a single smack. "You don't go here?" she repeated, the slight raising of her voice making it seem more like a disbelieving sentence than an actual question.

"Do I *look* like I go here?" I knew it was a mistake the minute I said it, but it was too late. That morning I had taken special care with my outfit, choosing a pair of chocolate brown pants in faux suede and a lavender button-down shirt with three-quarter sleeves. Hardly executive wear, but certainly not what I remembered girls wearing to *my* middle school.

"Kinda," she said, squinting at my hair, which was pulled

neatly back into a bun, and then at the toes of my shoes. I glanced down. I had completely forgotten that I had worn my Converse today—the ones that were faded black with frayed shoelaces and holes in the soft canvas. They were the only shoes I owned besides flip-flops, and I wasn't *so* far out of middle school that I didn't remember that backless shoes were footwear-non-grata on campus.

It must have been those shoes. "I'm carrying a purse," I pointed out defensively. Okay, so I'd seen five-year-olds at the mall with purses, but I only started carrying one myself a year ago, when I realized I was always misplacing the crumpled money shoved into my pockets.

"So?" she sneered, holding up a purse of her own. And hers probably *hadn't* been bought at Wal-Mart for $8.99 on sale, which meant that it was more expensive than mine. "Whatchu got in yours?"

I rummaged through the main pocket. "Money, old receipts, that sort of thing," I said. How had I gotten myself into this?

"How much money?"

It was tempting to tell her to mind her own business, but I couldn't very well back down now. "Five . . . fifteen dollars," I said, fudging the amount a little. I didn't want to look pathetic in front of a middle schooler.

"I've got thirty," she boasted. "Any credit cards?"

This was starting to get really uncomfortable. "Uh . . . my debit card. But it has a Visa logo on it, so technically it can count as a credit card."

She held up two plastic rectangles. "I have a *real* Visa card, 'cause it's everywhere I want to be," she said, paraphrasing the commercial with scary accuracy. "I also got a Citibank card for my rewards. What else you got?"

"A cell phone?" I offered, no longer sure of the superiority of my purse's contents.

She dismissed my cell phone with a wave of her own. "Me, too," she said, "*with* a Kanye West ring tone."

Mine was a lame, tinny version of *Für Elise* that was one of the default ring tones. "Oh, yeah?" I taunted, fully caught up in our contest now. "Well, I have this!" I held up my container of birth control pills as though they were a gold medal at the Olympics. She had no way of knowing that they had been essentially useless to me so far.

The girl scoffed. "The pill? Please. I've been on it since I got my period two years ago."

She had been on the pill since she was *eleven*? She must have been eating a lot of hormone-injected chicken. I read an article somewhere about how most meats nowadays are injected with so many hormones, girls start developing freakishly early. Meanwhile, I played with Barbies until I was almost fourteen, although I claimed it was only because the younger girl down the street forced me to.

Finally I stumbled upon it—my saving grace. The one thing in my purse that there was no way this little pip-squeak could even touch for several years. With a flourish, I brandished my driver's license.

45

"Bet you don't have one of these," I said and smirked.

She snatched it from my hand and studied it for a long moment before handing it back with a shrug. "Whatever," she said. "I just wanted to know if you knew where a room was."

"What room?" I asked automatically, even though there was no way I would be of any help to this girl. That's even if I wanted to, which I'm not sure I did at this point.

She squinted at a card in her hand. "Room one-thirty-four-A," she read. "I'm supposed to go to some stupid mentoring thing there. The guidance counselor is making me."

"Room one-thirty-four-A?" I repeated dumbly.

"Yeah, that's what I said. You know it?"

"No . . . but that's where I'm going, too. I'm one of the mentors."

It was hard to tell which one of us was less thrilled.

The program was already in full swing by the time the girl (turns out her name was Rebekah) and I found the room. It met once a week and had been doing so for the past month, and so it was *really* in full swing by the time Rebekah and I joined the group. Total, I counted approximately ten other mentors and roughly the same number of middle school girls.

"Go ahead and take a seat on the floor," a very large woman with very large curls said, smiling over at us. "Right now we're just discussing teenage pregnancy."

Great. I would have hated to miss the really good stuff. I sat cross-legged on the floor. Rebekah shot me one final snotty look before settling down across the room.

The large woman—I guess this was Linda—handed me a folded-up piece of paper. "What is this?" I asked.

"This is your life," she answered cryptically before moving on to pass out more of the sinister little papers.

"What did you get?" one of the girls asked me. She was so tiny she could have passed for a seven-year-old with badly brushed red hair. "Mine says . . . something about a *fffff-d*?"

I glanced at her paper. "PhD," I corrected. "It's a degree you get, in school." I noticed that there were other things on her paper: the number 24, the word *no*, and the word *yes*.

"Like a grade?" she asked. When she wrinkled her forehead, her freckles bunched up together.

"Not like an A-plus or a C, no. But like a level of school, yeah." I tried to think how to clarify. "You know how seventh grade is higher than sixth grade?" I asked.

She nodded eagerly. "I'm in seventh grade."

Could've fooled me, but I moved on. "Well, getting a PhD is, like, the very highest level of all, after high school and college and even after more school. You have to finish"—I did some quick arithmetic in my head—"about twenty-three years of schooling before you get a PhD. And it's a really cool thing."

"'Cause it means you're smart?"

I shook my head. "Because it means you worked hard."

It was clear she didn't understand the distinction. I guess it was a little too early to begin the lecture about innate characteristics versus behavior, and how it's more positive to emphasize behavior because it, at least, can be changed. Maybe when she hits eighth grade I'll try again.

"My name is Molly," she said.

"Leigh," I replied before realizing that it sounded like I was just repeating the last syllable of her name back to her. "My name is Leigh," I clarified, giving her a smile as I unfolded my own paper. Mine listed: Master's, 26, yes, and no. I totally didn't get this assignment.

"Okay, everyone!" Linda clapped her hands together and twenty females turned to face her. "In this scenario, those papers are your lives. Imagine that you have an unexpected pregnancy, and you have to face the challenges that go along with a new baby. The first part is the amount of education you have. The second part is your age. The third part is whether your parents approve, and the last part is whether the father is involved with you and the baby. I'm also going to be handing out a worksheet to help you guide your responses."

I looked down at the paper in my hand. *This* was my life? As far as I could tell, the only bad part about it was that the father was no longer involved. Although with the divorce rate being what it is, who knows—maybe that was for the best. At least I'd have complete control over my child's upbringing. No father to undo my punishments and slip desserts under the table. If you looked at it in a certain way, it might even have been a really good thing.

And my parents approved? Uh, yeah—I'm twenty-six, with a *Master's*. It's weird, but I doubt that, in real life, my parents would bat an eyelash if I announced I was pregnant. My mom would just want to know what sign the baby would be born under, and my dad would start mixing up some crazy prenatal potions to increase my spiritual connectedness to the fetus or whatever.

I glanced over at Molly's. She had even more education than I did, and she was two years younger! In order to receive a PhD when she was only twenty-four, she would have to have been, like . . . eighteen when she graduated from college. Which meant she was only fourteen when she graduated from high school. Which meant that, potentially, she could have entered grade school when she was a year old. And what, her parents don't approve of her passing along her genius IQ to a baby whose father is, by the way, totally supportive and involved? This assignment was ridiculous.

"So . . ." I started to say, but Linda came by and thrust another piece of paper at me. I glanced over the questions before my hand shot up in the air.

"Um, Linda?"

She turned around, an inquisitively friendly but long-suffering look on her face. "Yes?"

I looked at the questions again. "It's just that . . . I don't understand how we're supposed to answer these."

Her smile was frozen on her face. "How do you mean?"

Rebekah and Molly were both staring at me, along with the rest of the mentors and the girls. Now that I was looking around the room, I vaguely recognized several girls among the mentors from school. Even Ellen, my academic archnemesis, was sitting toward the back in a crisp pinstriped skirt, looking at me as if I were insane.

(And if you're thinking that two months is too little time to have an academic archnemesis, you should know that Ellen was the only person in Intro Psych who actually read the first chapter *before* the first class. Who does that?)

"Well . . . like, for example, the first question."

Linda shuffled the papers in her hands, turning one right side up until she could read along. "How will you handle day care?" She blinked at me. "It's a perfectly legitimate question, one which many new moms have to face."

"I realize that." I tried to give her my best I'm-not-being-difficult-I-promise smile. "But I have a Master's, and I'm twenty-six years old. I'm sure I'll just hire an au pair or put my kid in a pre-Montessori school. Or, hell, my parents approve, so I'll just foist the ankle-biter off on them."

I'm pretty sure I'm not supposed to say, "hell." Or call children ankle-biters. Or, for that matter, express any kind of disenchantment with this mentoring program (at least not until the second or third meeting).

Linda's mask was starting to slip. She was clearly not enjoying this.

The girls were, however. They were laughing and discussing their own fake lives with a renewed interest. A weird combination of their enthusiasm and Linda's blatant disapproval really egged me on. I felt like I was back in middle school again.

Linda's smile was completely gone. "Teen pregnancy is a serious issue," she said.

"I *know*," I stressed. "I saw *Juno*. I just think maybe we should stop worrying about whether Jennifer Aniston regrets not having a baby with Brad Pitt and focus more on the girl in the Lifetime movie *Fifteen and Pregnant*."

Linda's mouth was something right out of *Honey I Shrunk the Lips*. "I'll tell you what . . ."

She paused expectantly, and it was a few moments before I realized that she was waiting for me to fill in my name. "Oh, it's Leigh."

"Well, Leigh, I'll tell you what. Since you seem to know so much about the subject, why don't you take charge of the next meeting with what you think is an effective presentation on teen pregnancy?"

This was my punishment? Some people may hate public speaking, but not me. I really love it. It's not that I'm super great at it—I just like the feeling I get when I'm winging it. I imagine it's like the thrill thieves always say they get, when they're about to steal a really valuable piece of art or something.

"Okay," I said.

Linda blinked again. "Fine. Since that's settled . . . I will see you girls next week."

The room was a bustle of thirteen-year-old girls rushing

toward the door. The mentors followed only somewhat more sedately, and Ellen stopped as she passed.

"Leigh," she said. "Why are you here?"

I shrugged. "Just doing my part."

"No, you're not," she spat. I had never seen her this openly hostile before. She always seemed so in control. "You don't even care. You're just here to goof off, while *some* people"—her expression made it very clear that she meant herself—"are here to develop crucial leadership skills and make a difference."

And have something else to put on her college transcript, of course. "Whoa, Tracy Flick, calm down." I held up my hands in what I hoped was a conciliatory gesture. "You do realize that it's possible for *both* of us to be here, and for both of us to make a difference?"

She gave me a confused look. Clearly, she was not an *Election* fan. "Whatever. Just stop disrupting the group, and stay out of my way."

She spun on her heel and slammed through the double doors. I couldn't believe this. How had my extracurricular turned into twenty paces at dawn?

> **RELATIONAL AGGRESSION:** A strategy
> for attaining social advantage by manipulating others'
> social alliances. According to research, males tend to
> be more physically aggressive, while females are more
> relationally aggressive.

"I'M thinking about becoming a vegetarian," Ami said, pushing a rubbery piece of chicken around her plate.

More than eighty-five percent of Stiles's student body is vegetarian, so part of me wanted to convince Ami to stay a carnivore. We were a dying breed (who also contribute to the premature death of other animals . . . so, yes, I see the irony). But another part of me couldn't blame her, since the meat options in the student union sucked. Most colleges had students lobbying for more fruits and vegetables. We had meat-eaters camping out in front of our salad bar, shouting, "If it's red and bleeding, it's what we should be eating!"

"You realize that if you become a vegetarian, you can't have the chicken quesadilla at Taco Bell anymore," I said.

Ami paused. "Well, then, I'll give up red meat."

"No double cheeseburgers," I pointed out.

"Hell." Ami popped a piece of chicken in her mouth. "What's the point?"

"Oh my God," I said.

"I know, but I like fast food," Ami said, "in all its greasy glory. You said it yourself—all that trans fat crap is just propaganda anyway, invented by—"

"No," I said. "Not that. Sydney Belcher is walking toward us. I think she's going to *sit* with us."

"Who is Sydney Belcher?" Ami glanced over her shoulder

"She's a senior psych major," I hissed, "and *stop looking!*"

Just then Sydney reached our table, a scarily purposeful gleam in her eye. "Hey, Leigh," she said.

Sydney is not just another psych major. She's *the* psych major, and she also happens to be my TA for Intro Psych. It's not even that she's that great a student. Yeah, she was president of the Psychology Club, but I heard that the last club-sponsored event was two years ago, when they rented *Kinsey* and played it in the teaching auditorium. Sydney's also presented at more major conferences than most professors, but everyone knows she just goes so she can flirt with graduate students. Still, she's incredibly intimidating. I only interacted with this girl out of fear and the kind of awed respect you might give a person of God.

"Who's your friend?" Sydney asked, pulling out the chair beside me and giving me a wide smile. I breathed a little sigh of relief. It was always hard to figure out which end of the bipolar spectrum you were going to get with her. I started to introduce Ami, but Sydney cut me off.

"So, what are you doing for your final project in Intro Psych?"

Sydney was staring at me expectantly, and my mind raced furiously to figure out what to say. When was that due? I thought we had until the week of final exams to turn it in, but maybe there was something I didn't know.

"Um," I said, "adjective usage in Internet personals." Briefly I considered the possibility that everyone else had already turned in their final projects. Should I have already finished?

"Great," she said. "Well, I'd like to get all of my students together. You know, for kind of a study group type of thing. Are you in?"

I would rather have my cuticles cut again. I'm not much for group stuff to begin with, but with Sydney acting as moderator, this particular group had trouble written all over it. "Sure," I said, and then something compelled me to add, "in fact, I was just thinking how cool it would be if someone set up something like that."

Sydney just blinked at me. "Well, it'll be fairly small. Just me, you, Joanna, Ellen, and Jenny. You know Joanna, Ellen, and Jenny . . . right?"

I had only interacted with Sydney a handful of times, and yet I saw right through her. This was classic Sydney—she'll reintroduce you to people as though you're completely incapable of knowing anyone without her influence. She does this even when it's a small school and the people in question are in *my* year. No doubt in a few weeks she'll be introducing me to Ami. *Oh, Leigh, do you know Ami? She's studying to be an art major. Isn't that awesome?*

Talk about Narcissistic Personality Disorder.

"Yes, I know them," I said, and smiled through gritted teeth. "Actually, just last week Joanna and I went surfing together."

Sydney arched her overplucked eyebrows. "*You* surf?"

No, but I knew Joanna did. Joanna was the quintessential California girl, all tanned skin and bleached hair, her conversation liberally peppered with words like *bodacious* and *radical.* I think I even saw her Rollerblade once. In reality, my experience with her was limited to the time I borrowed her pen.

"Sure, I surf all the time. When the waves are right, of course," I added, with a toss of my head that indicated that a surfer of my caliber had to be very discriminating about waves. "I would love to get together with Joanna, Jenny, and Ellen. It's such a shame about Ellen and her fiancé, though."

Sydney leaned in, an avaricious gleam in her eyes. "What happened?" she asked, practically salivating.

It's common knowledge that Ellen's fiancé is a complete bastard, and that they'd be broken up by now if Ellen didn't have this control-freak need to keep up appearances. So I felt pretty safe dangling that particular gossipy bit for Sydney. Surely *something* was going on with Ellen and her fiancé, even if I didn't happen to be privy to the salacious details.

I glanced around as though scanning the area. "I probably shouldn't say," I murmured regretfully. Out of the corner of my eye, I saw Ami hide a smile behind her hand.

For a second it felt satisfying, like popping a pimple, but I should have known better than to mess with Sydney. Not finding satisfaction discussing Ellen's love life, she turned to mine. "You're still with your high school boyfriend, right? Andrew something?"

Cautiously, I nodded. "For over a year now," I said, the response almost automatic. *Oh, how long have you two been together?* —*For over a year now.* "Andrew Wieland. He's a philosophy major."

"Wow," Sydney breathed the requisite follow-up, although her tone was unimpressed. "Yeah, I think I met him once. He just seemed so . . ." She trailed off, twirling her fingers with their overly long fingernails as she searched for a word.

"So . . . what?"

"*Dry*," she finished. "Although I'm sure you're perfect for each other." So apparently I'm dry, too, now. "Does he room with Nathan McGuire?"

"Yes," I replied tersely. This was the part of going to a small school that nobody tells you about. Sure, you can walk anywhere on campus in less than ten minutes, and yeah, it's nice that classes are no bigger than thirty students. But everyone knows *everything* about everyone. It's like a huge game of telephone, or a sewing circle.

She fluttered her lashes, spidery with mascara. "For a freshman, he is *fine*," she gushed.

"I suppose he is," I bristled. "If you like that sort of thing."

That sort of thing being dark hair, green eyes, and a tall, muscled leanness that could rival any teen heartthrob. I've seen him shirtless, remember. But he's got the social skills of a weird, math-obsessed two-year-old.

"Well, *I* think he's hot," Sydney reiterated, in case I was somehow confused the first time. "Is it true that his dad died a couple years ago?"

I was surprised, but I didn't want to show it. "Um, yeah. I think so."

Sydney made a face that could've just as easily been "that's interesting" as "that's too bad," and then she flipped her long, dyed-black hair before flicking a glance at her expensive designer watch. "I'd love to stay and chat, Leigh, but I've got a meeting for that research project on mating rituals in California sea lions." She laughed, a high-pitched sound that rang in my ears like tinnitus. "How do I end up doing all this stuff?"

You volunteer for it, Sydney.

"I'll keep you posted about the group," Sydney said, already dismissing me as she rose, smoothing her too-short skirt. "And you keep *me* posted about Nathan."

Yeah, I'll let you know when he decides to have a lobotomy. I grinned at the thought, not caring if Sydney thought it was for her. "Sure will."

Sydney strode off like a high-heeled stork, her chin thrust in the air. Sydney wears heels with everything—jeans, shorts, *especially* miniskirts. The worst part is that she obviously doesn't know how to walk in them, since she never bends her knees and instead uses her arms to propel her, pumping at her sides like a determined power walker. Her head is craned forward like an overeager giraffe, and somehow she manages to thrust her chest (truly her pride and joy) out at the same time. Put together, it makes her look very, very funny.

"That's sad about Nathan's dad, if it's true," Ami said after Sydney had gone. "And Sydney's right—he *is* kind of fine."

"Shut up," I said, but I was smiling. In some sick way, I really enjoy people like Sydney. She's like a walking case study. For *what*, I have no idea, but it's fun to try to figure it out.

> **CIRCADIAN RHYTHMS:** Our most familiar endogenous circadian rhythm controls wakefulness and sleepiness.

I CAME home that evening to find an e-mail waiting from Dr. Justus, my history professor. If it were up to me, I would never take a nonpsychology class in my entire four years, but apparently there's something called "well-roundedness" that they encourage here. Plus, I can't technically enroll in any other psychology classes until I pass Intro Psych, and there's no way Dr. Harland would let me sign a contract for one class.

The e-mail was addressed to me by my full name, as though I might confuse the e-mail sent to my inbox with one for another Leigh.

LEIGH NOLAN,

YOU WERE MISSED IN CLASS TODAY. PLEASE NOTE,
HOWEVER, THAT YOUR ABSENCE DOES NOT EXEMPT YOU
FROM TURNING IN THE CRITICAL ANALYSIS PAPER DUE
MIDTERM. I'LL LOOK FOR IT IN MY BOX TOMORROW.
JUSTUS.

"Shit." I stared at my computer screen in disbelief as Ami
came up behind me, crunching chips loudly in my ear.
"Remember how I skipped my history class because I didn't do
that paper?"

"I thought you skipped because the dollar theater was
showing *Dirty Dancing*."

"Well, yeah," I said. That movie is genius. Everyone flips
out over the "Nobody puts Baby in a corner" line, but my personal favorite is when Baby shouts out Johnny's name in this
superbreathy voice, and then has NOTHING to say. She just
stands there, like an idiot. "But now apparently I'm supposed
to have my critical analysis paper done and in Dr. Justus's box
by, like . . . tomorrow."

Ami leaned over my laptop, the chip-crunching silenced
for a few moments while she scanned the e-mail. "What's a
critical analysis? Like a book report or something?"

Every now and then I get annoyed with how little real
work Ami does. She's the only freshman I know who has two
days off a week, and she's announced on multiple occasions
that her goal is to avoid writing a single paper or taking

61

even one final exam while she's in college. And she's *totally* exploiting the contract system, since she found an adviser who would let her get away with a lot of dubious "tutorials." It's fine until moments like this, when I realize how little she knows about fundamental research skills. I mean, this is coming from a girl who thought MLA style was a fashion movement.

"It's basically just a critical paper," I explained, "that analyzes people or events and their historical significance. At the beginning of the semester, we picked topics, and somehow I ended up with a paper on Albert Speer, the 'good Nazi.'"

"Who says he's the good one?"

"Nuremburg," I said with a straight face.

Ami nodded as though that made total sense. "And you've done . . . how many pages?"

I grimaced at her.

"Zero?" Ami's eyebrows shot up. "You haven't even started?"

"I've done my research, if that's what you mean," I said, affronted. "But if you're asking how much I've actually written . . ."

Ami shook her head. "Weren't you supposed to have been working on this for the past two months? I knew you were a procrastinator, but man."

I glanced back at the e-mail on the screen, the words burning into my retinas. Then I started typing.

Dr. Justus, thank you for the reminder. Although
I am eager to read your comments on my critical

analysis, I unfortunately am out of town and thus
can not drop it off in your box until next week.

Ami coughed on a piece of chip. "What if he sees you around campus? I assume you're not skipping the rest of your classes. What if he talks to one of the other professors? And you know he'll just ask you to e-mail the paper to him."

Reluctantly I deleted the last sentence of my e-mail. As much as I hated to admit it, Ami was right. Rule number two of lying is to make it as airtight as possible. Which just goes back to rule number one: never get caught. That lie had too many holes in it to be a safe bet. My fingers rested over the keyboard as I thought, until finally I began typing again.

Although I am eager to read your comments on my critical analysis, my computer has some sort of virus that has wiped out all of my documents. Campus computing is working on getting them back, but it's uncertain right now if I will be able to recover them all.

"Oh my God," Ami groaned. "You are so ridiculous. What next, Leigh? Why not 'a dog ate my homework' or 'I must have had the paper in my other backpack'?"

Impatiently, I deleted the last few lines. "So, what do you suggest?"

"I don't know . . . why don't you just e-mail Dr. Justus and tell him you'll put it in his box tomorrow?"

I swiveled to face her in my desk chair. "Oh, I get it," I said excitedly. "And then by the time he gets back to me to tell me he never received it, I'll act really confused and troubled and insist that I left it for him. By then, I'll have written it, and I'll just offer to give him another copy."

Ami put her hands on my shoulders, her inky black gaze holding my gray one. "Or you could just do it."

"Write it tonight?"

"You don't fool me for a second, Leigh. Every time you have any assignment to do, you do this. You obsessively research and outline and then, the night before, you freak out and start making up stupid excuses about why you didn't do it or making plans to drop the class. But you always pull through, write a cutting five-page review of a book you didn't read, and turn it in the next day. You're like a machine."

I grinned at her. "I do thrive on this, don't I?"

"So much it makes me sick," Ami said with a smile. "Now, get to work."

Ami can be encouraging when she wants to be, but inevitably her own lack of work drives her to become the biggest distraction. In the first hour I was working on my paper, she asked me if I wanted to go out for ice cream, walk down to check our mail, and paint her nails. Eventually I called Andrew. As expected, he was studying, too, and told me to come on over.

"You can set up your laptop on the bed, if you want," he said when I got there.

I glanced around the room. Andrew's twin-size bed was covered with laundry and papers, and there were stacks of library books on every conceivable surface. The floor wasn't much cleaner, with half-packed boxes still strewn about.

"Is there anywhere else I could work?" I asked doubtfully. Working while hunched over my laptop, dirty laundry piled up behind me so the headboard wouldn't dig into my back, was hardly my ideal way of doing things.

"You mean like the desk?" Andrew gestured pointedly to the papers scattered over its particle board surface, even covering half of his computer keyboard. "That's kind of where I'm working, Leigh."

"I guess I'll just work out in the common room or something." I sighed, giving him a smile to let him know I was trying to make the best of it. "It's probably better that we aren't in the same room, anyway. Less distractions that way."

Andrew wrinkled his nose at me. "The coffee table is actually a little sticky right now—a little accident involving duck sauce." His face brightened. "But hey, why don't you just use Nathan's room? He's out for the night, and I'm sure he won't mind."

Like that wouldn't be weird. "I don't know. . . ."

But Andrew was already ushering me out of his room and into Nathan's. "Come on," he said, "he won't even know."

I had only ever seen a sliver of Nathan's room through the

open door before, and I have to admit, I was curious. The first thing that struck me was that it wasn't as neat as I thought it would be. Not that it was a disaster, but in my mind, a math major with a stick up his ass should be at least a little OCD. But, like Andrew, Nathan had a pile of library books by his desk, stacked perilously high. He must have been in the middle of changing his guitar strings, because his guitar was lying, unstrung, on his bed, with coiled-up strings tossed carelessly next to it. And on the floor was a crumpled Velvet Underground T-shirt that I recognized as the one he had been wearing yesterday.

"Are you sure that Nathan won't need his room?" I asked.

Andrew chuckled. "Yeah, I'm sure. Nathan's got a hot date tonight. I wouldn't be surprised if I don't see him for the next week."

"Really? I didn't know he was seeing anyone."

Andrew shrugged. "It's relatively fresh. Remember Heather, the girl who spent orientation week drunk in the courtyard, yelling about how much she liked sex?" He didn't wait for my response. "She's Nathan's hot date."

"Oh," I said. There were a lot of Heathers (and not of the cool, dark-comedy movie kind), so that didn't really narrow it down. A *lot* of girls had acted out a variation of the one-woman "I like sex" show. I'm all for women's liberation, but . . . gross.

"Anyway, if you need anything, just poke your head in my door." Andrew leaned over to give me a quick kiss on the forehead. "Oh, but try not to do it too much—okay, hon? I can't afford to get sidetracked right now."

With that, Andrew left, closing the door behind him. If it felt weird to be standing in Nathan's room with Andrew, it felt even weirder to be standing there alone with the door closed. His walls were covered with posters of bands—most of whom I'd heard of, but a couple I hadn't. Tom Waits, Gang of Four, the Velvet Underground . . . I peered closer to read the fine print on a Sex Pistols poster for the *Great Rock 'n' Roll Swindle*.

Feeling like an intruder, I carefully moved some papers off his desk to make room for my laptop. There were lined papers covered in incomprehensible numbers and equations, sheets listing chord formations, and an envelope from a Patricia McGuire (his mother?). I was particularly surprised to find that Nathan was a doodler, and even more surprised to see that he mostly doodled . . . cats. There were little cartoon cat faces, a cat chasing a mouse, cats playing with yarn . . . Who knew that Nathan McGuire corresponded with his mother and had a serious thing for cats?

I think in Jungian dream analysis, cats represent the anima, or a guy's feminine self. Whatever *that* means.

I sat down and opened up my laptop, resolved to work. After all, I had left my own room because of Ami and her constant distraction. One e-mail I did *not* want to write to Dr. Justus (who's kind of gruff and old) was one with the truth.

Dear Dr. Justus, I just wanted to write to apologize for my failure to turn in a critical analysis paper. See, first there was this girl who just carried a watermelon, and somehow ended up dancing with the hired-help bad boy at a summer resort. Then I was in my boyfriend's roommate's room, and I just had to snoop around a little. You know, check out his DVD collection, whether he wears boxers or briefs, whether he keeps bodies of humanities or social science majors in a crawl space under his bed . . . that sort of thing.

(Boxers, by the way. And he has a lot of music DVDs, although I did see the first season of *Flight of the Conchords*. No crawl space . . . that I could find, anyway. But these math majors are tricky.)

After several hours, I had only ten pages and was already starting to flag. The glaring red numbers on Nathan's alarm clock read 1:15. It felt so much later.

I stood up, enjoying a satisfying crack in my back as I stretched. For the past half an hour I hadn't heard any more typing sounds coming from Andrew's room, and when I knocked at his door there was no answer. Quietly, I slipped in.

He was sleeping! Andrew "I can't afford to be sidetracked" Wieland had actually fallen asleep! I couldn't believe it. And unless he always shuts down his computer and changes into pajamas while he works, he had gone to sleep on *purpose*. I wanted to shake him. How dare he go to sleep when I still had ten more pages to write?

He looked so peaceful while he was sleeping, though. Instead of waking him up, a part of me considered curling up next to him and getting some sleep myself. I was so tired. . . .

Ten pages. That's what I had to keep telling myself. Ten pages and a Works Cited page. Then tomorrow I'd skip British and American drama (I swear, this is not becoming a habit, but that class is seriously lame) and sleep all day. All I had to get through was tonight.

I had been working steadily for another half hour when the door flew open and Nathan walked in, looking just as startled as I was.

"What are you doing here?" I gasped after I recovered my breath.

"What am *I* doing here?" he repeated incredulously. "This is *my* room. What's your excuse?"

As if the whole scenario wasn't surreal enough, I couldn't believe I was actually experiencing the classic "what are you doing here" argument that is the staple of sitcoms and romance novels. But there I was, sitting in Nathan's desk chair at *his* desk, while he stood in the doorway staring at me like he was seriously considering the state's policy on involuntary commitment to a mental health facility.

"I needed a quiet place to work," I tried to explain. "Ami was distracting me, and then I came here, but Andrew needed his desk to work, and there was some issue with duck sauce, and Andrew said you wouldn't be home tonight, so . . ."

It was only then that I really took in Nathan's appearance. He and Heather must have gone to the Olive Garden or something, because he was definitely way more dressed up than I'd ever seen him, wearing a crisp white shirt and dark green cargo pants. I didn't think he owned anything but band T-shirts.

He also looked really tired. The cuffs of his shirt were rolled up and the top button unbuttoned, and his dark hair looked like he had been running his fingers through it all night. Or Heather had.

"I'm really sorry," I said, gathering up my books. "I'll be out of your hair in just a minute." One thought about hair, and it was turning me into a babbling idiot. "Out of your room, I mean."

Nathan gave me a bleary-eyed look. "How much more do you have to do?"

"Ten pages? And a Works Cited page."

"And when do you have to turn it in?"

I was taking contemporary European history, so maybe I was mistaken, but I could have sworn that the Spanish Inquisition ended hundreds of years ago. "Um . . . tomorrow."

His green eyes widened. *Tomorrow?* he repeated. "Nothing like the thrill of last-minute, huh?"

"Well, thanks for letting me use your room. Or, not *letting* me, exactly, but not freaking out more that I used it. Or . . . you know . . ." I realized I was rambling again, and I probably looked like a moron, because I was using my chin to hold all my books in place, and I couldn't open my mouth all the way or else the books would topple over. "So anyway, I'll be going home now. Thanks again and . . . I'm sorry."

Nathan stopped me at the door, and for some reason I started thinking about his cat doodles all over again.

"Listen," he said, reaching for the books. "We both know that if you go back to your room, Ami will be there and she'll want to watch *Pretty in Pink* for the hundredth time. You'll never get any work done there."

All I could do was gape at him. "*Pretty in Pink* is a good movie," I protested feebly.

He gave me a crooked smile. "Yeah, but it's no *Sixteen Candles*, you have to admit. And you have ten pages left to write."

"And a Works Cited page," I added, still feeling a little overwhelmed.

"The point is, I'll probably just crash anyway, so you can finish your paper here, since you've already started." He rubbed the side of his jaw. "I mean, if you want."

If I didn't know any better, I would think that Nathan McGuire—my boyfriend's roommate—who I'm pretty sure despises me—had just invited me to work in his room while he slept there. It was such a bizarre idea that I couldn't even wrap my mind around it.

"Forget it," Nathan said abruptly, stepping aside to let me pass. "I never should have offered."

"No!" The word shot out of my mouth before I could stop it. "I mean . . . I really appreciate it. I do have a lot of work to do."

His gaze swept over my face before he gave a terse nod and set my books back on the desk. "All right," he said. He crossed over to one of his dresser drawers, extracted some clothes, and left for the bathroom. I had barely hooked up my laptop again when he returned, wearing a soft gray T-shirt and flannel pajama bottoms. I sat there, not sure what to say.

"You can leave the desk lamp on," Nathan said, and then with a rustle of covers, he was asleep.

"Leigh!" The voice was low and urgent in my ear. "Leigh! Wake up!"

"Nathan?" In my half-asleep state, I thought it must be him. But then I cracked one eye open and saw Andrew's face, staring down at me. I shot straight up in my chair, my back protesting as I did so.

"What time is it?" I asked, peering at the alarm clock on Nathan's bookcase, which also served as his nightstand, his entertainment center, and, if the bottom shelf stacked with at least three pairs of Converse All Stars was anything to go by, his shoe rack. 11:17. I had a two-second panic attack until I remembered that I had finished at around five in the morning before finally falling asleep. Dr. Justus often checked his box right around lunchtime, which meant that I'd be pushing it if I stopped to print the paper on my own printer.

"Can I use your printer?" I asked Andrew.

For the first time I noticed how annoyed he looked. "Why don't you just use *Nathan's*?" he snapped.

I blinked. "I think I've imposed enough, don't you?"

"I don't know, have you? How do you think I felt when Nathan came out this morning to tell me that *my* girlfriend was asleep at his desk!"

It took me a few seconds to register that Andrew was jealous. Andrew—normally so levelheaded and cool—was actually *jealous!*

"I'm sorry," I said, trying to keep the smile out of my voice. "I was working, and I just lost track of time. It was no big deal."

Andrew grunted. "Well, it was obnoxious to hear how smug he sounded when he told me to wake you up and make sure you had finished your paper. As if he knows what's best for *my* girlfriend."

Even though we've been dating over a year, I still get a small thrill when I hear the words *my girlfriend* come out of his mouth, especially when he emphasizes the first word the way he was doing now. I had been awake for five minutes and already he had called me that twice. I kind of liked this possessive thing.

He sighed. "I'm sorry, Leigh. I shouldn't have put you in this position. I really didn't expect him to come home last night. Heather must be losing her touch if she—"

"Don't worry about it," I cut him off. "Like I said, it was no big deal."

Andrew reached out to touch the side of my face. "I know," he said. "I just thought that if you were going to spend the night, it would be with me."

It was the first time he'd brought up me sleeping over in a while, and I knew I had to tread carefully. "I want to spend the night with you, Andrew," I said softly.

He smiled, his brown eyes warm on my face. "Really?"

"Really," I assured him.

Andrew pressed a kiss to my lips. "Well, then, let me hook up my printer for you."

> **SOCIAL FACILITATION:** The idea that
> being in a group enhances performance of simple tasks,
> but actually hinders performance of more complex ones

UNFORTUNATELY, I only had the chance to grab three hours of sleep between my almost all-nighter and my big teenage pregnancy presentation at Simms Middle School. I was tired and kind of clammy, and the liter of Mountain Dew I'd downed earlier made me weirdly jittery and in desperate need of a bathroom. But at least this time, I was ten minutes early and I knew where to go. I was even wearing a pair of Ami's dress flats for the occasion, though her feet were a size smaller than mine and the shoes were starting to seriously pinch. Somehow I thought that the whole "don't have sex or you might have babies" message would be less convincing in a pair of beat-up Cons.

It took me a while to come up with my approach. After all, the D.A.R.E program was based on loads of research and years of application, and it still was pretty ineffective in preventing drug use. In fact, there was a whole group of kids at my school who thought it the height of irony to wear the old-school D.A.R.E T-shirts while lighting up a joint. Then again, these are the same kids who sit in the lounge and laugh uproariously over the latest reality show about people racing to win a million dollar prize or sleeping with the same guy in the hopes of being selected as his one true love in the end.

It was hard to figure out what I could possibly say in half an hour that would warn a group of preteen girls against getting pregnant. If this were one of my classes, I would just throw together a PowerPoint presentation and call it a day. But I'm pretty sure that the average middle school girl is more interested in watching Christina Aguilera dip to number four on *TRL* than in sitting still for a half-hour slide show presenting data and research.

Ellen was already there when I arrived. She glanced at my hands, nearly empty except for a small pile of index cards. "Aren't you supposed to give some sort of presentation today?"

As if she hadn't been hassling me about it for the past week. "Yes," I said shortly.

Ellen raised her eyebrows, but at least she didn't say anything else. A few of the other mentors started filing in, and then the final bell rang and the girls starting arriving as well.

Rebekah shot me a deadly look, but Molly smiled at me as she sat down on the floor.

"Are you going to talk today?" she asked. "You're funny."

I was touched in spite of myself. "Well, thank you," I said, fighting the urge to stick my tongue out at Ellen. I bet the girls found her as funny as watching C-SPAN. Last week, when we went around the circle and introduced ourselves, Ellen listed her research interests and the fact that she worked part-time as a file clerk at a law firm downtown. Everyone else had just discussed their pets or their favorite colors.

At that point, Linda came in and officially started the meeting. We had a couple new girls, so it was determined that we would go around the circle *again*, only this time she decided to focus our introductions.

"Today, why doesn't everyone say their name?" she suggested, looking around the room with bright eyes. "And then after your name, say . . . what you would name your firstborn child!"

Way to discourage teenage pregnancy there, Linda. I bet D.A.R.E. never had to deal with this kind of crap. *We'll just introduce ourselves, and while you're at it, tell everyone your drug of choice.*

Not surprisingly, when it was her turn, Ellen said she didn't want any kids. "My fiancé and I are just too driven," she said with a breezy shrug.

Ellen would never make it as the heroine of a romance novel. In romances, the protagonist is always this very maternal, warm woman who doesn't mind when the hero's small niece blows her nose on a very expensive silk dress. Then the hero sees how different she is from his ex-flame, who freaked out when the kid sneezed on *her* designer dress, and he falls in love.

Finally it got around to me. "Rocky," I said. "After Rocky Balboa, the Italian Stallion."

Everyone laughed, but I wasn't totally kidding. Anyone who's watched any of the Rocky movies would be proud to raise a son named Rocky. I mean, who can't get behind a namesake who defeated Ivan Drago and communism all in one amazing fight? Nobody who loves America, that's for sure.

Once the blatant encouragement of procreation was wrapped up, Linda finally turned to me. "So, Leigh," she said, that trademark fake smile pasted on her face. "Last week you had some interesting things to say about teen pregnancy. Would you like to share them now?"

"Sure," I said, standing up. "But first, can I have two volunteers?"

Molly's hand shot up. I noticed Rebekah was examining her nails as though spoilers for the latest CW show were written in her polish. I desperately wanted to pick her, but I *had* said "volunteers." And unfortunately the research methods portion of Intro Psych had already drilled it into my head that experiments were now supposed to have *participants* rather than *subjects*. Stupid semantics.

"Molly," I nodded my head in her direction. I looked around the room, and my eyes alighted on a slightly overweight girl with dirty-blond hair. I think she said her name was Kathy—or was that what she wanted to name her kid? I couldn't remember.

"And, uh . . . you," I said, pointing at Kathy or future-mother-of-Kathy. "Okay, you two can stand up here with me.

"Now, last week we talked about the effect an unwanted pregnancy might have on a made-up life, but let's talk today about what you might do right now if you had a baby.

"What I have here"—I shuffled my index cards—"are scenarios that you might find yourself in if you had a baby. Molly, would you pick the first one, please?"

Molly glanced uncertainly at me, as though already regretting her decision to volunteer. Finally she selected one of the cards from the very end and turned it over to read it.

"There's a big test tomorrow, and you have to study. Unfortunately, your two-month-old won't stop crying," she read, before looking back at me. *"What would you do?"*

"Anyone?" I looked expectantly over the crowd of blank faces.

Finally a girl whose name I remembered was Tawnya raised her hand. "I'd ask my mom to watch him, 'cause I got schoolwork to do."

I shook my head. "Your mom is tired of having the baby foisted on her, and she's busy watching her favorite reality show. You're going to have to handle this one."

Another girl raised her hand. "Just ignore it. The baby'll stop crying."

"What if he needs to be fed?" I asked. "Or changed? What if he's sick? And what if he doesn't stop crying—will you be able to concentrate on your homework?"

The girls started shaking their heads, catching on. Encouraged by their interest and the disgruntled look on Ellen's face, I let Kathy/mother-of-Kathy pick another scenario, which involved having to miss a party because you couldn't leave the baby. After that we did several more scenarios in a row, until I was confident that the girls were beginning to understand a small sliver of the responsibility that a child represented.

Finally, Rebekah raised her hand. The entire time, she'd been sitting in the back, blowing her long bangs out of her eyes and staring at the ceiling.

"Yes?" I smiled at her.

"What about abortion?" she asked.

I froze. "Abortion?" I repeated.

She nodded. "Yeah. If a baby's so much trouble, why not just abort it?"

Ellen raised her hand (totally superfluously, of course, because she just started speaking without waiting to be called upon). "Isn't it true that, by week eight, a baby's major organs have already begun to form?"

"Um," I said, "I don't really know." So far, we'd only made it through the sensation and perception and cognitive psychology portions of the Intro Psych book. Developmental wasn't until after Halloween.

"It's true," Ellen said. "By week five, they have a spleen."

How was I supposed to read ahead and know these things when I hadn't even bought my textbook yet? And yes, I know that makes me a horrible student, but seriously, why would I spend a hundred dollars on a book when I can use Wikipedia for free?

"Thank you, Ellen," I said, my voice sickeningly sweet. "As Ellen has just so aptly demonstrated, education is *very* important. Ultimately, it's every woman's decision what to do with her baby and her body, but the best thing that you can do is educate yourself and know what you're comfortable with."

Linda's eyes looked like they were going to pop out of her head. "Okay, well maybe we can talk about that another time," she said. "But we have other things to do, so let's just—"

But there was an earnestness about Rebekah's face that told me the question wasn't just her way of heckling me. I wasn't going to back down from this one. "Because you're a minor, it would be your parents' decision, too. I know it sucks, but that's the way it works."

Trying to redirect the issue of abortion back toward teenage pregnancy, I addressed the entire group. "Abortion is a choice legally available to you, but remember that it is *not* the same as taking precautions to prevent a pregnancy. For example, if you're seriously considering having sex, you should go to a clinic and—"

Rebekah cut me off. "Would *you* get an abortion?"

Shit. "I . . . don't know," I said. "I really don't know."

Linda shot in front of me, gathering the index cards from Molly and Kathy/mother-of-Kathy and shooing the girls back to their seats. "All right," she said, her voice high-pitched. "I think that's about all we have time for today. We wouldn't want you girls missing your buses. See you next week!"

The session erupted in a shuffling of backpacks and a jostling to get to the door, and I turned to Linda in confusion. "They still had five minutes," I said. "And it seemed like they were actually really listening."

"You were *encouraging* them to have sex," she hissed, "with all your talk of abortions and clinics and pills."

I blinked. "I was trying to give them honest information," I said. "If it's already occurred to them to have sex, they're going to whether we talk about it or not. At least if they had some information they might be better able to protect themselves."

Linda snapped her teeth together. "Well, it's not something we talk about here."

She stalked off, leaving me standing there with my index cards, completely flummoxed. I guess the hypothetical babies that we're always talking about just popped up out of the flower patch or something. So far this mentoring program made absolutely no sense.

"Nice going," Ellen said, passing by with a smug smile.

Ellen would definitely be the other woman in a romance novel. She'd be the one who tried to sabotage the heroine at her job but was eventually caught cheating and taking all the credit for accounts that the heroine had actually put together. She'd get fired, and meanwhile the hero and his beautiful, honest employee would make passionate love on his mahogany desk.

My lips curved upward into my own superior little smile, but it quickly faded as I remembered the truth of the situation. The truth was that I wasn't beautiful or honest, and I felt a little silly instructing a bunch of thirteen-year-old girls how *not* to get pregnant when I couldn't even figure out how to have sex in the first place.

I guess it's weird that I'm the only college-age girl in the UNIVERSE who can date someone for a year and *not* have sex, but let me explain. Even though I know it's a completely cheesy, teen-flick kind of thing to do, Andrew and I had planned our first time together to be on prom night. But what those movies never show is the part where your friend ends up crashing your hotel room because he had an older brother pick up three cases of hard lemonade and now he's crying over a girl who dumped him TWO years ago, at summer camp. They also neglect to tell you that, if your boyfriend ends up visiting his grandparents for a month after graduation and you spend a lot of time scrubbing bathrooms at a B&B, it becomes incredibly awkward to broach the topic of sex *again*, once that night of teen abandon has passed you by.

It seemed like going to college would make the whole thing way easier, but it just introduced a new set of complications. I know tons of people who get "sexiled" on a regular basis, and roommates who've set up elaborate systems of beads around the doorknob or a special magnet stuck to the metal doors to indicate that they're taking full advantage of their newfound freedom. But Ami and I had talked about it on one of our first nights, and we both agreed that it was rude to kick someone out of her own room, and it was totally weird to have any overnights when the other one was there.

Andrew had his own room, but it didn't solve the problem of the beds. All the beds were twin extralongs, which are basically regular twin beds that have had a sliver cut off the width and added to their length. Or at least, that's how it seems. I slept over at Andrew's room just once, in the first week of school, and I ended up sleeping on the floor just because I kept rolling off the edge. Since then, he hadn't brought it up again, and I always invented some reason why I'd rather go back to my own room, anyway.

In college, some people created insane opportunities to have sex whenever and wherever they pleased. (I'd even read some anonymous student's blog about doing it up against the washers in the laundry room, which just gives me more reason to be irritated when people take my clothes out before they're done and stack them on top.)

Meanwhile, Andrew and I? We spent all our energy figuring out how to explain why we *weren't* having sex.

How pathetic.

NEED FOR ACHIEVEMENT: A personality trait that is high in people who tend to be concerned with achievement and have pride in their accomplishments. These people avoid high risks (because there is a chance of failure) and low risks (because they won't generate any sense of achievement).

SYDNEY called to let me know that the Intro Psych study group would meet at her condo, which was located at the edge of a lush golf course about twenty minutes from school. I heard. somewhere that Sydney's father is this big-time market analyst who makes, like, a thousand dollars a minute consulting for corporations. So I shouldn't have been surprised that Sydney's condo was as nice as it was, but it still blew my mind that someone only three years older than I was could live like she does.

Sydney opened the door almost before I knocked, as though she'd been waiting. "Leigh! You're not late! Come on in."

85

I'm not a nut for being punctual or anything, but I'm not one of those people who buys into the whole concept of "Stiles Time," either, which is supposedly how this college warps your sense of time until you're chronically ten minutes late for everything. So I put Sydney's comment down to random bitchiness and stepped through the door. "Nice place," I commented.

Sydney dismissed her thousand-dollar furniture and state-of-the-art entertainment system with a flick of her wrist. "I recently redecorated the study," she said. "Here, let me show you what I've done with the place."

Reluctantly, I started to follow her, and caught myself when I stumbled over a huge lump on the floor.

It was a cat. And not just any cat. This was the biggest, meanest cat I'd ever seen. It looked like it could crush an armadillo in its jaws, and it had the beady eyes of a crocodile. It was more than a cat. It was a Linda Blair movie.

"Oh, that's Sir Wug," Sydney said. "Careful. She's in perpetual heat."

Like mistress, like cat. *"She?"*

Feeling another pair of beady eyes watching me, I noticed Ellen perched on the couch, the straight line of her back barely grazing the cushions as she regarded me with displeasure. I guess she was still upset about the whole mentoring thing.

"Hey," I said, to test it out.

"Hello," she replied icily. Yeah, she wouldn't be giving me a BFF locket anytime soon. Although I still didn't understand why she was taking my role in the mentoring group so personally.

"Um . . ." I said to Sydney. "Did she already take the tour?" As vile as Ellen was, I did *not* want to be alone with Sydney.

"Sydney showed me around earlier," Ellen said, and I thought I saw her shudder.

It didn't take me long to realize why. Let's just say that the only thing Sydney has in common with Martha Stewart is her penchant for cheating. Mostly her decor consisted of naked pictures of herself that were supposed to seem "artistic," but instead just looked like she really, really wanted to show off her body. Which isn't that great, and I'm not just being bitchy. Her boobs looked really weird.

For the pièce de résistance, Sydney ushered me into her study. "As you can see, I got a new Mac," she said, gesturing to the small laptop on her desk. "I had had my old one for over a year, so it was getting a little slow."

Probably from all those naked pictures she was loading onto it. Right next to the laptop, where I'm sure she wanted me to see it, was a glossy 5x7 of her butt in profile, right where it starts to curve into the top of the leg. I averted my gaze.

"Is that a new desk chair?" I asked, as though I cared. It was leather, and looked much nicer than the barely padded chairs they gave us in the dorms. Our chairs didn't have wheels on them, either, so if you lived on the first floor you could totally hear the person above you scraping their chair back and forth on the linoleum.

"No, I've had that. And the desk and bookshelf were here before."

Okay, someone would have to explain to Sydney that "redecorating" did not mean having Daddy buy you a new laptop and putting a picture of your naked body on your desk. I just wasn't going to volunteer to be the one to do it.

"They're nice," I said lamely. "Maybe we should go back to the living room and see if Joanna and Jenny are here yet."

Luckily, Sydney just shrugged and we left her study, which had been starting to give me the creeps. After only ten minutes in her condo, I had this weird crawling sensation on my skin, as if a stray piece of hair had come undone from my ponytail and was brushing against my back. Maybe it's the fact that everything feels vaguely '80s, even despite the brand-new Mac and wide-screen HDTV. It wasn't in that cool *Napoleon Dynamite* sort of way, either. More in an uncomfortable, greasy time warp way, kind of like that Strokes video for "Last Night." Some things just shouldn't look that authentic.

Joanna and Jenny had just arrived, and so we spent a few minutes in the living room making awkward small talk that mostly revolved around A) Sydney's thesis (on whether bumblebees will give preference to light or sound, or something equally lame), B) our classes, and C) our opinions of professors. Joanna and I spent a few moments commiserating over how difficult it was to make an appointment with Dr. Harland before Sydney cut in.

"All right," she said. "We should really get to work. So does everyone have their stuff?"

I pulled out my Intro Psych notebook. Ellen had brought a small accordion-style file with papers neatly organized by the different areas of psychology. Ellen and Joanna also both had their textbooks. I knew Ellen would be a card-carrying member of the "suckers who buy textbooks" club, but I hadn't expected Joanna to buy into the hype.

Only Jenny's hands were empty, her eyes wide and stricken. "I forgot," she said, her voice the merest thread of a whisper.

I've heard Ellen refer to Jenny as GAD Girl, referring to the acronym for Generalized Anxiety Disorder. I wouldn't go *that* far, but sometimes I do wonder how Jenny dresses herself in the morning. We haven't even gotten through one whole semester yet, and already she seems like she's one midterm away from madness, one deadline from a nervous breakdown.

Supposedly the Intro Psych TAs have a bet going on about whether she'll finish out the year, which I think is kind of mean. Also bad money sense for those rooting for Jenny, because she has a better chance of having a piano fall on her head than of making it through the finals.

Sydney rolled her eyes. "Just sit there and listen," she said. "That's probably what you would have done anyway."

Jenny nodded meekly, her face redder than her hair as she slumped back on the couch. I tried to give her a slightly encouraging smile, but her head was down and it didn't look like she was going to make eye contact for the rest of the night.

"So, first off," Sydney said, addressing the rest of us, "let's just start by getting to know each other. Why don't you guys tell me about where else you applied, and why you chose to come to Stiles."

Ellen leaped to answer, ticking off a list of schools that made my jaw drop. Pretty much every school in the United States that contained the word *university* in its name was on her list, including all the Ivy Leagues.

"I got into Yale, actually, but I chose Stiles for its uniquely independent approach to education."

"The fact that Yale costs, like, fifty thousand dollars per semester probably had something to do with it," I muttered.

Ellen's eyes challenged me. "Sorry?" she said, but she didn't sound very sorry.

As if I were going to give her exactly what she wanted— a rational reason to hate me, instead of the numerous *irrational* ones she seemed to harbor now. "That's just a lot of schools," I said. Her parents probably couldn't afford Yale after they declared bankruptcy from the thousands of dollars in application fees, SAT prep classes, and transcripts for the application process alone.

Maybe there were diminishing dollar signs in my eyes, because Ellen got my drift perfectly. "My parents pay for anything school-related," she said with a toss of her head. "They believe that my education is the most important thing in the world."

How nice. I wondered if they considered her fiancé

"school-related," since as far as I knew he was living in Ellen's dorm rent-free and she paid his car insurance.

"What about you, Leigh?" Joanna asked. "Where did you apply?"

"Just Stiles," I said.

"*Just* Stiles?" Ellen repeated. "That's stupid. What if you hadn't gotten in? You wouldn't have gone *anywhere.*"

Sydney's eyes sharpened. "Was Andrew already going to go to Stiles? Was that why you applied?"

This was a no-win question. If I said no, then it looked like Andrew and I didn't care about staying together. If I said yes, then I looked like a typically sappy girl who planned her life around her high school boyfriend.

"He'd looked into it." I hedged, hoping she would drop it. Truthfully, Andrew had mapped out his college plans by the tenth grade (as you can see, not a lot had changed). By the time we started dating, he was already set on Stiles. I didn't really care, and the school had pretty convincing brochures (if they don't offer a class, you can start it yourself!) so I decided I'd apply there, too.

"So what about grad school?" Sydney asked. "Are you guys planning on going to the same school?"

"I'm not ruling anything out," I said. "We'll just have to see how it goes."

I noticed that no one was asking Ellen what her fiancé planned to do while she studied in Pennsylvania or Hawaii or Wisconsin or whichever of the fifty states she would apply to grad school in. I didn't know a lot about him, except that he worked at the three-cent copy place and that he and Ellen were constantly bickering.

Which, unfortunately, I can kind of relate to. And to think, I used to be so smug about my relationship with Andrew.

"I think that's radical," Joanna put in, nodding her approval and effectively silencing Sydney. "There's no need to make any hasty decisions at this point."

From the first day of Intro Psych, I marked Joanna as someone I wanted to meet. She's just . . . interesting. For one thing, she's one of the biggest girls I've ever seen. And I don't mean in that euphemistic "she's not fat, she's big-boned" sort of way. I mean that she's really just a *big* girl. Her legs are these sturdy, tanned columns beneath her boardshorts, gleaming with health and energy. Seriously—I don't know if she oils them or what, but they totally gleam. She's almost six feet tall, and she has this incredible white blond hair, which I'm pretty sure is real, since her blue eyes are framed by strikingly white eyelashes. I've always had this weird sensation that in another life, Joanna was a tree.

My New Agey parents would be proud.

"So, what about Nathan? What's his deal?" Sydney asked, her eyes getting that weird glint again.

"Who's Nathan?" Ellen glanced from me to Sydney, not liking being excluded. Jenny briefly lifted her head, as though she were interested, but her scraggly red hair quickly fell back to cover her face.

"Are you kidding me? He's only, like, the *hottest* freshman."
Sydney sighed dramatically, and I rolled my eyes. Couldn't she
find a guy her own age?

"He's Andrew's roommate," I explained, since I didn't
think the description "hottest guy" would produce a police
sketch artist's likeness anytime soon. "He's planning to be a
math major."

Joanna wrinkled her nose. "So hot but a little boring,
huh?"

I could think of a lot of things to call Nathan, but oddly,
"boring" wasn't one of them. "More like self-righteous," I said,
and immediately felt a twinge of guilt. Not that I had any reason to feel guilty—I'm sure he'd said worse about me. And just
because he helped me out when I was in a tight spot with my
paper didn't mean it was a betrayal to talk behind his back.
Right?

"Well, I wouldn't exactly be asking him to give a guest
lecture," Sydney said with a lascivious smirk. "I'm sure we
could find more interesting things to do."

Gross.

"Okay, Mrs. Robinson," I said. "Let's get back on task."
Never thought I'd be saying *that*.

"Actually, I don't really need any help in Intro Psych,"
Ellen said. "I took AP psychology in high school."

I had taken that class, too, *and* AP statistics. But I was here
because I'd been coerced into it by Sydney's conversational
wizardry (and also, because Stiles didn't believe in letting you

"test out" of anything, a fact which I was totally cursing right now. Invent your own classes, my ass).

"So why did you bother to come?" I asked. Which, given the fact that I was here for pretty dubious reasons myself, was a little snarky. Like I cared.

"I don't like to be left out," Ellen said. Well, I guess admitting you have a problem *is* the first step toward getting help. "And I have some questions for Sydney. You're applying to grad schools now, right? Do you have any tips that will help me when I apply in three years?"

Seriously, there's something in the water at this school. I know that Stiles is "uniquely independent" or whatever, and it *has* been ranked number five in the list of top small public liberal arts colleges with tuition under ten thousand dollars a year in the United States. But still.

Sydney practically beamed with pleasure at being the center of attention. Again. "Well, usually your grad school application consists of your transcripts, letters of recommendation, personal statement, and CV."

"Wait," Ellen said as she hurried to scribble it all down. "What's a CV? And what goes in your personal statement?"

It's not like she's going to write it now, for crying out loud. But of course, Sydney rushed to answer. "Your CV is like an academic résumé. And the personal statement is usually a recounting of your biggest research experience, a sob story about what you've gone through to get to grad school, or a combination of the two."

I hate personal statements. I had to write one for Stiles, and it was exactly like Sydney said—basically, you were supposed to discuss a hugely impressive research opportunity you've had or weave some tear-jerking tale about your life. Considering the fact that my biggest research experience in high school was the year I spent learning everything I could about Olga Korbut (how cool is it to be the first woman *ever* to perform a backflip on the balance beam in competition?), that left only the sob story.

When I was seven, a bee stung me while I was swinging from the monkey bars, and I fell and broke my arm. When I was fifteen, I lost my position as homeroom representative in a struggle over my refusal to say the Pledge of Allegiance every morning. (So you know, it's not that I'm against America—I simply have issues with blind nationalism being taught to young children.) And just last year, my favorite 0.7 mm rolling gel pen was discontinued, and every pen I've tried since either bleeds through the page or fades away in thin, spidery script.

Somehow I didn't think any of those things qualified as personal statement–worthy "obstacles." And unless something happened to me in the next three years that was tragic (yet inspirational), I was pretty much screwed for my grad school application.

"Obviously, your CV is where you can list all your accomplishments," Sydney continued. "So if I were you, I'd start writing them all down over the course of the next three years, so you make sure you don't forget any."

From the way Ellen's pen moved furiously over her notebook, I was sure that she was already starting to list all of her accomplishments of the last two months. The sad part was, she probably had done more in that period of time than I'd done in all of high school.

In high school, I had made it almost an art not to involve myself in *anything*. I didn't join National Honor Society, even though that meant I was one of only two people in the honors program not to wear a white scarf at graduation. (The other was Norm Erwin, who wore the same pair of jeans every day for four years, complete with ketchup stain, so clearly I was in good company.)

The accomplishments I'd listed on my application to Stiles: the *sobresaliente* award in Spanish (I have no clue how I earned this, since I used to speak in a deliberately funny accent so I wouldn't have to try a real accent and risk embarrassing myself), eight years of violin (I played in first grade and then in eighth, so it's kind of true), and president of the Scrabble club (sometimes friends would come over to my house to play, so it totally counts).

"Well, so far I have membership in psychology club," Ellen said, glancing down at her list, aka the *Kinsey*-watching club. "And of course, there's always mentoring."

She shot me a deadly look, and I decided to fan the flames.

"That's right," I said. "I'll probably put that down under 'leadership' on my CV. You know, since I single-handedly led the last session and all."

"Single-handedly poisoned the youth of America, maybe," Ellen said. "I can't believe you even acknowledged that girl's question, much less answered it. I would have just told her it was inappropriate and moved on."

"*That girl* is Rebekah," I said. "And it was a good question. She deserved an answer."

Impatiently, Sydney gestured to the papers in her hand. "So you're helping kids with their self-esteem and crap. Grad schools eat that up. But don't forget about other stuff. Like, awards and honors. After three years, you better have *something* to put under there."

I was assuming that being appointed first-chair violin didn't count. I started to remind everyone that there was *more* than enough time to worry about all this stuff, but then I caught a glimpse of Ellen's face. There was a little smirk playing around her lips, as though she sensed my discomfiture and was enjoying it.

"Well, I did enter the California Collegiate Writing Contest," I blurted. It was totally true. I mean, all I'd done was recycle an old AP psych paper from high school, but it was something, right?

Sydney looked at me skeptically. "Was it for creative writing or research writing?"

"Research," I said, rolling my eyes as if to say, *what else?*

"Awesome," Joanna said. "What was your paper on?"

"Cognitive influences on bulimia." Wow, that sounded impressive as hell. I was starting to feel pretty good about this whole contest thing. I'd entered as a lark, but maybe I had a shot at winning.

Up until then, Ellen had been watching this exchange with interest, but now she broke in, that small smirk turning into a full-fledged smile. "I thought that contest was only for upper-classmen."

Why couldn't I ever remember to read the fine print? You'd think I would've learned my lesson when I ended up costing my parents three hundred dollars in AOL bills because I failed to read the whole "service will automatically be billed, even if not used, until cancellation notice is received" bit.

Oddly, it was Jenny who spoke up. "Actually, it's not," she said softly. "There's an underclassmen division, too."

"Oh." Ellen was deflated, but only for a second. "Well, I'll probably just wait to enter it next year. You know, when I've actually *done* something at this school to write a research paper, instead of just rehashing some immature high school crap."

She was totally on to me.

Just when my anxiety was starting to go from a limited symptom attack to a full-fledged panic attack, Joanna glanced at her watch and stood up. "Sorry, dudes," she said. "But I really have to go. I have a yoga class over on campus at six, and I have some stuff to do before then. But thanks, this has been really helpful."

I wondered if she meant that. It seemed to me that all this had been was an excuse for a lot of underhanded competition and bitchiness. We hadn't even cracked open our Intro Psych textbooks. Well, those who actually owned the textbook hadn't, anyway.

"Oh, and one more thing," she said, flicking her white blond hair carelessly over one shoulder. "Some of my surfer friends are throwing a totally wicked party at the beach this weekend. It's kind of a Halloween bonfire thing, but without any stupid costumes or anything like that. You guys should all make it out if you can."

Sydney shrugged. "As long as there's alcohol and boys, I'm there."

Ellen wrinkled her forehead. "I don't think I can afford to take any time away from my schoolwork," she said. Jenny muttered something about being in the same boat. I can't think of two people *less* in the same boat. Even if they were both on the *Titanic*, Ellen would have commandeered the first lifeboat while Jenny went down with the ship.

"Leigh?" Joanna turned to me. "Of course, you're welcome to bring Andrew."

"And Nathan," Sydney put in, but I ignored her.

"Sure, I might come," I said, gathering up my things in case Sydney had any ideas about continuing the meeting. "I'll have to see what Andrew's plans are for this weekend, but I'm free."

"Radical," Joanna said. "Well, I'll see you there!"

By this point, everyone had started to get ready to leave, and Sir Wug raised her head, annoyed at the disruption. I said my quick good-byes and tried to make it to the door before

Ellen had a chance to catch up with me, but it was no use. I was attempting my trick on the car door, juggling the folder in my hands, when all of my papers slid out and scattered across the parking lot.

I knelt down to pick them up, and before I knew it, Ellen was at my side. She didn't help me collect them, but instead just stood there, her own file folder clutched defensively across her chest.

"Good luck on the contest," she said. "You'll really need it." And then she spun on her heel, stalking off in her ugly square-toed shoes. Was it only a week ago that I feared Sydney as the worse of two evils, judging Ellen to be the less devious one?

Now I wondered if perhaps I had misdiagnosed the situation. Because if ultracompetitive psych-major monster was its own separate *DSM-IV* category, then Ellen was a much more serious case than Sydney.

I scooped up the last of the papers and dropped them on my green vinyl seat, sighing as I started the engine. I still was apparently the *only* person at Stiles who didn't have her entire future mapped out, and now I also had that stupid contest to worry about. I felt like I was all-in in a poker game, waiting for Ellen to call my bluff.

But would I have a winning hand?

> **HAWTHORNE EFFECT:** The tendency of people to behave differently if they know they are being observed

FOR someone who lives less than ten miles away from some of the most beautiful beaches in the world, I don't go to the beach that much. When I was a kid we took a trip to the beach, and I just remember being annoyed by the smell of sunscreen, the squawk of seagulls, and the way that the sand would cling to my wet feet. Then, of course, if I tried to wash them off in the ocean, they would just get wetter and the sand would cling more. Talk about a no-win situation.

Ami, Andrew, Nathan and I all decided to carpool together to the party, and since I was in one of my "support Gretchen" moods, I insisted we take the Gremlin. Ami called shotgun, much to Andrew's annoyance. I couldn't really blame him for being annoyed, since Ami's barely 5'2" and would be a whole lot more comfortable in my tiny backseat than Andrew. But you can't argue with the rules of shotgun.

"Aw, crap," I muttered, noticing the two yellow slips under my windshield wipers. Now I had *another* thirty dollar fine to pay. And they were threatening to tow.

"Why don't you just buy a decal?" Andrew asked. "It's what they're meant for, after all."

Andrew made it sound so easy. "To-may-toe, To-mah-toe," I said, letting him slide in behind my seat before climbing in myself. The Gremlin's front seat is a bench seat that must have been adjustable at one point, but isn't any longer. So I have no choice but to drive as though I'm some sort of gangster—leaning way back, one hand resting lightly on the top of the steering wheel and the other on the open window. I probably look pretty cool until people pull up next to me and realize I'm blaring Cutting Crew on the eighties station.

"Have you heard back about that contest yet?" Ami asked as I turned onto the main thoroughfare to the beach.

"Not yet," I said. "I think the results aren't supposed to come out until sometime in early November."

"Cross your fingers you won it," Ami said and snickered. "Or else Ellen will flay you alive."

Not that I needed that reminder.

"I think it's great that you're taking a little interest in

making the most of your college experience," Andrew said. "Even if it is for the wrong reasons."

Luckily I didn't really have to respond, because we pulled into the beach parking lot and I swung Gretchen expertly into a small space between two SUVs. Already I could smell the sweet tang of salt water and feel the gentle breeze on my face, and I smiled as I stepped out of the car.

The fall is a beautiful time in California. Okay, so the leaves don't change color or anything, but who needs it? Once you've seen one red leaf, you've seen them all. Fall takes the edge off California's heat, softens the colors a bit, and gives everything this sparkling serenity.

Just then a bird pooped about two centimeters away from my bright yellow flip-flop, and I sprang back in surprise. Maybe I was laying it on a bit thick when I said *serenity.* California in the fall is dry and hot, and let's face it—there's something very autumn-ish about multicolored leaves that you just don't get from a swaying palm tree.

In the distance I could see a group of people who looked like they could be Joanna's friends, and we all started trudging toward the beach with our towels and bags. Andrew has a tendency to walk a little fast, and Ami stopped to fumble through her bag for sunglasses, leaving Nathan and me to stroll through the soft sand together.

It was several moments before he spoke. "I've never ridden in your car before," he said.

Why would you have? I wanted to ask, but all I said was, "Oh."

I waited for the inevitable follow-up. *Having no air-conditioning in California is ridiculous. Why don't you buy a newer car that isn't such a clunker? We could have just taken my car, you know.* I've heard it all before. In the first couple of weeks, Ami complained a lot about my car (although she does like the "cute retro" way it looks). Eventually, I stopped midtrip to the art supply store and told her Gretchen wasn't taking her anywhere until she apologized. Since then, Ami's been very respectful.

I was so busy anticipating Nathan's words that it took a while to realize what he had actually said.

"It was fun."

Ami caught up with us, and she started chattering about some project she was doing that involved stringing shoelaces in a grid across the school courtyard. But I was still glowing from Nathan's compliment to Gretchen the way a proud mother would beam over her child.

I spotted Joanna, and she waved. "You came!" she called. "Awesome!"

"Who's that?" Ami whispered, leaning in.

"That's Joanna," I explained. "She's cool. Jenny probably won't be here, and I doubt Ellen will show, either. Sydney said she was coming—you remember her. Watch, she'll be the only one wearing stilettos at the beach."

"Joanna kind of looks like Hulk Hogan. You know, if he were a woman."

Which was an extremely difficult image to get out of my head, but somehow I managed to greet Joanna normally.

"What did you think of the Intro Psych study group the other day?" I asked her.

She shrugged. "It was all right," she said. "What about you?"

"Worth it for the group dynamics alone," I said, my gaze seeking out other people I knew and finding Sydney standing there, just as I thought she would be, wearing a small bikini top, a sarong, and three-inch heels.

Signs that Sydney was definitely a narcissistic personality: Grandiose self-importance, check. Fantasies of unlimited success or power, check. Believes she is "special" or somehow deserving of excessive admiration, check, check.

Unfortunately, she saw me, too. Or maybe it's more accurate to say that she saw Nathan. She stalked over toward us with her familiar stork walk and a determined look in her eye.

Andrew stood next to me, an idle hand draped around my shoulders as he surveyed the crowd. Andrew's strange about parties. He always acts like he's above them, but once he finds new people who haven't heard his theory about what constitutes a soul, he's in his element. After all, we did meet at a party.

"Leigh!" Sydney greeted me warmly. It occurred to me that my past few interactions with her had been largely pleasant. While I know that the laws of probability don't really support the idea of being "due" a certain outcome, I've also always learned that past behavior is the most obvious predictor of future behavior. Given that, the odds of her niceness continuing just didn't seem very high.

"I don't think we've met," she cooed to Nathan, her fingers brushing against his forearm. "I'm Sydney. I've heard a lot about you."

Oh, that's right. Narcissistic personalities are also very interpersonally exploitive. I remember now.

"Really?" Nathan shot me a look out of the corner of his eye.

Sydney tittered. "Don't worry—I don't believe all of it. I'm sure you're not as self-righteous as Leigh claims."

Nathan turned to face me fully, the wind ruffling his hair. There was a quietness about his face that caused a weird twisting sensation in my gut. "That's good to hear," was all he said.

I wanted to say something, to protest that my words had been taken out of context, but the truth was they hadn't been. I felt horrible, but I couldn't think of anything to do or say that would make it better.

Andrew dropped his arm and squeezed my waist. "Let's go walk by the water," he said, pulling me away. I glanced at Nathan one more time, but he had turned his full attention to Sydney and was listening intently to a question she was asking about statistical analyses for her thesis. Sydney is a lot of things, but stupid is not one of them. I didn't buy for one second that she needed help to run a simple chi-square, especially from a freshman.

Ami seemed to be clicking with a group of surfer guys,

and with her and Nathan both occupied, Andrew and I split off and headed toward the water. I had shaved just earlier that day in anticipation of the beach, and now the salt water stung my legs as we walked in comfortable silence.

"You know," Andrew finally said, "I've been doing a lot of thinking."

Since Andrew's always thinking, I wasn't surprised. But I looked up at him, an expression of polite curiosity on my face. "Oh?"

"I think you should stay over tonight," he said.

I stumbled slightly on a seashell protruding from the sand. "You do?"

He nodded. "After all, what's the point of college if you can't have your girlfriend spend the night?"

I wasn't so sure that I wanted this to be some kind of rite-of-passage thing, but a small thrill still went through me at the very idea of sleeping over. "What about the bed situation?" I said, more to gauge his reaction than anything else.

"Well," he said, giving me a sideways smirk. "Maybe we'll just have to get a little closer, won't we?"

"I would love to," I said, smiling up at him. Before I knew it, he leaned down and pressed his lips passionately on mine. I kissed him back, trying to put all my feelings into that fusion of our mouths, as though somehow my lips could tell him something I couldn't put into words.

I'm not sure if it worked, though. Eventually he pulled back, and instead of commenting on the messages of love he had just received via the kiss, he took his shirt off and threw it on the sand. "Let's go for a swim," he suggested.

Andrew dove into the water before I could reply, but I was still reeling from the thought of spending the night with him. He could have suggested we get dental work done and I probably would have blindly followed him at this point. I slipped out of my jean shorts and T-shirt to the boy-cut bikini I wore underneath, wading out to meet him.

We swam for a bit—mostly Andrew did, since I have a thing about putting my head underwater. I saw *Jaws* a few too many times as a kid, and so it's hard for me to swim underwater without having my eyes open. And chlorine wreaks enough havoc, but salt water is the worst. At one point Andrew dunked me under, ignoring my squealing protests, and I sputtered as I broke the surface.

"What was that for?" I choked.

Andrew shrugged. "You need to have some fun, Leigh. You're always so neurotic."

Okay, so maybe I'm a *little* uptight. On the first day of Intro Psych, we took the Myers-Briggs personality test. I scored really far on the Judging side, which means I prefer schedules and lists and plans. But I'm also the girl who never starts a paper until the last minute and who drives a car that makes no pretense of reliability. If there's anyone in the relationship who's uptight, it's gotta be Andrew.

I didn't call him on it, though. We had been having such a good time up to that point that I really didn't see the need to start a childish argument. "Let's head in," I said instead.

The sun had almost completely set, and dusk settled in as Andrew and I strolled up the beach. I heard talk of a bonfire, and a few of Joanna's surfer friends were gathering up driftwood and piling it on the sand. Nathan and Sydney were nowhere to be seen.

"Where's Nathan?" I asked.

Andrew glanced idly around before shaking his head. "Probably just off somewhere. How would I know?"

I should have just let it go at that, but something made me press on. "He was talking with Sydney earlier, and now I don't see either one of them," I said. "Isn't he still with Heather?"

"Christ, I don't know." Andrew turned to me with an exasperated sigh. "It's not like I'm filming a friggin' biopic on the kid. Why do you care, anyway?"

I didn't *care*. But I didn't think there was anything so wrong with wanting to keep tabs on the people I had to drive home.

Ami ran over from where she had been chatting with several very cute, shirtless surfers. "Oh my God," she breathed. "Those guys over there are *so* fine. Dumb, but fine. Do you know what one of them said when I mentioned Anne Frank?"

"What?"

Ami dropped her voice to a beach-bum baritone. "He said, 'Isn't she the one who makes those crazy folders? Those panda bears always freaked me out, man.'" She chuckled. "Can you believe that? He actually thought that Anne Frank was *Lisa Frank!*"

This was coming from Ami, who has had *many* such moments herself in just the short time I've known her. Once she asked if Portuguese was just a dialect of Spanish. This was particularly disconcerting, considering Ami's last name is Gutierrez, she speaks fluent Spanish, and she visits extended family in Nicaragua every year. So you'd think she should know.

"Why were you discussing Anne Frank, anyway?" I asked. Not the usual topic of conversation for a kooky artist and a bunch of surfers at a beach party.

"I was just trying to figure out what she did when she . . . you know . . ." Ami looked at me expectantly, as though I could read her mind. But as much as it would thrill my parents, telepathy has never been one of my talents. It didn't work in the first grade when I hoped to figure out what my teacher could *possibly* be thinking with those polyester pantsuits, and it wouldn't work now.

"No . . . what?" Went on dates with Peter? That's what I used to wonder about when I read the diary in eighth grade. I'm sure they just hung out in his room a lot. Trying to hook up in the secret annex must have been harder than beating the last level of Donkey Kong. And that's pretty hard.

"Had her period." Ami laughed. "Like, did she have to use towels? Because that would be totally gross."

I was speechless for a few moments. "You have the weirdest pickup lines," I finally said.

Andrew snorted. Whether it was at Ami, me, or the fact that this conversation was even happening, I couldn't tell. "I'm going to go help with the bonfire," he said, and walked away.

I waited until he was out of earshot, and even then I lowered my voice and leaned in to make sure no one but Ami could hear my next words. "Andrew asked me to spend the night tonight."

Ami's eyebrows shot up. "He did, huh?"

Her tone made me wary. "Yeah. He did."

"So you're going to?"

When your boyfriend of a year asks you (after multiple false starts, which Ami and I had totally analyzed to death) to spend the night with him, you don't exactly say no. "Of course," I said, but I could hear the defensiveness creep into my voice.

"Do you really think that's such a good idea?"

"Um . . . yes?"

Ami took me by the shoulder, steering me farther away from the party, even though we were already isolated. "You realize that if you spend the night over there, you're probably going to . . . you know."

Okay, this time it didn't take a mind reader. It was only the same thought that had been circling in my head like a vulture over a fresh carcass from the moment Andrew brought up the subject. "Would that be so bad?" I asked. "It's not like I'm hooking up with some random guy. I mean, this is *Andrew* we're talking about."

Ami nodded slowly. "Right . . . *Andrew*. Do you really think it's going to be special with him?"

I couldn't believe I was hearing this. "Look," I said, getting angrier now. "I am fully aware that you and Andrew are not going to form a mutual admiration society anytime soon. But he's my boyfriend, and if we decide to take this step, I think it's our decision and you need to respect that."

"*Dios mío*," Ami muttered, a clear sign I wasn't the only one getting agitated. "All I'm trying to say is . . . doesn't it ever bother you, the way he treats you? And why do you think sex will make it any different?"

Of course I had known we were talking about sex. But for some reason hearing the actual word made it seem so much more immediate, and I felt my heart start to race. Was it from excitement? Or fear?

"There's nothing wrong with the way Andrew treats me," I said. So we didn't *exactly* have the five to one ratio of positive to negative interactions in the relationship recommended by marriage therapists. But it was probably at least two to one. Maybe even three to one if he wasn't stressed about his schoolwork.

Ami rolled her eyes. "That's what Tina Turner said about Ike," she said, "and at least she got roses when he was being a jerk."

That was so unfair. "Why can't you just be happy for me?"

"I wish I could be." Ami sighed. "Believe me, I really wish I could."

"Well, don't hurt yourself trying," I said. I spun on my heel—a little awkwardly, since we were standing in incredibly soft sand—and stalked toward the bonfire, which was in full force now.

Andrew had found a couple of girls (I think they were humanities majors, the sluts) who were hanging on his every word regarding the true nature of altruism. When he saw me coming, he stopped talking and rose quickly, leaning over to press a firm kiss to my lips.

For some reason, it reminded me of the rare times that my parents would crack down and tell me to clean my room. Usually I would bring a book in there and sit cross-legged on the floor amid the mess, reading. When my mother would poke her head in to check on my progress, I would always spring up guiltily and throw the book under the bed. There were times when I knew she had probably been standing in the doorway for thirty seconds before I, totally immersed in my book, was even aware that she was there. But still I would chuck my book across the room and start shuffling papers, as if it might actually fool her.

It was just Ami's comments that were getting to me, I told myself. They were making me paranoid and oversensitive, and creating trouble where there was none. My relationship with Andrew was not only solid, it was actually moving forward. Finally.

"What's Ami's problem?" Andrew asked, glancing back at Ami, who was still standing huffily apart from everyone else.

He snickered. "Did someone break it to her that she might have to write a paper with *legitimate* sources, and not just ones from the Internet?"

Normally I just would have reeled off a lie to explain away the situation, but at that moment I saw two silhouettes walking toward the fire. I squinted into the distance, pretty sure that the two figures were Nathan and Sydney. Were they holding hands? The way they blurred together in the shadows, it was impossible to tell.

The two silhouettes came upon the circle of people surrounding the fire, and I saw that it *was* them. Unlike everyone else, Nathan hadn't bothered to wear a swimsuit. Instead, he had on his usual uniform of jeans and a band T-shirt, this time Radiohead. They weren't holding hands, but Nathan laughed at something Sydney said as they found a place on the sand across from Andrew and me. Then Nathan pulled one leg up to his chest, linking his hands casually around his knee as his eyes scanned the crowd.

I realized I was staring and tried to look away, but Nathan's gaze stopped on me, and the smile faded from his face. Seriously, if looks could kill.

Okay, so Nathan hated me. What else was new? And Ami was mad at me—she'd get over it. If not tonight, then by graduation for sure.

At least I had Andrew. I snuggled closer to him, and he casually draped his arm around my shoulders. "I love you," I said.

He looked down at me, and for a second I was afraid he wasn't going to say it back. It wasn't the first time I'd told him I loved him, but there was an extra edge to my voice this time that would have been hard to miss. But then he smiled. "I love you, too."

I didn't care what Ami said. Tonight was going to be perfect.

INTIMACY v. ISOLATION: A crisis
during young adulthood over finding love and settling
down. If this crisis is not favorably resolved, the young
adult will begin to avoid commitment, resulting in alien-
ation from others.

ANDREW and I drove back to his apartment in silence.
When I told Ami we were leaving, she said she would just
catch a ride with Joanna back to campus. I wanted to remind
her not to accept a ride with one of the surfer guys—no matter how cute they were. I wanted to laugh with her about
Sydney, whose ass was now demonstrating the ancient water-
sand conundrum after she toppled over in those tall heels.

Mostly, I wanted to talk to Ami about the possibly huge
implications of the night to come without her talking me out of
it or telling me anything I didn't want to hear. But if the pinched
look on her face was anything to go by, I was on my own with
this one.

I had also pretty much stranded Nathan at the beach. Andrew had been in such a hurry to leave, and the last thing I wanted to do was bother Nathan while he was with Sydney. So Andrew and I just left. I've never done anything like that before. And even though I was sure Sydney would be more than thrilled to give him a ride, it was still a crappy thing to do.

"That was a good party," Andrew commented, interrupting my thoughts, and I started.

"It was," I agreed after a pause. "We should do stuff like that more often."

Andrew grunted noncommittally.

"Not like all the time or anything," I clarified. "And of course school will come first." When Andrew made that sound, it usually had something to do with worrying about his six-course load.

"Maybe."

Those two syllables hung in the air for a few minutes. It was dark, and I was driving, so I couldn't really look at his face to see what he was thinking. "Andrew?"

"Yeah?" he asked absently.

I really wanted to ask where he saw our relationship going, or if he thought we could make it through the whole four years together. But it just seemed like a really awkward time to bring it up. So I just said the first thing that popped into my head.

"Is it true that Nathan's dad died?"

"Yeah," Andrew said. "Why do you ask?"

"No reason. I just heard something about it, and I guess I wondered."

For a few minutes it didn't seem like Andrew was going to say anything else, but then he spoke again. "This kid in my theory of knowledge class actually went to high school with Nathan," he said. "Apparently, everyone thought Nathan was really weird, because he only took a morning off for the funeral. That was it. He came back that afternoon, like nothing had happened."

"Oh," I said. "Well. People deal with grief in different ways, I guess."

"Obviously," Andrew said. "Pete was in Nathan's biology class, and one day, like a *month* after the funeral, Nathan just put his head down and started to cry. And not just a little bit. He was *sobbing*. Pete said it was really embarrassing."

I totally bought Nathan the unfeeling robot, but this was a new image of him. I didn't have a whole lot of time to think about it, though, as we reached the suites parking lot and the same anxieties about tonight came rushing back. As I unbuckled my seat belt and climbed out of Gretchen, I was still formulating the approach I would take to have a serious conversation with Andrew about our relationship. And by the time Andrew unlocked his front door and guided me inside, my heart was pounding, my palms felt sweaty, and I *still* couldn't form the words I wanted to say.

Nathan's guitar was leaning against the couch, and I brushed my fingers gently against the smooth wood. "You know,

I've always wanted to learn to play guitar," I said, fully aware that a babble was coming on but powerless to stop it. "When I was younger I played violin—I wasn't bad, either, if you consider being able to play Minuet in A Minor a musical tour de force. But the teacher was always on everyone's case, saying, 'You can lead a horse to water, but you can't make it drink,' and I was, like, well, 'a group is only as good as its leader—'"

Andrew cut me off. "Leigh, I know about your eighth-grade orchestra days, remember? I didn't ask you over here to talk about that," he said, in an attempt, I think, to sound sexy.

I knew that, of course. What wasn't so clear to me was why he *had* invited me. As much as I'd agonized over why he hadn't asked up to this point (we were still settling in, his classes were crazy, and I *know* his mom gave him a speech about how she's not paying for him to live in sin), I was questioning why he'd done so now.

We had been together for over a year, after all, and since coming to college, we'd had all the freedom in the world to do what we wanted. And yet, months had gone by without Andrew even *hinting* that he would like me to spend the night. I'd told myself it was for the best, since I toss and turn for hours before I fall asleep under the best conditions, and even more if I have to sleep in the same bed with another person. When I was nine I visited my cousin, and we had to share her water bed. It had been one of the most excruciating nights of my life.

"So why did you, exactly?" I asked.

Andrew crossed over to me, bringing a hand up to cup my cheek. "Come on, Leigh," he said. "You know why."

He started to kiss me, and all questions flew from my head as I leaned into him, my eyes fluttering closed. Andrew's kisses always make me feel like I'm taking a warm bath, one of those where your whole body relaxes and you feel yourself just sinking into it. I could taste the slight tang of the beer he'd sipped earlier, and even though I don't really like beer, it tasted kind of good on his lips.

In one deft motion, Andrew slipped the thin T-shirt I was wearing over my head, leaving me standing in my jeans and bikini top.

"What about—" I started to protest, but Andrew cut me off.

"He won't be home for hours," he said, "and even if he walks in, who cares?"

For a second I had the uneasy feeling that Andrew almost *wanted* Nathan to walk in, but for the life of me I couldn't figure out why. "*I* care," I said, pulling back from him. "Let's just move this into your room, okay?"

Andrew sighed, but he took my hand and guided me back to his room. There were a few awkward moments while I stood, still in my bikini top and totally conscious of the smell of salt water that clung to it, as he cleared his bed of papers and books. In a romance novel, he would have taken his arm and swept everything off in one passionate arc, but I really couldn't see Andrew ever doing something like that.

Instead he scooped up the books, stacking them neatly by the bed, and shuffled all the papers together. One caught his attention and he stopped to read it before I cleared my throat.

"Right," he said, and tossed the papers on his desk before reaching to take me in his arms again. I pressed against him, both of us standing while we kissed, until Andrew eased me back onto the bed. I felt his hand go to the button on my jeans, and I stiffened.

"Wait," I tried to say, but it came out sounding more like *mmph* as Andrew's lips crushed mine. For some reason I kept thinking about that last mentoring program, and the many questions the girls had asked. *What about abortion?*

Andrew slid the zipper down, and I tore my mouth from his. "Wait," I said, squirming beneath him, and then finally, "Andrew, wait!"

He raised himself up on one elbow, looking down at me with a combination of glazed passion and annoyance. "What?"

I licked my lips, trying to figure out how to phrase my next question before deciding the blunt approach would work best. "Um . . . do you have a condom?"

I could tell by the blank look on his face that he didn't. "Aren't you on the pill?" he asked.

I'd gone to the gynecologist right before the whole prom thing. Andrew and I had talked about it, and he was super-supportive of my going. He even looked up side effects and all that, and told me that the pill is supposed to help clear up skin, too. Way to go, science.

But then, the morning after what *should've* been one of the most momentous nights of our lives, you know what he said? "Do you know how many idiots had sex last night? Nothing like the anticlimactic aftermath of the oldest high school ritual to tank a relationship, huh? I'm so glad we didn't end up making that mistake."

And that was the last I'd ever heard of it. Until now.

Now Andrew was looking at me expectantly, waiting for my assurance that everything was taken care of. "Yes, but . . ."

"But what?"

This would be so much easier to do if I weren't lying beneath him, half naked. "The pill doesn't protect one hundred percent," I said cautiously, "and it doesn't protect at all against STDs."

Andrew's brows drew together. "You think I have an *STD*?" he asked incredulously.

I suddenly had a whole new respect for what we ask of thirteen-year-old girls. To expect them to actually discuss these kinds of things in the heat of the moment and practice safe sex was a lot harder than I had thought. And it wasn't just that I was worried about what my boyfriend would think, either. There was also a part of *me* that wanted to say: You know what? I'm tired of being the last virgin holdout when everyone else my age just wants to have fun.

"I don't think you do," I said, "but I just don't think it's safe unless we have a condom."

There. That hadn't been such a bad way to put it.

Certainly better than the whole *no glove, no love* claptrap. But Andrew wasn't buying it.

"Come on, Leigh," he said, not for the first time tonight, although this time his voice sounded a little whinier. "We've been together for a long time. Don't you think you can trust me?"

I didn't know. I had no idea if I trusted Andrew. Which could only mean one thing—*I didn't trust my own boyfriend.*

"Please, Andrew," I whispered, wishing I could find some kind of glitch in the universe that would allow the floor to swallow me whole.

For a few minutes Andrew just lay there, suspended above me. But then he rolled away, leaving me staring at his bare back.

"So, what?" he asked. "You want me to go to the store or something? I can pick up a condom if it's so important to you."

My eyes were burning, and I squeezed them shut. After a few moments I said, "Maybe it's just not the right time."

I felt the bed shift as Andrew turned to look at me. "When is it ever?" he snapped, as though somehow it was *my* fault we hadn't had sex up until now.

I can tell you one thing. A girl doesn't spend thirty dollars a month on birth control just to be a tease. And it is *not* easy to find one convenient time to take the damn thing, either, especially when you're a college student who keeps weird hours.

But if I was the one who wanted to take our relationship

to that level, why was I balking now? All I could think of was Ami's earlier question. *Do you really think it's going to be special?*

Suddenly I knew the answer—*no.* Not tonight, at least. I was reminded of the vague uneasiness I'd felt earlier at the party. It almost seemed like Andrew was out to prove something—what or to whom, I had no clue. But I wasn't so sure I wanted to be part of it.

"Please," I repeated now. "Let's just go to sleep, okay?"

I reached out tentatively to touch his back, but he shrugged me off. "Fine," he said. "Turn off the light."

He lay down, his back still to me, and I stared down at him for a few minutes before I stretched across him to switch off the lamp. "I really do love you, Andrew," I whispered into the darkness.

But he had already gone to sleep, or maybe he just didn't answer, and eventually I settled in next to him. I wished I could fall asleep that easily. I wished I had remembered to grab my shirt, which was still out in the living room someplace.

Most of all, I wished I could go back to that moment by the beach and just say, *Maybe another night.* And then leave it at that.

When I woke up the next morning, my back aching from sleeping on the edge of the bed, Andrew was gone. It was a Sunday, so I had no idea what would have compelled him to get out of bed before noon, but I tried not to dwell on it as I rifled through his dresser for a T-shirt to borrow. I pulled on an old "You Otter Give Blood" shirt before poking my head out the door, ensuring the coast was clear before stepping out into the common area.

Nathan's door was closed, but then, it usually was. I wondered if he had ever come home last night, but I quickly shoved the question out of my head.

It was possible that Andrew just stepped out for a moment and would be coming right back. In that case, I didn't want to miss my chance to talk with him. While I waited, I grabbed a box of Cinnamon Toast Crunch from the coffee table and a pint of milk from the minifridge.

I had almost finished my bowl when Nathan came out of his room, shirtless again. I mean, I know it's technically his apartment, but doesn't he have any common decency at all? He stopped when he saw me.

"You're still here," he said, more of a statement than a question.

There wasn't much to say to that. "Yeah . . ."

His eyes darted briefly behind me, and I realized that, to my utter mortification, my T-shirt from yesterday was probably still lying on the floor. But if it was, Nathan didn't comment, his gaze settling instead on the bowl in front of me. His eyebrows pulled together. "You're eating my cereal," he said.

I glanced down at the Cinnamon Toast Crunch, now just soggy broken-off pieces and cinnamon-speckled milk. "Sorry. I didn't know."

He snatched the box off the table. "No, you *didn't* know,"

he said, his voice heated. "You just assumed. You spend the night and suddenly you think you own the place."

That was hardly fair. "I do not. I was hungry, that's all. I'll buy you another box, if that makes you feel better."

Nathan rubbed the back of his neck, as though the conversation were giving him a headache. "I don't care about the stupid cereal," he muttered.

Then why make such a big deal of it? I assumed he was still mad at me because of the whole "self-righteous" comment and the way we left him at the party. "Look, about last night—"

But Nathan cut me off. "I don't want to hear it, all right? It was bound to happen sooner or later. Just don't eat my cereal," he said. "Okay?"

Unable to think of anything to say, I nodded.

With that, Nathan returned to his room. I didn't think he was still mad, since he shut the door quietly behind him. But I could hear him playing his guitar aggressively through the wall, each chord a jangling assault, and it sounded like he was pretty in touch with his core emotion. Somehow I didn't think he was writing a song about those cats he seemed to love so much.

Quietly, I rinsed out the offending cereal bowl, grabbed the evidence of last night's fiasco from the carpet, and slipped out the door. I ran down the steps and got into my Gremlin, driving out of the parking lot much unhappier than when I had driven in, but a lot wiser, too.

I had learned three things over the past twenty-four hours.

A) A girl should always carry her own condom. B) Sleeping in a waterbed with a relative you don't know very well is still *way* more comfortable than sleeping next to the boyfriend you just turned down for sex. And C) never *ever*, under any circumstances, touch a guy's Cinnamon Toast Crunch.

> **CONFOUNDING VARIABLES:** Variables
> that could differentially affect the dependent variable,
> usually as unintended independent variables

BY the time the next mentoring session rolled around, I was both dreading and anticipating yet another foray into the strange workings of the adolescent mind. (Okay, I know I'm only, like, five years older than these girls, but I've never watched *Hannah Montana*, and believe me, that makes all the difference.) On the one hand, last week hadn't been particularly enjoyable, what with the censorship and all. Then again, it would be kind of nice just to have the distraction.

As if the whole debacle with Andrew weren't enough, apparently we were supposed to pick our final paper topics for Intro Psych. Sometimes I think that professors don't understand that, just because students *pick* topics in early November, it doesn't mean they'll do any work on the paper until the week before it's due. Or at least, I won't. Ellen was the first one to raise her hand for *her* topic (portrayal of thinness in television commercials, by the way, which *totally* kicks ass. Now there's no way I can do something about stupid Internet personals).

At least Ami and I patched up our differences. Maybe Ami noticed how subdued I was that next morning, or maybe she just decided it was pointless to fight, because she eased right back into our normal pattern with very little disruption. Unlike me, Ami doesn't dwell—she just bounces right back.

I wasn't so sure if I could. Things with Ami were fine, and even the Intro Psych paper wasn't *really* a big deal. But I felt more conflicted than ever about Andrew. Ami thought he was kind of a jerk, and most everyone else told me that a long-term relationship from high school would never last through college. Then I would remember the good times, like when Andrew bought me a three-foot-tall stuffed bear, just because. Or the time that he stayed up all night with me, helping me study for the European history AP exam. And it wasn't like I didn't have my shortcomings—like the way that sometimes, when I get upset, I just shut down and stop communicating. But now, I'd lost the energy to fight about our relationship, or to fight *for* it. I wasn't exactly thrilled about the way he'd acted or the things he'd said, and he still hadn't formally apologized for any of it.

But then I thought—does he really have to? I may not be that good at calculus or trigonometry, but this was a simple arithmetic problem that anyone could solve. Boy and girl date for a year + boy asks girl home + girl is on birth control = sex. So why did I overthink it? Why did I have to go and throw in a bunch of variables that weren't there?

I tried to clear my head of my own problems so I could be a clean slate for whatever thirteen-year-old issues I had to deal with today. So far all we'd discussed was pregnancy, and I couldn't see any opportunity to get in any good body-image questions. Unless maybe I couched my real questions in mentoring-friendly ones, like *When you have a baby out of wedlock during your senior prom, are you scared of getting fat?*

Linda brought the group to attention with a clap of her hands. As with every other meeting up until now, she asked us to go around the circle and say our names. Since last week she wanted everyone to say their mythical first baby's name, this week she asked us all to include a brief story behind our own first names. I knew I had to come up with a lie quickly, because the truth was just way too damaging for me to spill.

See, one thing I don't usually tell people, something I've fought since grade school to keep *anyone* else from knowing, is that my first name isn't actually Leigh.

. . . It's Tuesday.

That's right, Tuesday. I've heard it all. Over the years I've been called Wednesday Addams's illegitimate sister, been sung the ' Til Tuesday song "Voices Carry," and even suffered through ill-thought-out references to Ruby Tuesday.

The worst of it is that I was actually born on a Thursday.

My parents, always more counterculture than I'm comfortable with, were going through a "Days of the Week" zodiac phase at the time. Apparently associations with Thursday include abundance, beliefs, wisdom, and understanding—all things my parents were confident they would cultivate in me. So they named me Tuesday to remind me to develop my other side, the one that can be bold and adventurous, brash and strong. Obviously I haven't had the best of luck so far, or I wouldn't be in the mess I am now.

It could have been worse. I could've been named Pisces or, if they were going through their Chinese zodiac phase, Sheep. Worse still, if they had discovered the Mayan calendar at that point I might've been called Galactic Activation Portal (apparently I am one—who knew?).

Now, as we went around the circle, each girl stated her name for what felt like the billionth time (which didn't mean I remembered them any better). Although I finally verified that Kathy was the name of the girl and not her prospective child, so that's a plus.

Then it was my turn. "My parents chose Leigh because it could be a girl's or a boy's name," I said in a partial truth. "They didn't want to know which I was until I was born, so they figured it would be easier just to pick one name."

I never totally got how people could do that. I'm all for

surprises, but the sex of my baby? Yeah, not a good thing to spring on a woman who just went through hours of agonizing labor.

All I can say is, thank God I was a girl. Can you imagine a boy named Tuesday Leigh? He'd probably grow up to be a middle-aged man with a room full of stuffed animals and a predilection for typing out actions with asterisks. *Grins.* *Comforts.* *Eats a sandwich.*

Well, maybe that's a little harsh. But he'd be messed up, anyway.

After everyone had a chance to talk, Linda made an announcement. "Today we're going to enter our second phase of the program." She looked around expectantly, as though we were all supposed to start whispering excitedly about the mysterious second phase. When that was obviously not going to happen, she continued.

"What I'm going to do now is pair you off, so every mentor has a mentee and vice versa. For this first session, you can just get to know each other—your likes and dislikes, hobbies, what's going on in your life. You'll be together all semester, so it's important to find some common ground."

At this point I'd really rather have had a Mentos than a mentee, but it didn't look like that was an option. I waited patiently for Linda to finish. "So when I tell you to, just find a partner who you're going to want to work with—"

I knew Linda already considered me her worst nightmare, but I couldn't let this go unchecked. "Uh, Linda?" I said, raising my hand. "Do you really think that we should pick our own partners?"

"What is it this time, Leigh?"

I couldn't say what was going through my mind, not with her looking like that. But her approach would lead to some people getting picked last, which is bad enough on a mandatory PE kick-ball team, when you know you can't kick the ball for crap, but much worse in a situation like this. Who wants to know that no college-age girl volunteered to guide them? And who wants a room full of thirteen-year-olds rating them second best at giving guidance?

"I just think it might be better if you picked," I said. "Since you have more experience with this kind of thing."

Linda beamed. "Well, all right. Let's see, then . . . Leigh, you and Rebekah can team up."

Then again, maybe I should have gotten off my high horse and just let Linda do it her way. Rebekah grimaced at me from across the room. Trying to hide my reluctance but probably failing, I picked myself up off the floor and moved over next to her.

"What's up?" I asked casually, then wondered if she'd think I was trying too hard to use hip lingo. It's impossible to tell how old these girls really think we are. Then there are times, like when I had to explain to Molly who Pearl Jam was, when I felt positively geriatric.

"Nothin'."

At least it wasn't totally monosyllabic. "Nothing, huh?

That's . . . cool." I winced. I was the worst mentor ever. "What'd you do today?"

"Not much."

I noticed she wore an Oakland Raiders T-shirt, and I figured I would take what I could get. "Are you a Raiders fan?"

She drew her brows together before glancing down at her shirt, obviously just making the connection. "Not really."

What happened? When I first met this girl, it was like I couldn't shut her up. Now, getting her to talk was like pulling teeth. I searched my brain for other California football teams. "What about the San Francisco 49ers, then? Or, um, the Rams? They're in L.A., right?"

Rebekah rolled her eyes. "Not for a jillion years," she said.

"Oh." I wished there were another way to get her to talk that *didn't* involve me looking like a dumbass. What was I thinking in the first place, talking about football? All I knew about the sport was that it looked like it hurt a lot.

I really wanted to ask her about the question she'd raised last meeting: *What about abortion?* If only she knew how much that question had haunted me for the past week.

But somehow I doubted that a girl who acted like the most mundane details about her day were state secrets would be dying to have a gabfest. And yet I was strangely determined to make this meaningful. It would take some guerilla tactics— maybe if I spilled something first. After all, what did I really have to lose? This girl was already looking at me as though I were some kind of pocket lint.

"Um . . . so I have this boyfriend," I said. "We've been dating since high school, and he's really awesome. Like, he's practically a genius."

"You want a medal?"

"No, that's not what I'm saying." I blew a couple strands of hair out of my face. "I mean, we've been having some problems lately. I just don't know what to do about it."

"What kind of problems?" she asked. She could've been saying, "Fine, tell me about the history of mental institutions in the U.S. if you insist," for all the interest she was showing. Then again, now that she was asking me point blank, I didn't know what to say. The whole reason I'd brought this up in the first place was to build intimacy and rapport, kind of like a good therapist does with a patient. Although it would *definitely* be inappropriate for therapists to start sharing details about their personal sex lives.

Whatever. It's not like I was licensed yet. I may as well get this kind of thing out of my system.

"I almost lost my virginity a few nights ago," I blurted, the words tumbling out of my mouth so fast there was no taking them back. I could feel my face turning red.

Myriad emotions crossed Rebekah's face—interest, disgust, disdain—before she settled on nonchalance. "So?" She shrugged. "I'm not your hairdresser, and you ain't my best friend, so it's none of my beeswax."

"I couldn't go through with it," I said.

Finally, a flicker of interest. "Oh, yeah?" she said. "Why not?"

"No condom, for one thing."

Rebekah made that smacking sound with her lips again, the one that sounded like the perfect onomatopoeic expression for 'scorn.' "I get it," she said. "Safe sex, don't do drugs, rah-rah-rah."

I shook my head. "This isn't an after-school special, if that's what you're thinking. But I couldn't get it out of my head that something might go wrong."

Suddenly Rebekah sat up straighter. "Wait a sec," she said, "just a few weeks ago you were on the pill. You showed it to me. So, what's up with *that*?"

Perfect. She couldn't get into R-rated movies yet, and suddenly she was Nancy Drew. But at least she was engaged in the discussion, and maybe there was a chance she'd open up a little. "I was—I am," I corrected. "But that's not one hundred percent foolproof, you know. And there's still—"

Linda had been strolling around the room, and she chose that moment to pass by Rebekah and me. She raised her eyebrows at us, and for a minute I worried she had heard the whole thing. I didn't need a sixth sense to tell me she wouldn't exactly do a jig over the idea of us talking about sex.

Then she moved on, and I let out my breath. I waited until she was across the room before leaning in to finish my sentence. Rebekah leaned in, too.

"There's still the problem of, you know, STDs," I whispered. "And some of them aren't curable, either."

Rebekah snorted. "In ten years we'll all have STDs," she said, blowing it off as though she were saying *Taco Bell will come out with the eight-layer nachos.* "Who was this guy you were hookin' up with, anyway? He a player?"

"No, we weren't hooking up. I told you, he's my boyfriend since high school. For over a year, actually." There, that should impress her. In middle school, we used to refer to people who were together for longer than a week as "married."

Another snort, this one louder. "That don't mean he's not a player."

Such cynicism in one so young. This is the point where most people would lament today's youth, waxing poetic about innocence lost or something like that. A part of me did find it sad. But another part of me found it almost . . . refreshing. Can cynicism be refreshing?

"Well, we've been together awhile," I said. "And he's not a player . . . I don't *think*, anyway."

"So what's the problem?"

Trust Rebekah to cut to the chase. "I told you," I said, feeling a little defensive now. "He didn't have a condom, and even though I doubt he has any diseases and there's very little chance I'd get pregnant, it just seemed like a bad idea to take the chance."

Rebekah stared at me for a long time, and then she shook her head. "Nu-uh," she said. "You're a liar."

"No, I'm not," I said automatically, although I didn't even know which part of the story she objected to.

Rebekah cocked one scarily arched eyebrow at me. "Oh, yeah?" she challenged. "So your boyfriend, who you've been with for a while and who you say ain't a player, wants to do it with you. You're on the pill. But you chicken out. Ain't no way that was just 'cause you were worried about a little ol' STD."

Okay, so I didn't really think that Andrew had any communicable diseases. Rebekah had seen that for what it was—a badly constructed veil to cover up the real issue. What that issue might be, *I* didn't even know yet.

"I guess I was scared," I admitted. "But I don't know why."

Rebekah nodded sagely. "I was scared, too, my first time."

Her *first* time? "How old are you? Thirteen?"

"Fifteen!" Rebekah corrected, affronted. "I started school late and was held back a bit, that's all."

I realized I didn't know this girl very well at all, and so far my plan to get her to open up had yielded more about *my* sex life (or lack thereof) than hers. "So when was your first time?"

"Last year," she said. "In the woods behind a Kmart by my house. It wasn't the greatest. The second time was better."

"Oh." I didn't know what else to say. "Same guy?"

"No." Rebekah cleared her throat, as though uncomfortable. "This boyfriend of yours, he ain't a player, but is he all right?"

She didn't give me an operational definition for "all

right," but I assumed she was asking whether or not he was good to me. "Yeah," I said. "Sometimes—most of the time. I love him a lot."

"And what about him?"

I looked at her, as if to say, what *about* him?

Rebekah twirled her finger impatiently. "Does he love *you?*" she said, as if to a child.

I froze. "He says he does," I said slowly. "But I . . . don't know."

Linda clapped her hands to bring everyone back to attention, and I barely registered anything else as she adjourned the meeting and dismissed the girls. Rebekah scooped up her backpack and hesitated, as though unsure if she should say something else. But then she mumbled a brief good-bye and ran out the door, leaving it swinging behind her.

I came out of my daze only when Linda came to stand by me. "Leigh?" she said. "You can go home now."

I looked up at her. "Why are these girls here?" I asked.

Linda paused, as though not considering the question so much as my motives for asking it. "They were referred by their guidance counselors," she said finally. "For being 'at risk.'"

"At risk for what? Teen pregnancy?"

"Not necessarily. Just at risk for . . . developing problems."

I guessed we would get to the other problems later, once the unit on teen pregnancy finally concluded. I still didn't feel like I was any closer to understanding Rebekah, and I was starting to feel further away from understanding myself.

I gathered my stuff and headed out in the hot afternoon sun toward the parking lot. I got into Gretchen and started her up, oblivious of the searing heat of the ignition as I turned the key.

Rebekah clearly had her own problems, and I was determined to figure them out. But I still couldn't believe I had been that honest with someone I barely knew, who hadn't even entered high school yet. After deciding I wanted to study psychology, it was only now that I had even *begun* to get the point behind therapy.

> **CONFIRMATION BIAS:** The tendency to seek evidence to support one's hypothesis rather than to look for evidence that will undermine the hypothesis

AMI was the one who discovered the results of the contest. She instant-messaged me from her desk, which was right next to mine. This is one of those things Ami does. She'll IM me to tell me we should walk to the campus store and get Dippin' Dots, to tell me when she's tired and going to bed, and to refer me to funny links she finds on the Internet. She does this even when leaning back in her chair, turning her head, and *talking* to me would work just as well. Better, even, since everything she types looks like it's gone through a scrambler.

Her message was one word, or rather, almost-word: COGNARULATIONSS. I looked over at her and rolled my eyes, but I typed back. THANKS . . . FOR WHAT?

It was only a few seconds before Ami's reply popped up. She's a fast typist, just not a good one. WINING 2END IN THE CNTETS.

That one took me a while to get. When I finally deciphered it, I swiveled my chair in one swift, outraged motion.

"Second place?" I said. "*Second place?* How could I get second place?"

Ami held up her hands in surrender. "Don't shoot the messenger," she said. "I thought second place was good. Just think, you weren't even going to enter until you threw something together in, like, an hour. So, second is not too shabby."

"You don't understand," I pressed. "I talked a big game at that stupid psych clique meeting that I was going to win it. This is a catastrophe."

Ami shrugged. "Politics," she said. "Everyone thought Andreea Raducan would get the gold medal, too, until she tested positive for drugs."

For my persuasive writing sample for English composition class, I'd written about the 2000 Olympics scandal involving the Romanian gymnast who won the gymnastics all-around competition, only to have her gold medal stripped when she tested positive for some common substance found in cold medicines. It totally traumatized me when I was a kid, but for some reason, Ami loves this story, and tries to work it into a lot of conversations where it doesn't really apply.

"I didn't take *drugs*, Ami," I pointed out. "Not even

accidentally. Where did you read about the contest, anyway?"

"Here, I'll send you the link." Ami rapidly typed out a new message and sent it over to me. After correcting the spelling of one of the words, I was directed to a campus news site.

There it was: "Students take Second and Third Places in State Writing Contest." I clicked on the article and skimmed it just enough to know that, sure enough, I had won second place in the underclassmen research division for my paper on cognitive-behavioral therapies for treating bulimia. At least Ellen hadn't won anything, but still. The jackass who had taken first was some Northern California girl for her paper titled "Religious Imagery and Symbolism in Joseph Conrad's *Heart of Darkness.*"

Was she kidding? I had read *Heart of Darkness* in, like, tenth grade, and it didn't take a genius to catch the reference to asceticism that appeared on the first page. I believe the exact words were that Marlow "resembled an idol." What do you need, a two-by-four?

"I'm so dead," I muttered.

Ami came to stand behind me, reading the text over my shoulder. "Don't be such a drama queen," she said. "So you didn't win—big deal! You still get to go to a sweet awards ceremony in San Francisco. With . . ." she squinted at the screen. "Some guy named Li Huang. Who is Li Huang?"

I didn't have the faintest idea. Apparently he had won third place in the underclassmen creative writing portion for his poem, "Cherry Blossoms," and he was the only other person from my school listed.

"You realize his name is Li, right?" I said. "We're going to be name twins. Oh, my God, I am *so* dead."

Ami sighed. "I thought Chinese people switched their names. Is he Chinese? If he is, he'd be going by Huang, not Li."

"Still," I said. "Someone will pick up on it, and we'll be Leigh and Li for the rest of the trip. We'll sound like a moving company, or a personal injury law office or something."

"When is the ceremony?"

That was the other thing. The awards ceremony was *this* weekend. That meant in only a few days! Who gives only a few days' notice? I guess they figured that people would be so overjoyed by winning their stupid contest that they'd just cancel plans.

"Maybe if you could come with me," I said. "Then the whole thing wouldn't be so bad."

Ami pursed her lips, considering it. "I'd totally do it," she said. "But what reason could we possibly give for me crashing the party? It's not like *I* won anything."

I checked my e-mail and, sure enough, there was an e-mail already sent by Tim Dell, our special events coordinator/admissions officer/director of student affairs. (When I say Stiles is a small liberal arts college, I mean *small*.) I had never personally interacted with him before, but I guess he was the one who handled this kind of thing.

Dear Leigh and Li (hey, isn't that funny!)

It was already starting.

First off, congrats on your achievements! I'm sure both of your works were stellar to receive such recognition! As you may have already gleaned, the awards ceremony is coming up on us fast— which means we must act quickly!

"Is this guy on speed?" I asked.

I figure we can all caravan to San Francisco together—who can say road trip! Don't worry about hotel accommodations—I've already booked two rooms at the hotel that's hosting the ceremony. Leigh, you can stay in one and Li and I will stay in the other. Don't you two get mixed up, now!

"I think I'm going to be sick."

Anyhoo, e-mail back with whether or not you can make the ceremony—although I expect you both to be there! It's not often we are so honored— much less twice honored!

Yikes. A road trip with this guy was going to be like watching a cheerleading competition on fast-forward. I was more determined than ever to get Ami to come with me.

"Look," I said, "it even says right there in the e-mail—I have my own room. So, what would be the problem with you staying with me?"

"Hey, like I said, I'm all for it," Ami said emphatically. "But I'm not so sure about this Tim guy. Don't you think the school would care that they were giving a free trip to someone who wasn't even supposed to be there?"

I glared at Ami. "You just don't want to be cooped up in a van with Tim 'anyhoo' Dell."

"Well, yeah." She shrugged. "Who would?"

Neither Ami nor I was superexcited at the prospect of spending a whole weekend with my name twin and the most exuberant forty-year-old man on earth, but I did eventually wrangle a way for her to come to San Francisco with me.

At first, Tim, who I thought couldn't be down on *anything*, wasn't really going for it. He seemed very reticent in a reply e-mail to my question regarding Ami, evidenced by the fact that there was only one exclamation point in the whole thing. And it had come at the end, after the word *thanks*. Not a very promising start.

But then I reminded him that it wasn't like I'd be sharing a room with him and my name twin, anyway, and that it was probably dangerous for a girl to stay in a hotel room by herself in the City. That's right, I capitalized it. As if Stiles were totally rural, being just outside of Los Angeles and all. Ha.

So Ami was coming to San Francisco with me, which was the only thing that made the trip palatable. I was even beginning to look forward to it a little as a welcome break from everything else in my life.

The night before we were to leave, I went over to Andrew's to say good-bye. We hadn't spoken much since the night of the party—a brief conversation or two on the phone, a single uncomfortable cup of coffee grabbed at the Toad's Monocle a few days ago after we ran into each other. He said he had just been really busy, and I claimed the same, and I wasn't sure if neither of us was lying or if we both were.

Nathan was the one to let me in the suite again. Only this time, he was wearing a shirt. I didn't know if I was disappointed or relieved.

"Where's Andrew?" I said, holding my purse in front of me as if it were made of Kevlar and the common room were unfriendly gang turf. Which, face it, it kind of felt like right now.

"Shower," Nathan said. He sat down on the couch, and he seemed almost surprised when I took the chair across from him.

I blushed as I realized what he must be thinking. It wouldn't be that abnormal for a longtime girlfriend to just poke her head in the bathroom and say hi. Maybe he even thought I would want to join Andrew in the shower. I wondered suddenly what Andrew had told him about our relationship. I wondered what, if anything, Andrew had said about our one aborted attempt at sex. Did Nathan think it was weird that here we were, freshmen in college, and Andrew and I didn't even sleep in each other's rooms?

Because I did. Think it was weird, I mean. But the alternative had just seemed so much stranger.

"Congratulations, by the way." Nathan's words jolted me out of my thoughts, and it took me a few moments to realize he must be referring to the contest.

"Thanks," I muttered. I didn't bother to ask how he knew about it. After that article, everyone seemed to know about it.

"You must be pissed," he said. And then, at my blank face, added, "since you told all those girls that you were going to win it."

How did he know that? I assumed it was from Sydney—that girl had a big mouth. Then, as if reading my mind (or my uncomfortable posture), Nathan said, "You mentioned it in the car on the way to the party." Now it was his turn to look ill at ease. "Never mind. All I meant to say was, congratulations on the second-place thing."

"Fake it 'til you make it, right?" I said. It was supposed to sound like a really cool, breezy thing to say, but it came out sounding a little bitter. Nathan started leafing through a Fender catalog as though I had ceased to exist.

Finally, Andrew emerged from the shower, looking like some kind of Ralph Lauren towel commercial and smelling like the sandalwood soap he uses. He paused as Nathan and I both looked up.

"Leigh," Andrew said. Try as I might, I couldn't analyze his tone. Was he happy to see me?

"Hey," I replied. Then, because the sight of him in a towel was a little distracting, I cleared my throat. "Um . . . is it a bad time?"

"No," he said, and then as if to emphasize his point, he repeated it again. "No, not at all. Let me just get changed and I'll be right out. Okay?"

"Okay."

Andrew changed quickly, sparing me much more interaction with Nathan. When he came out of his room, he inclined his head for me to come to him. I rose from the couch and slid past him, but not before I caught his words to Nathan.

"Oh, I almost forgot," Andrew said, one hand braced against the doorjamb. "Sydney called earlier. She wants you to return her call ASAP."

Andrew was one of those people who pronounced it "a-sap" instead of saying each individual letter. I don't know why, but that had always kind of irked me.

Nathan didn't even glance up from his guitar catalog, making me wonder whether he was going to call her back or not. Certainly he didn't seem in any rush, but maybe he was just playing hard to get. Do guys play hard to get?

Andrew's hand on my back guided me into his room, but I was still agonizing over Nathan and Sydney's supposedly budding relationship. If Sydney and Nathan hooked up, did that mean she was going to be over at the apartment all the time? Was I going to have to hear sex noises? Were she and Nathan going to do it before Andrew and I did?

I was starting to feel a little sick.

"So," Andrew said. He sat at his desk, flipping open a textbook as though he'd much rather read about man's eternal struggle than talk with his girlfriend. "What's up?"

It took me a few moments to remember why I had come in the first place. "I guess you've already heard about the contest."

Andrew got that wrinkle in the middle of his forehead that he gets when he's trying to remember something. "I don't think so," he said. "Did you tell me about it?"

Maybe everyone *didn't* know about it. "No, I didn't . . . I just thought maybe you would have read about it or something."

Andrew shook his head. "You know how busy I am, Leigh," he said. "Did you win?"

"Kind of," I said. "I got second place."

He smiled, reaching out to cup my knee. "Well, that's still good."

"Yeah," I said lamely. "Anyway, I'm leaving tomorrow for this awards ceremony in San Francisco. I just wanted to let you know."

"Oh, okay." Then his eyebrows rose, as though hitting upon an idea. "Do you want me to come with you?"

The idea was so sweet I felt immediately guilty for not having thought of it myself. I just hadn't predicted that Andrew would *want* to come.

"I don't know," I said. "Maybe if—"

"Because, you know, I've been thinking," he said, taking my hand in his. "I know things that night didn't go the way either one of us planned."

You can say that again.

"But I know I can make it right," he continued. "I even went out and bought a box of condoms—ribbed. That's what the guy at the store said girls would like."

That should have excited me, or aroused me, or something. But the word *ribbed* coming out of Andrew's mouth, along with the knowledge that he had actually consulted with some slimy convenience store clerk on what *girls* (plural!) would like, just made me feel . . . sleazy. I jerked my hand back in an unconscious gesture of repulsion.

"It's not about the *condoms*," I said, my voice dropping on the last word in mortification. "It was never about that, not really."

"Then what, Leigh?" Andrew threw up his hands in disgust. "I just don't get you. We talk about having sex and we agreed we were ready six *months* ago, and then you get all touchy about the condom thing. Then I get the condoms and you tell me it's something else. So what is it?"

Maybe I *was* building this up too much. People lost their virginity all the time, just fooling around on a golf course like in this one romance novel I read, or having one drunken night with someone random. Maybe if I just did it the one time, I would realize how stupid I was being and be able to let go of these inhibitions. The very thought put a metallic taste in my mouth.

"Let me ask *you* a question," I said quietly. "Why now?"

"What?"

Patiently, I repeated myself. "Why now? Like you said, we've been going out a long time. And you never really showed much interest in getting me into bed—in fact, I started to wonder if you wanted me at all."

I didn't realize how true it was until I said it. Most of the last year had been spent wondering what was wrong with me that, after a date, Andrew seemed satisfied with a ten-minute make-out session before dropping me off at my house. It's not like I wanted to do him on his heated seats, but shouldn't he want *something* more?

Now suddenly it was like sex had reached DEFCON 5, and we had to act immediately or fear total nuclear meltdown. It made no sense.

"Of course I wanted you, Leigh," Andrew sighed. "I still want you. I just want to be able to have sex with my girl-friend without you turning into a psycho every time it comes up."

He still hadn't answered my question, but I didn't really care anymore. Suddenly I felt like if I didn't get out of that room I would choke. I could feel how neurotic I was being, but

I couldn't stop it. And I just couldn't watch him turn into more of a jerk.

"Maybe this weekend will be good for us," I said. "We'll both take time away and reassess everything. I'll try to work out whatever's preventing me from taking this step. And while I'm doing that, you figure out why it's so important that we do this *now*, after a year of waiting."

I moved to kiss Andrew, before deciding that it might be awkward, given the situation, and so I turned away at the last minute and ended up kind of slobbering on his chin. Clearly, this was *less* awkward.

Closing Andrew's door behind me, I stepped back out into the common room. Nathan was on the phone. I was about to excuse myself quietly when I heard him say, "Sure, I'll be there."

Was it just me, or did he glance at me and slightly angle his body away when he said that? You'd think he was on the phone with the Rosenbergs, the way he was murmuring into the mouthpiece.

"It's no problem at all," he said. This time he definitely gave me a look that could be considered "squirrelly," to quote Ami. Apparently there's a guy in her touch art class who gives her that look whenever she starts talking about how her painting reflects her vaginal space. After the first time, she kept it up just as kind of an experiment, and so now her professor wants her to join FMLA (the Feminist Majority Leadership Alliance, or, as Ami called it after one meeting, Fem-La-Di-Dah) and perform in *The Vagina Monologues*.

"Meet you at eight, then," Nathan continued. By this point, I was openly staring. "All right. Bye, Sydney."

He hung up the phone, and I just gaped at him. Sydney? *Sydney?* I hadn't expected him to actually return her call. I knew I wouldn't have. He was going to hang out with Sydney?

Wait. Were they *going out?*

Nathan cleared his throat. "It's, uh—" he started to say.

Just then Andrew's door flew open, and I turned. Andrew was standing in the doorway, blinking at both of us.

"What's up?" he asked Nathan. Then, to me: "You're still here?"

"I was just leaving," I said. At that point, you couldn't have paid me to stick around.

ADAPTATION: The process by which people learn new information, composed of two complementary processes. In assimilation, people interpret new information with their existing schemas. In accommodation, they modify schemas to incorporate new information that doesn't fit.

HOW Linda at Simms Middle School found out about the contest, I have no idea. But at the mentoring meeting before I left for San Francisco, she seemed totally determined to make me into some kind of heroine for college-bound youth.

"Our very own Leigh won second place in a statewide contest," she announced, beaming. It was as if the session when I'd practically forced the girls into having premarital sex (according to her) had never happened. Linda was all psyched to make me an example. "Why don't you tell everyone how you did it, Leigh?"

"Uh . . ." Even though I'd stood up in front of everyone

two weeks earlier, somehow this seemed way worse. "Hard work, mostly."

From the back of the room, I heard a snort, and I just knew it was Ellen. I'd recognize that nasal disdain anywhere.

Then again, maybe a little shameless self-promotion never hurt anyone. "Mostly, it was sheer perseverance. Even if people doubt you, or call you a liar, remember that you can achieve anything you want. Well, almost anything. You know, if there wasn't some stupid girl who wrote some cookie-cutter piece-of-crap essay about *Heart of Darkness*."

And there it was: the widened eyes and pinched lips, as Linda remembered that I was not to be trusted with public speaking. "Okay," she said, placing her hands on my shoulders and practically forcing me to sit back down. "That's right; you can do anything you set your hearts on. Including being a mother, but let's wait another ten years or so before you set your hearts on *that*."

If subtle segues were a martial art, Linda would be a black belt.

"Still," Linda continued, "a couple of weeks ago, it seemed like you all had a lot of questions about raising a child, and started to see just a sliver of the responsibility that a baby represents. So I thought, to give you a better idea . . ." Linda reached behind her, into a large cardboard box. "Babies!"

For a second my heart stopped, as I imagined a box filled with actual human babies. Oh my God, I thought, she went to some unsuspecting, underdeveloped country and pretended to be a celebrity so she could bring home a box of their children.

But then she pulled out a baby doll, and my heartbeat returned to normal. At least, until I got a good look at its face. Now I knew what Chucky would've looked like as an infant.

"There are only five of them, so you girls are going to have to take turns," Linda said. "But these dolls will help you realize how much work real babies are. Just like real babies, these dolls cry, eat, and wet themselves. When they cry, you'll need to soothe them. And if you're too rough with them, they'll be harder to soothe."

Okay. I think I had one of these dolls when I was a kid— a little more darling and a little less Damien, maybe, but still.

"Now, don't be too rough," Linda said, handing the first baby to Kathy, "because these dolls cost five hundred dollars each."

Five hundred dollars? My Wets-Herself Wanda had cost, like, two dollars at a garage sale. For that kind of money, we could've bought a year's supply of birth control for each girl. Or, at the very least, we could've bribed them to keep their pants on.

I watched Linda pass another baby to Rebekah, and I half expected Rebekah to sneer at the whole exercise. But instead, she cradled the little robotic demon child in her arms, turning to a friend to say, "I'll name him Tyrone. After his daddy."

Just when I thought it couldn't get any worse. I rolled my eyes and glanced across the room to see Ellen doing the same thing. It was fleeting, but for a second we were actually on identical wavelengths.

"All right," Linda said once all the babies had been assigned. "There are five babies. I'd like to form five groups around these babies, so if you don't have one, please find a girl who does and join her group. Try to spread out evenly."

This time, I actively chose Rebekah, plopping down on the floor right next to her. She was rocking the baby, a beatific smile on her face. I saw where the baby got his demonic DNA from.

"Whatever happened to bags of sugar?" I asked no one in particular. "Or eggs?"

"Try the grocery store," Ellen said, forming a little circle with Rebekah and me. Molly, who had just come to join us, giggled.

"No, I meant—" I started, and then shook my head. "Never mind."

Linda outlined the main rules of having the babies: A) don't be rough (again, she mentioned the money, and again, I thought that I wouldn't trust a middle schooler with my troll collection, much less a *five-hundred-dollar* baby); B) although the school has said they'll allow the girls to bring the babies to class, if there's any disruption, the babies are to be given to the guidance counselor and picked up at the end of the day (bet the counselor will love that); and C) don't leave the baby unattended, and don't entrust the baby to anyone else's care (except school officials, obviously).

Which is totally artificial, if you think about it. I mean, even young single mothers can hire babysitters, can't they? Whatever. There was so much else wrong with this scenario I guess it was a question of picking your battles.

Apparently, we were just supposed to sit in a circle and talk about babies, without any misguided direction or blatantly inappropriate guidance. It was a total free-for-all. I cleared my throat, trying to think of a way to maybe broach the subject of body image in adolescents (is there a delicate way to ask about compensatory behaviors like taking laxatives, or is that one of those things you have to warm up to?), but Ellen cut in.

"So, Leigh," she said with a smirk. "Second place, huh?"

I shrugged. "Politics," I said. "Sometimes gymnasts have their gold medals stripped, even when everyone knows it's all the Romanian team doctor's fault."

"What?"

"Forget about it," I said. "So, Molly, how's school been?"

"Okay," she said. "What's a Romanian?"

Rebekah glanced up from her robo-baby, and for a second I thought her attention had actually been grabbed by the mention of Romania. Because *that's* the icebreaker I've been waiting for—Eastern European gymnastics powers. Yeah, right. "Weren't you gonna do it with your boyfriend or some-thin'? What happened with that?"

Ellen arched an eyebrow at me. I've always been jealous of people who can do that. "Wow," she said. "Sounds like you've been doing some great mentoring. Way to go, Leigh."

Molly's head swung between the two of us like she was watching a tennis match. "Do what?" she asked. "What are you guys talking about?"

Seriously, why is she even here? This mentoring program can only corrupt her. Especially my group, since sex seems to follow me wherever I go. And, yes, I get the irony.

"Anyway," I said. "I think we should get back on task. Who here wants to have a baby, like, right now?"

"I don't," Molly said, wrinkling her nose. "They're smelly. And loud."

"So wait," Ellen said. "Have you and Andrew never done it?"

"Babies *are* smelly," I said. "And loud. Good call, Molly."

"Who's Andrew?" Molly asked. "And done *what*?"

Rebekah rolled her eyes. "Have sex, retard. You in kinder-garten or somethin'?"

If it meant I could go into labor at this exact *moment* and not have to participate in one more second of this conversa-tion, I would totally have a baby. Of course, that would mean I would actually have to have sex in the first place.

"I just can't believe that," Ellen said. "Haven't you been dating for, like, a year? My fiancé and I have only been together for six months, and we—"

She broke off, I guess remembering our audience. Or else remembering that it's no fun to be on the *giving* end of juicy information.

"Oooh, snap," Rebekah said. "Even the girl with the stick up her ass is gettin' some."

"Excuse me," Ellen said, "I do *not* have . . . that is, I'm not uptight."

"I don't even know what that word means," Molly said. "Does it have something to do with the fact that you dress like my mom? 'Cause if so, then you *are* uptight."

"Stay in school, Molly," Ellen barked.

Okay, this was totally getting out of hand. "Just chill, okay? That goes for everyone. Sex is not a competition, all right? I'm not looking to 'get' any. Which might be my whole problem, but you know what? It's not your business."

"It's *my* business," Rebekah said. "You the one who made it my business, last week."

"Oh, yeah?" I tried to do my best eyebrow arching at her, but I'm pretty sure all I did was squint one of my eyes shut. "Then do you care to explain your abortion question?"

Rebekah jutted her chin out. "No," she said.

"Awesome," I said drily. "And, Molly?"

"Yeah?"

"A Romanian is someone from Romania," I said. "It's a country in Eastern Europe, famous for its gymnastics, Gypsies, and Transylvania."

"Oh," she said. "Like the devil?"

"That's Tasmania," I corrected. "Transylvania is the place where vampires supposedly come from. Also, Rebekah's demon baby."

Rebekah glared at me, and at that moment Linda declared the mentoring session at an end. In just a half hour, I'd taught Molly some relatively useless geography, told Ellen to shut up, and insulted Rebekah's fake child.

And I used to think I wouldn't be any good at mentoring.

> **DREAM ANALYSIS:** A technique that examines
> dreams, holding that the defenses are relaxed and the
> mind is freer to express forbidden wishes and desires
> during dream states

FIVE minutes into the road trip, I knew it was going to be an excruciating couple of hours. This revelation came, not coincidentally, at the exact same time that Tim whipped out his Cirque du Soleil sound track and popped it in the van's CD player.

"It's not a road trip without music!" he trilled, turning up the volume on the tribal drumbeats and what sounded suspiciously like a piccolo.

Ami and I sat in the last backseat, with one extra bench seat between us and Tim, who was driving, and Li, who insisted on sitting up front. Tim asked Ami a bunch of questions, and Ami really played up her time in New York City to show how tough a bodyguard she'd be for me.

Which is a total laugh, considering that A) Ami's barely over five feet tall, and B) she only spent four days in New York City over the summer, and she mainly spent it shopping and going to see a musical version of some popular '80s movie.

"I think I'm going to have a breakdown," Ami said, pressing her fingers in her ears.

"Not if I get to it first," I said.

We spent most of the trip amusing ourselves by flipping through a *Cosmo* Ami had brought with her. There was a spirited debate over whether the "confessions" were real or fake—I said they were bogus, but Ami stood by them—and that deteriorated into an analysis of all confessionals in women's magazines.

I could see Tim eyeing us in the rearview mirror, and so I wasn't surprised when he reached to turn the music down.

"What are you girls up to?" he called out.

Considering at that point the magazine was open to a page of tips on getting the most out of your sex toys, I wasn't sure how to answer that question. "Um, not much," I said.

"You know, Ami, I spent some time in the Big Apple myself!"

"Oh, yeah?" she said, making a face at me.

"Have you ever seen those I Love New York shirts?" he asked. "But instead of the *word* 'love,' there's a big red heart? I bought one of those in the airport the last time I went. 'Cause it's so true!"

Is he serious? she mouthed at me. I shrugged.

"Uh . . . yeah," she said. "I heart NY. I bought one of those from some vendor on the street for, like, five dollars."

I choked on a laugh.

"Ooh, on the street! No wonder Leigh wanted you to come along," Tim exclaimed. "You're a woman of the world."

A weird guttural voice was now coming softly from the radio and, obviously eager to change the subject, Ami capitalized on it. "Is that French?" she asked.

Tim turned up the music a little. "Ah, Ami, obviously you've still got a lot to learn. But don't be embarrassed—a lot of people think that! It's actually a mystical language created entirely for Cirque du Soleil. I can understand this song, but alas, I am not yet fluent in all of it!"

What a freak. He turned the music back up all the way, and Ami and I went back to giggling in the backseat, although this time it was over Tim and his music rather than the *Cosmo* in our laps.

"I Love New York?" Ami whispered. "Really?"

"Hey, a girl who can buy T-shirts in midtown is the kind I need by my side in the big, bad world of Rice-A-Roni."

Ami giggled, turning the page from the sex toys article, but the next one wasn't any better. My own smile faded a little as I saw it.

"The Secret to Being Good in Bed." I didn't even have to

skim the article to figure out what it would say. For one thing, I'm sure a willingness to have sex at *all* was a prerequisite.

Although there were variations, all these articles basically boiled down to the same thing: self-confidence. Men don't care as much about technique in bed as they do about self-confidence and enthusiasm. They want a woman who's less concerned with sucking in her stomach and more interested in . . . well, you know.

It was the type of article that was meant to reassure those women who were already sex goddesses, while ignoring those who were nothing like that and had no clue *how* to be.

Just once I'd like to see an article called "Who Cares About Sex Anyway?" or "Caution: The Ultimate Aphrodisiac."

After a swift glance at my face, Ami shut the magazine and slipped it into her duffel bag. I'm sure she's dying of curiosity about what happened between Andrew and me, but I'm not ready to discuss it with her yet. In a weird way it was easier to discuss it with Rebekah, who didn't know the situation. I knew Ami was a little hurt by my not talking about it, but I couldn't help it.

Up in the front seat, Li was pointing at something outside the window, and Tim turned down the music again to figure out what was going on.

"Why that person standing outside with sign?" Li was asking, gesturing wildly toward a man on the curb. Ami and I both craned our necks to look out the window. It was one of those typical "grand opening" shindigs at some Mexican restaurant, complete with a man wearing a sombrero and a sandwich board that read EAT AT JORGE'S!

"He's advertising," Tim said, and I could tell by the tone of his voice that he didn't see what the big deal was, either.

This answer didn't appease Li. "Why they don't get real sign?" Li asked, flabbergasted.

"It's just for attention," I explained. "They hire a person to do it so people driving by will notice it more."

"Oh." For a moment Li was silent while he thought about this. "He get paid money?" he asked.

"Yeah," I said. "He gets paid money."

Even though I was staring at the back of his head, I could practically see the dollar signs light up in Li's eyes. One thing I'd learned in the half hour we'd been in the van was that Li was *very* concerned with money. It was, like, all he talked about.

"How much money?" he asked eagerly.

What was I, the census bureau? "I don't know," I said.

"Not much," Tim added. "But more than minimum wage, I would hope!"

Li made a pooh-poohing sound. "Not worth it," he proclaimed. "I only do for lots of money!"

During the trip Li asked how much money he could make operating a tollbooth, driving a delivery car, and selling rugs by the side of the road. He even made Tim tailgate a car that advertised how to "Be Your Own Boss" while he wrote down the phone number.

In my personal favorite query, he asked Tim how much

the college would pay him to be a professor. Tim was taking him seriously until it became obvious that Li wanted the college to hire him *now*, before he'd even graduated. Tim had to explain to him that you can't simultaneously be a student and a professor at the same school.

When we were only a few miles from the hotel, we had to make an emergency stop at a Kinko's. Tim sprang it on us that we would have to do a reading of our work at the awards ceremony, which neither of us was prepared to do. I wasn't in such bad shape. I'd brought a copy of my paper just to look over, and I was pretty good at improvising presentations. Since all I had to do was read an excerpt from it anyway, I'd be fine.

Li, on the other hand, started freaking out. He hadn't brought a copy of his poem, and there was only a slight hope that it had been saved in his e-mail somewhere. So on the back of the paper with the "Be your own boss" phone number, Li started trying to recompose the poem. I had no idea how the original one had sounded, but the new one was pretty hilarious. I wondered if the contest officials would realize he was reading a different poem.

We pulled into the Kinko's so that Li could check his e-mail and retrieve the original. Because of the delay, we weren't going to have the chance to drop by our rooms first, and Ami and I went into the Kinko's bathroom to change into our awards ceremony clothes. Of course in Ami's case, that meant some kind of crazy getup complete with leggings, a polka-dot dress, and huge silver earrings shaped like saxophones.

Whenever I check out Ami's dress style, I teeter for a few minutes between horror and admiration. This time I watched her pour some kind of heavy gold glitter eye makeup all over her eyelids before I finally settled on admiration. "I just don't know how you do it," I said, shaking my head.

Ami didn't pretend to misunderstand. "It's not as easy as it looks," she said. "Contrary to how it might appear, I don't throw on whatever I feel like. This is actually a very well-planned ensemble."

I was sure it was, although I had personally witnessed Ami tossing clothes out of her dresser drawers, flinging them over her shoulders like she was in some *I Love Lucy* episode, and then wearing whatever happened to land on top.

I'd borrowed Ami's flats again, but other than that, I looked pretty much the same as I always did. Slightly nicer long-sleeved shirt, with slightly nicer black pants. That's about as far as I'm willing to go for this thing.

Ami and I finally emerged from the bathroom to find Li asking the Kinko's copy guy how much he made working there. The pimply-faced kid was clearly uncomfortable, but doing his best to hide it. I decided to rescue him.

"Come on, Li," I said, gesturing to the paper in his hand. "Now that you have your poem, we should get going. We'd hate to be late to the awards ceremony."

Li's face brightened at the prospect. He was really hyped to read his stupid cherry blossoms poem. Not that I knew for a fact it was stupid—the reworking of it had been, but perhaps

169

it was unfair to judge based on a cheap copy done in fifteen minutes while sitting in a Dodge Caravan. I'm sure Sylvia Plath's "Ariel" would have sounded equally inane in such conditions.

Or maybe I was giving Li too much credit.

It wasn't long before we reached the hotel where the awards ceremony was being held, and we snuck in the back, hoping no one would notice that we were a little late. Luckily, the keynote speaker was just wrapping up his speech, which appeared to be something about the many different ways that we use writing. Like that hasn't been done to death.

They had to go through several categories before they got to us, so Ami and I amused ourselves by whispering snide comments about each contestant. Tim shot us quelling looks—or at least, I *think* that's what he was going for. It was hard to tell, since his face is so open and unlined, with eyes that always twinkle. It's hard to take a forty-year-old Boy Scout seriously.

One thing I noticed as people got up to present their papers—only the first- and second-place winners actually read excerpts of their work. That meant that I would still have to read, but Li wouldn't. I glanced over at him, expecting to see profound disappointment on his face. Hell, *I* was a little disappointed for the kid. He had just seemed so pleased to get the opportunity to read his stupid (or genius that sounded stupid when rewritten in a van) poem. But he just stared straight ahead, the smile on his face as wide and steady as though he were posing for a picture.

Finally it got to underclassman research. I sat up straighter in my chair, and Ami gave my arm a little squeeze.

The crane-looking woman behind the podium read out my name. "And in second place, we have Leigh Nolan with her essay entitled 'Food for Thought.' Congratulations, Leigh."

I was already halfway out of the row, Tim giving me the thumbs-up as I passed, but I couldn't muster a thumbs-up in return. "Food for Thought?" That's it?

The title of my paper was *supposed* to be "Food for Thought: Cognitive Approaches to Treating Bulimia." In that context, my title made sense—was clever, even. But without the subtitle, it didn't sound clever. It sounded like one of those idiotic online zines—the ones that list supposedly existential questions like: *Why does Hawaii have interstates?* or *Why do you drive on a parkway but park in a driveway?*

Weakly, I shook crane woman's hand and stepped behind the podium.

"The title—" I began—and then I had to stop to adjust the microphone. When I spoke again, it was weird to hear my voice boom out, ricocheting around the room, and I almost jumped back.

"The full title of my paper is actually 'Food for Thought: Cognitive Approaches to Treating Bulimia,'" I said. "I'll give everyone a second if you'd like to pencil that in your program."

I waited, but I didn't see anyone reaching for a writing implement of any kind. Finally I cleared my throat.

"All right, so I'm going to read for you the last section

of my paper, which discusses various cognitive aspects of bulimia," I said, and began reading. Despite the somewhat shaky beginning, I could feel the audience start to get into it—or at least, as into a research paper about eating disorders as you can get.

In my opinion, the study in the excerpt I chose to read was a particularly interesting one. Basically, it discussed bulimics' performance on a Stroop task, which is a task where words are presented in different colors. The participant is supposed to say the color, not the word, but sometimes, if it's a word that "interferes," they hesitate on the color or read the word instead.

In bulimics, there have been several studies that showed that they tend to perform worse on Stroop items that deal with body image. But a subsequent study found that bulimics also performed poorly when presented with other threat words that did not reflect eating or weight, such as "pain" or "isolation," thus suggesting some kind of emotional component to the disorder other than mere body-image distortions.

Because my paper was originally written for my high school psychology teacher and I had apparently not taken that into consideration when I adapted it for the contest, I had to ad-lib a little spiel about the Stroop task that had never been formally outlined in the paper. It's just one of those things that anyone affiliated with psychology should *know*, like Milgram's conformity studies or Freud's obsession with sex and mothers.

All in all, it went pretty well. I sat down to a round of

applause that, after I listened to the polite smattering the first-place winner got, made me feel as if maybe people had actually listened to my paper and *liked* it. For the first time, I started to think this contest had been a good idea even without the whole psych clique competitiveness thing.

Then they got to the underclassman creative writing awards. Crane woman called Li up, and Ami and I clapped as he rose from his seat. Then I noticed that he had something in his hand . . . his poem. Confused, I leaned over to whisper in Ami's ear.

"Is he supposed to present that?" I said. "None of the other third-place winners did."

She shrugged. "Maybe he just forgot to put it down."

We watched him reach the podium, where crane woman was holding out her hand for him to shake it. But instead of shaking her hand, he brushed past her and stood in front of the microphone. Li was actually going to read his poem! This was going to be incredible.

"Everybody, relax," he said into the microphone. He had no trouble speaking loudly into it, and immediately his heavy Chinese accent filled the room. "Close your eye, close your eye!"

I stifled a laugh. Everyone looked confused, especially crane woman, who still had her hand slightly stretched out as though expecting him to take it. Li repeated his demand for everyone to close their "eye," and reluctantly, some people obeyed.

"My poem," he said, stretching out the word to make it po-EM, "is called 'Cherry Blossoms.'" He held the paper in front of him, snapping it dramatically as he began to read.

"Cherry blossom fall from the sky," he began. *"Wrapped up in the most see-through butterfly. Cherry blossom catch on the wind. Cherry blossom want to be our friend. Cherry blossom . . ."*

It was just as bad as the van version. Maybe worse. Some of the lines were kind of pretty, and I have to give him credit for working in rhymes of "awesome" *and* "opossum," but mostly it was just meaningless. If this poem was worthy of third place, I shuddered to think of the runners-up.

What really made this version of the poem worse was its length. Every time it seemed to be wrapping up, it went on for another eight stanzas, and then it did it all over again. I had fully gotten over my amusement and moved into nodding off before Li finally stepped away from the podium. This time he held out his hand, and crane woman absently shook it, looking as though she had just been abducted by aliens.

Li sat down, and the second- and first-place winners presented their pieces, but nothing could compare to the moment when I saw Li push crane woman aside and order everyone to relax. For the rest of the ceremony, there was just no beating that for sheer entertainment value.

Afterward we all sat at a little table with plates of hors d'oeuvres. Ami laughed over Li's stunt and gave him serious props for his nerve, but he just blinked.

"What I do?" he asked. "I just want to read 'Cherry Blossoms.'"

Somehow that made it better. Li really seemed oblivious to the huge scene he had caused and the looks on the contest directors' faces.

"Well, it was a very nice poem," I lied.

"Thank you." He beamed. "But I want it to win first place. That why I enter contest—for the money."

The first-place winner was awarded one hundred dollars, the second-place winner won fifty dollars, and the third-place winner took home a free Mark Twain anthology. I could tell by the way Li looked at his anthology—as though it were a dead rat found behind the stove—that he was not too thrilled with one of America's finest writers. Or at least, not as thrilled as he would have been with one hundred bucks.

"Sell the book," I suggested. "Then you'll make money."

I glanced around, looking at all the uptight people from other schools trying to mingle while surreptitiously wiping sticky fingers on their pants or the dark green tablecloths. It struck me as funny that here we were, a table of three misfits from one of the smaller and lesser-known colleges, so insular and disgruntled that we hadn't won *first* place that we couldn't be bothered to interact with anyone else.

It occurred to me that throughout this entire day, I hadn't worried about the situation with Andrew at all. I'd known it would be a good idea to take a little break from each other—I just hadn't expected to be so successful at it.

Later that night, when Ami and I were sitting on the hotel beds in our pajamas, I considered talking to her a little about Andrew. But for some reason I still couldn't. We talked about a ton of other stuff—Li's stunt, school, even one of the surfer guys at Joanna's party who had gotten Ami's number but hadn't called yet. It felt good to advise Ami on her love life, since it took attention away from mine.

Finally, when pauses between conversation started getting longer and longer, we turned off the lights and went to bed. I could tell by Ami's soft snoring that she dropped off almost immediately, but I just lay there, staring at the shafts of light from the window blinds.

Then, all of a sudden, the wall started to shake a little. I turned to look at Ami, but she was dead to the world. Then I heard it. The people in the next room were having sex.

And not normal sex, either. The guy appeared to be making some weird growling noise, and the woman just kept repeating the same thing over and over: "*OhGodthatfeelssogood, ohGodthatfeelssogood, ohGodthatfeelssogood.*"

Perfect. I tried to put my pillow over my head, but I could still hear it. I felt like pounding on the wall and telling them to keep it down. And there was shorthand for *ohGodthatfeelssogood*—it was called a moan. It seemed to me that if she had the energy to repeat that whole sentence, maybe it wasn't as good as she was claiming. *Your woman's faking it!* I wanted to scream through the wall, just to shut them up if nothing else.

Eventually the sounds died down, and I drifted off to sleep, the pillow still over my head.

That night I dreamed I was walking along the beach, the sun peeking over the edge of the water. For some reason I knew it was sunrise rather than sunset, which made it more surreal, because we never see the sun rise over the water here. I was wearing a skirt as white and foamy as the waves, and my feet were bare.

In the distance, there was a figure walking toward me, wavering as though it were a mirage. But then it came closer, and I saw that it wasn't a mirage at all.

Seeing him, I felt this incredible swell of happiness. I ran toward him, my feet sinking in the soft sand. He stopped, smiled, and then the next second I was in his arms.

It was only weird later, when I woke in a cold sweat. In the dream, it felt right, the same way that I knew it was sunrise and that it felt normal to be wearing this superfloaty skirt that I would never own in my life.

His hands are on my waist, touching bare skin, skimming down my hips. I want to be as close to him as possible, and I arch my back and link my arms around his neck. I've never felt this way before, all warm and fluttery and alive. "Nathan," I breathe.

My eyes flew open, and I sat up like a shot, my tank top twisted and sticking clammily to my body. I looked at Ami, a wave of mortification passing over me. She was still sleeping, but it felt like the dream was a spotlight on me much brighter than the streetlamp slanting through the window blinds. It

177

seemed almost unbelievable to me that she couldn't see it, that it hadn't awakened her.

I dreamed about Nathan *kissing* me. I dreamed about *Nathan* kissing me. Oh, my God. Nathan *touched* me. I could still feel his fingers on my skin, feel the warm strength of his arms around me.

What had I been about to say? Before I woke up, I had just said Nathan's name, and somehow I knew I was on the brink of saying something else. Would I have said, *Oh, God, that feels so good?*

Where was a good psychoanalyst when you needed one?

RATIONALIZATION: The process of developing a socially acceptable explanation for inappropriate behavior or thoughts

WE weren't leaving until later the next day, so Tim gave us the morning and early afternoon to see a bit of San Francisco. Normally it would have been a blast, poking around shops with Ami, chatting and people-watching.

But I was still unsettled from my dream the previous night, and Ami, as if sensing my weird mood, was uncharacteristically quiet herself. Aimlessly, we roamed through one particular shop that was a smorgasbord for tourists. Under normal circumstances, Ami and I would have been having a ball trying on the brightly colored hats and mocking all the postcards. But instead, we were going through the motions, picking up kitschy San Francisco snow globes (filled with confetti instead of snow) and minimodels of trolley cars, with little real pleasure.

We left the shop without buying anything and strolled down the sidewalk, and I wished that I had thought to bring a sweatshirt. The chilly breeze coming off the nearby water cut through my Clean Communities T-shirt and whipped long tendrils of my hair around my face. Earlier, I had gathered my hair into a ponytail, but there were still those pieces that crossed obnoxiously over my eyes and stuck to my lips. Ami and I passed a hairdresser's shop, and I stopped.

"Here," I said. "I want to get my hair cut."

"What?"

"I'm sick of it," I said. "It keeps blowing in my face, and it's just a pain to take care of. I want it cut."

Ami put her hands on her hips. "Okay, I wasn't going to say anything," she said, "but you've been weird all day, and I am *not* going to let you cut your hair in a mood like this. You love your hair. *I* love your hair."

Andrew also loved my hair. For some reason, that only spurred me on. "My mind is made up," I insisted. "It's ridiculous to have hair this long."

"But you get all bent out of shape about Audrey Hepburn cutting her hair supershort in *Roman Holiday*. You always say you liked it better before."

"Yeah, but by the time we rented *Sabrina* and she did it again, I was totally over it, remember? It'll just take some getting used to, that's all."

Ami pursed her lips, obviously considering what to do with me when I was acting like a kid who wanted a new Barbie doll. "Fine," she finally agreed, surprising me a little.

"Okay," I said, giving her a sharp nod as if to say, *that's settled*. "Let's do it."

She grabbed my arm. "It's your hair, Leigh, and you can do what you want. But as your roommate, future maid of honor, and friend for life, I have to beg you to reconsider. At *least* wait until we're back home, okay? You don't want to get your hair cut at the"—she glanced up at the sign and made a face—"*Hair Factory*."

I opened the door, gesturing for her to go inside. "I know what I'm doing," I said confidently.

Once I was in the chair, a cover draped over me, and my hair wet and combed straight, my poise started to waver a bit. Did I *really* know what I was doing? Every woman, after all, is born with the instinctive knowledge that there exists no worse fate than a bad haircut. I wouldn't do anything drastic, I told myself. Just a few inches.

The hairdresser came to stand behind me, cracking her gum loudly. She had a weird, frizzy cut that was slightly longer in the front than in the back. I wanted to ask her if she had cut her own hair, but was scared of the answer.

"Whaddya want?" she asked. Her name tag said her name was Yvonne.

"Um . . ." I looked around the shop, hoping for last-minute inspiration from one of those posters they always have of gorgeous people with amazing hair. I saw a flyer advertising a program called Locks of Love, asking customers to donate hair to kids with long-term hair loss who need wigs.

That sounded okay. I could justify the haircut a little better if it was a charitable thing.

"How much hair do I have to cut off to donate to Locks of Love?" I asked.

I didn't know what I expected. Maybe that Yvonne would be so thrilled I was going to do a good deed that she'd wipe the bad attitude from her face. Instead she sighed, pushing the gum around her mouth with her tongue.

"Sheila!" she called to the woman at the next station. "How much hair do you need for that Locks of Love thing?"

Sheila paused in the middle of blow-drying to think about it. "Ten inches?" she said. "Maybe a foot?"

I looked at my hair in the mirror. I had that, easily. "How short would that make my hair?" I asked.

Yvonne took out a measuring tape, stretching it next to my hair. "We gotta give it a couple inches, 'cause it'll be shorter when it's dry," she said, "but right about . . . here."

Her hand was above my shoulder. I swallowed. "That's before or after it's dry?" I asked.

She moved her hand up to just below my chin. "There," she said. "Still wanna do it?"

Ami was sitting over in the waiting section, not too far from my chair. She shook her head. "Uh-uh," she said. "Don't do it, Leigh. Remember, go *gradual*."

But I had already asked about that program. Wouldn't I go to hell if I chickened out now, just because of a few lousy inches? And kids with diseases, that's pretty intense. I don't want that on my conscience. If the haircut was that terrible, it would always grow back.

"I have to agree with your friend," Yvonne said. "You have really pretty hair. It would be a shame to cut it all off."

I gritted my teeth. When was the last time a shop clerk said: *That's a really nice shirt you're wearing. I wouldn't buy another, if I were you.* Or a real estate agent: *What a charming home you have. You should live here forever and forget about selling it.* It was ridiculous.

And so what if my hair was pretty? Is there a law that says short hair can't be pretty, too? And don't sick kids deserve something pretty?

"Go for it," I said. "Take a whole foot if you need to."

Yvonne raised her eyebrows. "All right, if you say so."

She took out her sharp, silver scissors, and I almost backed out. There was that pit in my stomach, the one I always felt on roller coasters—you climb up and up, and the split second before you're about to rush back down, you're like, *No! I changed my mind, I want off!*

I know, I know. That's part of the thrill. But I actually hate roller coasters. When it makes that steep descent, I'm not the one screaming with excitement. I'm just screaming.

With deft motions, Yvonne plaited my hair into one long braid. She snipped a few of the shorter pieces in the front until they just barely covered my ears. *It's still not too late*, I told myself. *That could just be your bangs—bangs are back in style, right?*

"Having second thoughts?" Yvonne asked.

I almost nodded, but kept it still when I remembered that she had scissors in her hand. "No," I lied.

She shrugged and began to snip more hair from the front, until finally she hacked the top of the braid, just at the nape of my neck. Out of the corner of my eye I could see my latte-colored braid still in her hand, and I thought I was going to throw up.

I spent the next half hour with my eyes closed, scared even to think about what Yvonne was doing with my hair. She could have shaved the word *ice* in the side of my head and I would have been completely clueless.

I heard the blow-dryer go on, and I knew she was almost finished. She fluffed a couple of pieces here, combed out others there, and I heard the snip of the scissors as she trimmed some uneven edges.

Finally, she cracked her gum and said, "There ya go."

I opened my eyes. I couldn't believe it.

It looked . . . good. My hair has always been straight and shiny, but sometimes I wished it had a little more volume to it. Now the layers made it look like it was actually *styled*, curling just under my chin and swinging around my face. And my face, which I've always thought was a little too angular to be pretty, suddenly looked softer, glowing, even. I swear, it even made my skin look better.

What a difference a haircut could make.

"Here's your hair," Yvonne said, handing me the braid. "I'll get you the address for that program. You mail it yourself."

That was kind of a raw deal, but I was still powerless to argue against kids with diseases. I glanced down at all the hair I'd lost, but it didn't really freak me out the way it would have a few moments ago.

Okay, the braid itself did. Holding a hunk of your hair all braided up felt a little creepy, just a few steps away from moaning, "Precious," like that dude in *Silence of the Lambs*. But I didn't regret the haircut anymore. How could I, when it looked amazing?

I happily paid for the cut, adding a tip for Yvonne that was much more generous than what I would usually pay. Hey, I'm a college student. I don't *try* to be cheap. It usually just happens.

"Wow," Ami said as we walked back out onto the sidewalk. "Your hair looks *awesome*. How come you never thought to cut it before?"

I shrugged. "I don't like change," I said.

Ami nodded, not that she could relate at all to that. Her hair is even shorter than mine, with longer, almost shaggy bangs, but cut short as a boy's in the back. Just another thing that Ami could pull off that would make me look like a moron.

Then again, short hair suited me a lot better than I had ever thought it would. . . .

Easy, I told myself. Five minutes into having short hair and I was already planning to go shorter. I wanted to enjoy this length for a while.

I couldn't help swinging it as I walked, fluffing it with my hands and enjoying its brushing against my cheek. In first grade there had been a girl in my class who always wore this high, bouncy ponytail, and whenever she walked she would twist her whole body, making her hair swing like a jubilant pendulum. I always thought she was the biggest drip.

Now I was beginning to wonder if I'd misjudged her.

"So what do you think Andrew's going to think?" Ami asked, shooting me a glance from the corner of her eye.

"He'll like it," I said, wishing I felt as sure as I sounded.

Ami was silent for a moment. "You haven't talked to him all weekend," she said. "Are you two okay?"

In the world's most obvious change of subject, I looked at my watch. We had another twenty minutes before we had to meet Tim and Li. "Let's get ice cream," I suggested brightly, steering her toward a small dairy shop on the corner. "I could use something cold."

Not too long before, I had been complaining that it was too cold outside, but to her credit, Ami just went along with it. She ordered a cone of mint chocolate-chip, I got a cup of strawberry with rainbow sprinkles, and we sat on a bench to eat.

I let a spoonful of ice cream dissolve on my tongue while I considered my next words. "We didn't have sex that night," I said.

"I kind of figured." Ami peered at a rivulet of green ice

cream that was sliding down her cone as though it were the most fascinating thing she'd ever seen. "What happened?"

By now I'd abandoned the condom excuse, even though I still maintained that safe sex was an important issue. "I just got scared, I guess," I said. "There'd be no turning back from that, you know? And I wasn't sure I was ready to go there."

Ami looked at me. "So did you break up?"

"No, of course not," I said. "We're just taking a little breather, to reassess."

"To reassess whether you want to break up?"

"No!" I set my spoon angrily in my cup of ice cream, splattering strawberry on my hand. "We're not going to *break up* over something this stupid. I just need some time to think, that's all."

"What makes you think this is stupid?" Ami asked. "Sex is an important part of a relationship, you know. *Cosmo* says that a woman knows within five seconds if she wants to sleep with a man or not."

I rolled my eyes. "*Cosmo* doesn't know everything," I said. "Just look at all their so-called statistics—'Thirty-five percent of men have reported getting it on with a superior at work.' What kind of guys read *Cosmo*? The kind who sleep around with their bosses, that's what kind. It's a misrepresentative sample of the *Sex and the City* crowd."

Ami looked like I had just kicked a kitten. "*Cosmo* has a lot of valuable information in it," she said. "And *Sex and the City* was a revolutionary show."

I wasn't going to win this one, so why try? "Whatever," I said. "All I'm saying is that it's not that I don't *want* to have sex with Andrew. I just want everything to be right, and it didn't feel right that night. But we love each other, and soon, it will."

I tried not to think about the conversation I'd had with Andrew right before I'd left. *Ribbed for her pleasure.* Ick.

Ami's ice cream, untouched for several minutes, had started dripping in earnest, and she gave it a disgusted look before tossing it in the garbage. "Okay," she said. "Let me ask you this. Have you fantasized about it?"

A guilty flush spread over my face.

"You have!" Ami squealed, as though we were in sixth grade and playing a game of Truth or Dare. "Well, that's a good sign."

"Yeah . . ." I wonder what she'd think if she knew it hadn't been about Andrew. That stupid dream had been on my mind all day, and it almost seemed worth spilling it all to Ami just to get another opinion on it.

"Actually, I had a dream last night," I said cautiously.

"A sex dream?"

"Kind of. More . . . romantic, but yeah, definitely sexy." My fingers twisted nervously in my newly cut hair. "Did you hear the couple next door going at it last night?"

Ami's eyes widened. "You heard the people next door *having sex?*"

I nodded. "Yeah, it was really gross," I said. "But that's

probably what made me have this dream. That's the only explanation for it."

"Two strangers—*please* tell me it was only two—mating like rabbits through the wall may have been a part of it. But, come on. You and Andrew have been going out for a year without doing it; I'm sure you had sex on the brain anyway."

Sometimes, when the water was cold, it was better to just jump in. Wading just drew it out and made it harder. "It wasn't about Andrew," I said.

Ami blinked, but she recovered quickly. "That's not unusual," she said. "I've had sex dreams about faceless or random people before."

"Oh, he wasn't random, and he had a face," I said. I took a deep breath. "It was Nathan."

Ami's jaw dropped. Literally. Her mouth hung open for what felt like several minutes, and she started forming words, only to have it drop open again. From the way her lips kept coming together, I could tell she wanted to just say, "*What?*"

But then her mouth closed, and her eyes squinted, as though she were considering something. "Actually," she said after a while, "I could see it."

Now it was my turn to look stunned. "What?" I said. "Ami, that's crazy. Like you said, it's normal to have sex dreams sometimes, and it's been on my brain lately, and there was that couple next door—"

Ami cut me off. "That doesn't explain why it would be *Nathan*, and not Andrew."

I was starting to regret wanting a second opinion. "Look, I don't like Nathan, okay? I'm in love with his *roommate*, for crying out loud. Nathan and I can barely stand each other."

"You said it was more romantic," Ami said. "That's gotta say something. What exactly happened in the dream?"

I told her about being on the beach and seeing Nathan, running toward him and then kissing. I could feel my face grow hotter as I briefly outlined the kiss, leaving out the part about the bubbly feeling in my stomach.

"Whoa," Ami breathed. "That's major. The sunrise, that's like new beginnings, right? And a gauzy white skirt . . . sounds almost like a wedding dress!"

"All right, Stretch Armstrong," I said. "Cut it out."

"Fine," she said. "You're a psych major. What would the great Freud say about this?"

Non–psych majors always say things like "the great Freud," as though all psychology students worshipped the man. Don't get me wrong, I give him props for starting the whole movement into insight and whatnot—but seriously, what a crank.

"Freud would say the dream was a manifestation of my infantile sexuality," I said wryly. "He would put it down to the same pleasure-seeking impulse that babies have to touch their mouths and play with themselves."

Ami wrinkled her nose. "Ew," she said. "All right, well, maybe not Freud, then. What about the other people? What would they say?"

Dream analysis has never been something I've been particularly into, and we hadn't even gotten there in Intro Psych yet, so I had to struggle to remember what I had learned in AP psychology. "Adler thought that dreams were experiments of possible answers to immediate problems," I said after a beat.

"So, maybe Nathan is the answer to your current problem with Andrew. Maybe you secretly want to get with *him*, and that's what's stopping you from committing fully to Andrew."

I felt an uncomfortable clenching in my gut. "That's impossible," I said. "Maybe the dream is just about opening myself up to being physical in general, and Nathan has nothing to do with it. After all, Jung said that dreams weren't always unfulfilled wishes, and he often looked for the shadow in them. Maybe Nathan's my shadow."

"What's your shadow?"

"The part of ourselves that we don't like," I said somberly. "Maybe Nathan somehow reflects the most negative aspects of myself."

Ami wrinkled her forehead in a close approximation of her "psychology" look, with a healthy dose of "you're crazy" thrown in for good measure. She was on the verge of saying something else when Tim and Li walked up.

"We've been looking for you everywhere!" Tim cried. "I barely recognized you, Leigh—*great* haircut. Very chic!"

"Thanks," I said. In the intense conversation Ami and I had been having, I had quickly forgotten about my hair.

"Well, girls, we should be going," Tim said. "Wouldn't want to get back too late!"

I realized I hadn't bought any souvenirs. All I had to mark my trip to San Francisco was a second-place certificate, a braid of my own hair, and a churning in my stomach that could have been because I was slightly lactose-intolerant but was more likely because of that stupid dream.

"Can we just have a few more minutes?" I said. "I really wanted to buy something."

Tim made a production of looking at his SpongeBob SquarePants watch. "All right—five minutes," he allowed. "But then meet us right back here at the bench."

I ran to the store we'd been in before, Ami trailing behind me. Without taking time to look around, I grabbed one of the confetti globes of San Francisco and took it up to the cashier.

"Who's that for?" Ami asked.

"Andrew," I said. I wanted to buy it as a peace offering, but also because I wanted to have something in my hands when I went over to his suite. It would make it a little easier when I told him that I was finally ready to take the next step.

It was time Andrew and I had sex.

> **FIGHT OR FLIGHT:** The emotional experi-
> ence associated with the sympathetic nervous system and
> managed by the hypothalamus during high arousal. An
> individual must respond to a threat by either fleeing or
> going on the offensive.

OF course, it seemed utterly ridiculous later, when I was standing outside Andrew's suite, that a San Francisco confetti
globe was supposed to say, I want to have sex. I was trying to
figure out if there was any way to shove the whole thing in my
purse when Nathan opened the door.

In my fumbling with the globe, I must have dropped it,
but I was only dimly aware of the glass dome breaking open as
it hit the linoleum in the hall. Nathan and I just stood there,
staring at each other, neither of us reaching for it.

The dream was still fresh in my mind, and I felt my face
grow hot with the memory of what it was like to be held in his

arms. I know it's not like those things *really* happened, but seeing him now, standing so close I could smell the soap he used (Irish Spring?)—it almost felt as if they had.

So it was perfectly understandable that I would be staring at *him* so oddly, given the events of the past weekend, but he was returning my gaze. There was no way he could have known about the dream . . . could he? Maybe it showed on my face. Or maybe Ami had told him. None of this made logical sense, but somehow nothing seemed impossible, the way his gaze was so intent on me now.

"Wow," he said.

Oh my God, he knew. I had had impure thoughts about him, and he knew. It disgusted him, the fact that I had been so disloyal to Andrew. Even if not in the real world, I had betrayed Andrew in the dream world, and that's just as bad, right? I had tried to convince myself it wasn't, but who was I kidding? In my dream, I had let my boyfriend's roommate put his *tongue* in my mouth!

I licked my lips. "Okay, listen—"

Nathan reached out to touch my hair. Just a slight touch, flipping a strand over his finger, but I felt my breath catch. Maybe he knew about the dream but wasn't mad. Maybe he actually thought we could start something. Oh, crap, what if he wanted to start something?

"Your hair, it's . . ." There was a bemused look on his face.

I'm such an idiot. Of *course* that's why he'd been staring at me kind of funny—my haircut. I almost laughed out loud.

And here I was stressing about a stupid dream.

"It's what?" I asked, a weirdly breathless note in my voice. What did it matter what Nathan thought?

But I never got to hear the rest of his thought. At that point, Andrew appeared, pushing himself between Nathan and the door frame.

His gaze was on Nathan as he said, "Well? You going to let her in or are you two just going to stand there?"

Nathan moved out of the way, dark red streaking across his cheekbones, and I stepped into the suite.

Finally Andrew turned, his head jerking back a little when he got his first full view of me. "You cut your hair," he said flatly.

I reached a reflexive hand up to the silky strands. "It was too long," I said.

"I didn't think so."

Those four words, and already I could feel the self-confidence that had filled me with such happiness in San Francisco run down the drain. It angered me that he could make me feel this way, but it didn't stop it from happening.

"Don't you like it?" I asked, my voice small.

"Not particularly."

Nathan cleared his throat. "I think it looks great," he said. I glanced at him, only just remembering that he was still in the room, but he wasn't looking at me. He was looking at Andrew.

Andrew's jaw clenched. "Stay out of this, Nate."

I expected Nathan to leave then, or to at least retreat to

his room to play guitar the way he usually did. But he just stood there, glaring at Andrew. Finally, he turned to me.

"Your long hair was beautiful, but shorter, it's cute and spunky," he said. "It's very *you*."

He delivered the compliment almost aggressively, the words clipped. But somehow I didn't doubt his sincerity. Nathan thought my hair was beautiful? And was he saying that he thought *I* was cute and spunky? Even as the warmth of his words spread through me, I felt more confused than ever.

It shouldn't have come as a surprise that Andrew would react this way. While I hate change, he's pathologically phobic about it. Over time, he would get used to my hair, and then he would love it. But for right now, I would have to accept that he didn't like it.

It wasn't just my hair, either. There was a weird tension crackling in the room, as though there were a secret subtext and I didn't have my decoder ring. I wasn't even sure that I *wanted* to figure it out.

Then I remembered my original reason for the visit. "Oh!" I said, my voice falsely bright. "I almost forgot, Andrew. I brought you a sex present!"

It took a few moments for the reality of what I'd just said to sink in, that stupid smile still pinned on my face. I had just said, "*sex present*." I said it in front of Nathan, who was looking at me with a weird mixture of pity and something else, something I couldn't pinpoint. Did he pity me because I had just made a royal ass of myself, or because he knew about my massive insecurities when it came to sex?

But it wasn't even pity, either. It was more like the look you might give a kid who was sure they would win that contest on the back of a cereal box, when really you knew the odds were against it. It was the look of someone who knew something but didn't have the heart to tell you.

"Leigh." Andrew pinched the bridge of his nose as though he had a headache. "Why don't we go in my room, and we can talk in there?"

There was nothing unusual in that, so why did my insides twist? I followed Andrew into his room without glancing back at Nathan. I didn't think I could stand to see that look on his face again.

I had spent the entire drive over here rehearsing a little speech, and I decided to jump right in before I could be sidetracked. "I know these past few weeks have been hard," I began.

"You didn't call, Leigh," Andrew said. "You were gone for what, two days? And you didn't call once."

"Last I checked, I didn't have any missed calls from you, either," I pointed out.

"Don't do that. I'm sick of you making it all about me."

"It's at least half about you," I said. "You *are* half of this relationship, believe it or not."

Andrew sighed. "But I'm not the half that needs to be fixed."

At first I was speechless, so incapable of comprehending this attack that I couldn't even find the words. When I finally spoke, my voice came out in a whisper. "What's that supposed to mean?"

"Come *on*," Andrew said impatiently. "I'm talking about your massive insecurities, neuroses, complexes, whatever the hell you want to 'diagnose' them as. You can't just let go. You can't have fun. You can't stop analyzing anything for just *one* second and think about what *I* may want or what our relationship might need."

"You're talking about sex."

Andrew arched his eyebrows. "Among other things."

"Didn't you even *hear* what I blurted out earlier?" My breath escaped in a sad approximation of a laugh. "I bought you a stupid confetti globe in San Francisco as a peace offering, as a *sex* present, for Christ's sake. I wanted to show you that I *am* ready, that I want to take that next step in our relationship."

"It's not enough."

I knew he wasn't just talking about the globe. *What do you mean?* I wanted to ask, but I knew. And I didn't want to hear it. I couldn't stand the thought of all that subtext being put into words that couldn't be taken back.

Apparently Andrew had no such compunction, because he continued in the same voice he might use to tell an acquaintance the reading assignment for a class. "It's too late, Leigh. I needed someone who's a little more open, freer, more . . . sensual. At first, I thought if I just gave you time, you'd eventually get there. But it's just not worth the effort anymore. You know me, Leigh. I don't want to drive a Gremlin. I want the BMW, with a warranty and full maintenance."

Andrew's car analogy was so ridiculous it was almost surreal, but my mind was still hung up on the first words he'd said. I *needed* someone. Needed. Someone.

Needed. Past tense.

"So who's the BMW?" I asked.

For the first time since I'd arrived, Andrew looked ill at ease. "It's not what you think," he said. "Nothing has happened. We only just started talking over the last week or so, really. And we just have this amazing chemistry, you know? I've never met anyone like her—such a free spirit."

I couldn't think of anyone further from being a free spirit than Andrew. But right now I just wanted to know one thing. "Who. Is. She."

He hesitated. "Heather."

"Heather," I repeated, the name twisting in my gut like a knife. And why not? If there was one thing anyone knew about Heather, it was that she liked sex. No waiting for a year, no condom drama with Heather. I thought of that night, of the way he'd touched me right there on that bed, and I wanted to throw up.

"Like I said, nothing's happened," Andrew said, anxious for what—absolution? My heart was broken, scattered on the floor in little pieces that screamed out the name *Heather*, and still he cared only about himself. "Just hanging out, talking. I haven't cheated on you, if that's what you think."

"How does Nathan feel about this?" After all, Heather had been his kind-of girlfriend, even if he was going out with Sydney now. I don't know why the answer was so important to me, but it was.

Andrew blinked. "Nathan? There was nothing between them. They went out on one date, that was all, and Nathan said she wasn't really his type. End of story."

Apparently not. That was only the *beginning* of the story, as far as I was concerned. "So you're breaking up with me," I said flatly.

Andrew gave me that exasperated look again, as if frustrated that this was taking so long. "I thought that's what I was saying," he said, "when I was telling you that I think Heather is really more . . . what I'm looking for."

"You know this after a week," I said. I flinched as though I'd been punched, the realization hitting me in my gut. "You knew this a few days ago, when I left. But still you talked about making it work and buying"—I choked on the words— "ribbed condoms, because you knew that's what *girls* liked. You had her in mind, even then."

Tears were streaming down my face, the last sentence mangled in undignified hiccups that racked my body and left me gulping for air. Andrew tried to pat me on the back, as though I could be soothed, like one of those stupid robotic babies at the mentoring program. I shoved him away, knowing that if he touched me, somehow it would just be too much to bear. I wouldn't fall apart as long as he didn't touch me.

He tried to say something else, but I decided I was done listening. Flinging open the door, I stalked out into the living room. There was Nathan, sitting on the couch. The TV wasn't on, and I wondered if he'd heard the whole thing. He was sitting as straight as a sentinel, as though he were there to ensure that I would go quietly, and something inside me just snapped.

"Are you happy now?" I said brokenly. "I know you never thought Andrew and I should be together. Well, I won't be around to eat your precious cereal and ruin your college experience, and all because you couldn't keep tabs on your little sex-kitten girlfriend."

Nathan looked at me silently, as though this were just as hard for him as it was for me. Well, screw him. He had no idea what this felt like. He had gone on *one* date with Heather. Andrew and I had been going out for almost a *year and a half.*

Okay, just over a year—whatever. All I knew was that I didn't deserve this.

"Leigh," Andrew said, and I heard it again, that note in his voice that said *please don't cause a scene,* and not *I'm sorry I hurt you.*

I spun to face him. "*You* leave me alone," I said. "I don't want to talk to you, I don't want to see you, and I *definitely* don't want to hear any more of your pompous, self-centered crap. You're through with me, fine. Just leave me alone."

My fingers were clumsy on the doorknob, but even after I'd opened it I stopped short of leaving. There, scattered on the linoleum, I saw what remained of the San Francisco globe, now just shards of glass and bits of confetti around a little trolley car. I had the weird sensation of knowing I was about to lose it and yet being completely powerless to stop it.

"And this," I said, my hiccups now a cross between sobs and hysterical laughter, "this was for *you* and for our relationship and for our *first time*. But it's all broken, right? Everything's broken."

I knelt down, trying to scoop up the glass and confetti— for what, I don't know. Maybe it seemed symbolic, although all it really meant was that I was acting completely pathetic over a ten-dollar souvenir that could never be whole again. I guess that's symbolism for you, another term-paper topic to win a contest.

And then Nathan was there, crouching beside me. Through my tears, I thought maybe he was just trying to help me pick up the mess. But then I realized he had my hands in his and was guiding them toward him, away from the glass.

"Leigh, don't," he said, his voice husky and almost tender, but I didn't want it. I sprang up, jerking my hands back as though they'd been burned, and ran blindly toward the parking lot. I didn't look back, and this time, no one called after me.

> **LEARNED HELPLESSNESS:** A condition created by exposure to inescapable aversive events. This retards or prevents learning in subsequent situations in which escape or avoidance is possible.

IN high school, there was this girl named Kristy Salazar who was *always* being dumped. She never did the breaking up—she always had it done to her, usually in very public and hurtful ways. Once a guy blasted a song on his car's system about "ugly-ass bitches" or something like that. Another time, this kid actually raised his hand in class to announce that he no longer wanted to be with her. Most notoriously, her date to prom ditched her for his costar in the school musical. His *male* costar.

It would have been really tragic, except that Kristy was a complete drama queen. After each breakup she was inconsolable, carrying on in class as though her best friend had just died. And I started to realize—she's not crying because she was dumped. She was dumped because she won't stop crying.

I never thought I'd become Kristy Salazar, the girl who skips class and lounges around, a box of tissues glued to one hand. Before Andrew broke up with me, I'd just use toilet paper to blow my nose. But now, ever since what Ami was starting to refer to as the WWJD? Incident, I was a complete Kleenex convert. I had to be, for my nose's sake.

"You've got to snap out of it," Ami would say. "What would jerkface do?"

I sniffled. "Break up with his loving girlfriend for some sex maniac?"

"The same girl he compared to his BMW," Ami reminded me. "And no, but you're close. Jerkface would wreck the best thing he'll ever have, and all because he wanted to get some."

It reminded me of when I'd told my group at mentoring that sex wasn't a competition, and I wasn't looking to "get" any. How stupid. I burst into fresh tears, and Ami rushed to repair the damage. "Hey, there's one Coke left in the fridge. What would jerkface do?"

"Take it?"

"No," Ami said gleefully. "He'd pee in it, and *then* he'd take it."

I blew my nose. "That's the grossest thing I've ever heard." I paused, imagining the looks on everyone's faces if they caught Andrew doing something so crude and unsanitary. "And yet, oddly helpful."

That was the pattern for days—I e-mailed my professors and told them I was sick, which I figured wasn't exactly a lie. I did feel sick, except it was the kind of sickness that didn't go away with some Vitamin C and a couple of Advil Cold & Sinus.

I missed a psych clique—or Intro Psych study group, whatever—meeting, too. Joanna sent me an e-mail saying that all I missed was Ellen's talking more about her final project (she'd already coded over three hundred commercials and found a trend toward thinness in those for cars, alcohol, and clothes. Shocker). Jenny remembered her materials this time, but Joanna said she should have just left them at home, since all Sydney and Ellen did was rip her idea for a final project to shreds (something lame about the perception of symmetry in faces). Apparently, at one point, Jenny started crying so hard that Sir Wug actually got annoyed and left the room. Whatever works, I say.

Joanna didn't tell me any of the things I really wanted to know, and I didn't bother to ask. I wanted to know what had been said about me—with her nebulous connection to Nathan, Sydney surely knew about the breakup. And I think Ellen is friends with Heather, which just adds a whole layer of bitchiness to the kind of things they were no doubt saying behind my back.

Maybe it was because I didn't really care about the opinion of that stupid group, or maybe it was because I found it hard to care about anything, but even their potential trash-talking wasn't what was bugging me.

It was Nathan. The way I'd acted that day had been utterly cringeworthy, and the idea of Sydney and him laughing about it made my skin crawl. I also wondered how serious their relationship was—knowing Sydney, if they were together, she would have been gloating about it all over that meeting. But how could I possibly have asked Joanna about that? Hey, my ex-boyfriend's roommate might be hooking up with that psycho hose beast, and I feel oddly compelled to know about it.

So instead, I just avoided the group altogether, ignored Sydney's e-mails announcing the next meeting and the kind of materials we should be collecting soon. Who cared about a class that was only on the introductory level, anyway? Who cared about papers and final exams and transcripts? Who cared about Sydney's naked pictures and her stale cheese dip and her freaky cat? What did any of it matter?

Unfortunately, the one thing that I couldn't skip was the thing I most wanted to—the weekly mentoring group. How could I possibly advise a thirteen-year-old—or *fifteen*, whatever—about life and love and school and sex and all of the stuff I basically *sucked* at? I should be labeled "Leigh Nolan: A Cautionary Tale" and shown in every high school health class.

This meeting wasn't like the time Linda had us all join hands in a human pretzel and then work to untangle ourselves. At least that time, I barely had to say a thing, except for maybe the occasional "you go under, I'll go over."

Instead, this meeting was the Stiles campus tour, which had been hyped more than *Episode I: Phantom Menace* in the Star

Wars series. A few weeks ago, Linda had decided that the girls needed a tour of the campus to kick-start their motivation to do well in school and, naturally, not get knocked up. Meanwhile, she was also hoping that the chance to interact one-on-one outside of their school environment would encourage the girls to open up more.

So far, it didn't seem to be working. "So, that's the marine biology building," I told Rebekah, pointing. "That's where people study fish, and uh . . ." Wow, I was totally the worst tour guide ever. I can't believe all I could muster up about marine biology was that they "study fish."

Looking around, I saw all the other mentors chatting and laughing with their mentees. Even Ellen was smiling, and although I'm *positive* I heard her outlining the merits of one professor over another, her mentee actually seemed to be smiling, too.

Rebekah still hadn't responded to any of my overtures, and I continued to direct her attention to buildings I never went into and couldn't care less about. Was I stuck with a dud of a mentee? Or was she stuck with a lousy mentor?

"Where are all the babies?" I asked her, noting an astonishing lack of strollers or those slings that some people carry their babies around in. I'd have worried that if I put my baby in one of those I'd get hit by a car or something, and we'd both die. At least if I had a stroller, I could push my baby out of the way at the last second, thus sacrificing myself for the life of my small child.

"Home," Rebekah said.

Five single, teenage mothers roaming around a college while their infants were at home. How realistic.

"This is where most of my classes are," I said, gesturing to the small converted house that was the psychology building. "Um . . . do you want to go inside?"

Rebekah shrugged, which I took as a resounding yes. I opened the door and almost ran right into Sydney, who was leaving.

"Leigh," Sydney said, shifting the pile of notebooks in her arms. The books had caught on her shirt, and every inch she moved them meant another inch of bare flesh showing above the V-neck. Next stop on the tour: Sydney's boobs. "I was just finishing up some data coding for my thesis. What are you doing here?"

"Just, you know . . ." I realized that it would be incredibly awkward to acknowledge that I was mentoring Rebekah with her standing right there. But then, if I lied, Rebekah would totally rat me out on it. There was no loyalty there. "Wandering around."

Rebekah shot me a weird look, but I ignored her. Sydney was watching both of us with narrowed eyes. "Is this that mentoring thing you and Ellen were talking about? Where you hang out with underprivileged girls or something like that? Hey, like you said. At least it'll look good on your eventual grad school application."

I closed my eyes. What had that been, less than fifty

words? And yet she had perfectly summarized every single thing I did *not* want said aloud. I couldn't even look at Rebekah. It was official: I was the worst mentor *ever*.

"Why haven't you been coming to the study group meetings?" Sydney asked, the books hitching her shirt down farther as she adjusted them in her arms. This was *so* not PG-13. "Is it because of what happened with Andrew? I meant to tell you how sorry I was—Heather is such a skank. Really, Leigh, you shouldn't blame yourself. It could've happened to anyone."

Desperately, I looked for the rest of the group, hoping I could at least use them as an excuse to end this horrific encounter. But they were down by the self-sustaining ecosystem some environmental science major had built for his thesis years ago.

With my misery accomplished, Sydney turned her attention to Rebekah. "So, what do you want to be when you grow up?" she asked in a cheery voice.

"Not a bitch like you," Rebekah said, making that smacking noise with her lips. Had I ever not liked that sound? Now it was the sweetest thing I'd ever heard.

Sydney just stood there for a few seconds, in complete shock. Then her lips flattened into a straight line, and she turned to me. "Nice job, Leigh," she said. "Way to really mold our nation's youth."

Gathering her books close to her chest (thank God, now it was covered), she strode off toward her fully loaded Toyota Celica. I waited until she was speeding away before looking at Rebekah. "That was *awesome*," I said.

Rebekah dismissed it with a wave of her hand. "It's the truth," she said.

"Yeah, but still totally cool," I said. "You have no idea, that girl is like my worst nightmare."

"Whatever," Rebekah said. "She's not as bad as she thinks she is."

I realized we were still standing in the open doorway of the psychology building. "So, did you want to go inside?"

"Nah."

For a second I'd really deluded myself into thinking there was a moment of genuine bonding here. Obviously, I was mistaken. Now we were back to incomplete sentences and near-monosyllables.

I shut the door and started strolling toward the ecosystem. Rebekah jogged a little bit to catch up. "So you never did it, huh?"

Maybe polysyllabic sentences were overrated. I sighed.

"Never really got around to it," I said. "As you heard, we broke up."

Her fifteen-year-old eyes were all-knowing. "Because he was a player and you wouldn't do it with him," she said. It wasn't a question.

I didn't even try to keep the bitterness out of my voice. "Pretty much."

"Bastard," she said. Hearing the word come from her mouth shocked me a little, but it felt surprisingly good. I smiled for the first time.

"Yeah," I said. "Pretty much."

"Tyrone, he's the guy at the Kmart, you know?" She glanced at me, as though expecting I wouldn't remember, but I nodded. Her first time, and apparently the father of her five-hundred-dollar baby. I remembered. "He was the best one I ever had. Not the sex, I mean. He wasn't any good at that. But he was the best guy I ever could have had."

"So, what happened?"

Her eyes were very serious. "I got knocked up."

Jesus. A part of me had expected this, but it still floored me somehow, now that it had been said aloud. "And you aborted the baby?" I asked, thinking of her question a couple of sessions ago.

She shook her head, surprising me. "I was gonna. Tyrone didn't want me to. But then I lost the baby, and Tyrone couldn't never forgive me."

From the tremor in her voice, it sounded more like she couldn't forgive herself. "How did you get pregnant in the first place?" I asked. "I thought you said you were on the pill, too."

"My mom put me on after my older sister got knocked up," she said, "but I wasn't any good at takin' it. I just couldn't get it straight. But now I do, like vitamins. But Tyrone, he wants nothin' to do with me. Then I was stupid, I hooked up with his friend, trying to make him jealous, and now he ain't never gonna want me back."

That's right, the second time had been better. Apparently, Tyrone, for all his virtues, still couldn't stack up to his friend when it came to the physical side of the relationship. And yet he was the one Rebekah was still hung up on, the father of her lost child.

I wished I had something to tell Rebekah, some words of wisdom that would put it all in perspective. *Time heals all wounds,* maybe, or *everything happens for a reason.* But the words would have been empty, and for once, the ability to lie completely escaped me.

Rebekah and I joined the group by the ecosystem, and then everyone walked to the events center to meet the bus. Rebekah was about to step on the bus when I called her back.

"Hey," I said.

She just stood there, one foot on the step. The bus was idling, and the fumes made me want to gag. "Anyone who can tell Sydney off to her face," I said, "is someone any guy would be lucky to have. Seriously."

Rebekah rolled her eyes, but I swear I saw a smile touch her lips. She boarded the bus, and I waved as it pulled away.

I totally meant what I said to Rebekah, but I knew better than anyone that sometimes it's not enough to know that you deserve someone. It doesn't change the fact that you lost him. I mean, sure, Andrew and I weren't fifteen, I hadn't lost it to him behind the Kmart, and I didn't lose his baby or sleep with his friend. But what if Andrew was my Tyrone and I never got over him?

What if time *didn't* heal all wounds?

I was walking back from the events center when I ran into

him—Nathan, not Andrew. Somehow it was way worse to see Nathan. Maybe it was because all I could think about when I saw him was a movie playing through my head of that last day, of how pathetic I must have looked trying to pick up pieces of broken glass on the ground, babbling about my first time.

He didn't smile, but when our eyes met it felt like he had. I looked away, not wanting to see the pity I was sure would be there.

"Hey," he said. "How are you?"

Gutted. Hopeless, thank you for asking. Shattered, depressed, helpless—crazy with the thought that if I had just gone through with it that night, maybe I'd still have Andrew. Angry with Andrew, blaming him for those doubts, for making me blame myself. Mostly, I just felt sad.

"Fine," I said, tilting my chin. "How's Heather?"

The question was supposed to come out ultracivilized, as though I were the kind of girl who could casually refer to the home-wrecking skank who'd stolen her boyfriend. Unfortunately, it didn't come out like that, and I felt my bitterness and insecurity hanging between us like dirty underwear on a clothesline.

"She got hit by a bus," Nathan said. "She lived, but she's in a full-body cast and had facial reconstructive surgery using parts from a gorilla. Doctors say she'll never be the same."

I finally looked at Nathan and saw the small smile, the gentle light in his eyes. "That's a shame," I said through the lump in my throat. "And Andrew? Was he hit by a bus, too?"

This time Nathan didn't smile. "I wouldn't know," he said. "I don't live with him anymore."

Of course. Even though it's not like he and Heather were picking out place settings, it still had to be awkward to live with a guy who was dating the same girl *you'd* just gone out with. Word on the street was that Heather was a rather loud girl . . . maybe Nathan had gotten sick of hearing her moan *OhGodthatfeelssogood* through the wall. I felt a new wave of pain wash over me.

"Oh," I said. Then, feeling the inadequacy of that response, I added a lame "I'm sorry to hear that."

Nathan's eyes searched mine. "Really? I'm not."

I didn't know what he meant by that, but I really didn't have the energy to figure it out. So he and Andrew had a falling out—big deal. Andrew had been having a lot of those lately.

Nathan shifted his backpack to one shoulder, clearing his throat. "So, do you want to grab a cup of coffee?" he said, gesturing toward the Toad's Monocle, which was where I had been heading. "Or we could go to Dunkin' Donuts—my treat, of course."

It was a really nice offer, even if it *would* be pity coffee. But didn't he know how much it hurt just to look at him?

"I can't," I said with a small smile that I hoped looked apologetic. "I'm running late for class."

His gaze pierced me, giving me that uncomfortable feeling I always got around him, as though somehow he knew I was lying. But how could he? It's not like he'd memorized my schedule.

He swung his backpack around, unzipping the front pocket and rummaging through it until he came up with an index card and a pen. I watched as he scribbled something on the card before handing it to me.

There was some complicated math equation on one side of the card, and I stared down at it for a few confused seconds before flipping it over. In bold blue ink, he'd scrawled his name and his phone number, which I recognized as having a northern California area code. I frowned down at it, the ten digits of his phone number more cryptic even than the calculus on the other side.

"What's this for?" I asked.

Nathan shrugged, but the movement was jerky. "Just use it if you need it," he said. "Okay?"

"Sure," I lied. "Thanks."

He nodded. "See you around, Leigh."

"Bye," I said in a whisper that Nathan, already walking away, was not meant to hear. I slipped the index card into my purse, knowing as I did so that I would never, *ever* call him. After all, the ex-roommate of my ex-boyfriend, who probably moved out because *his* sex-crazed ex-girlfriend (okay, they only went on one date, but still) was now hooking up with the guy I'd planned to lose my virginity to at my senior prom? And, oh yeah, the guy who was the subject of a pretty intense dream I'd had only a few weeks earlier?

Not exactly at the top of my speed-dial list.

SEPARATION ANXIETY: The protest
and distress exhibited by a child at the departure of a
caregiver

AFTER three months at college, of course I missed my parents.
I mean, I have a soul. When I watched *My Girl*, I totally cried
when Vada ran down the stairs at Thomas J.'s funeral, saying
how Thomas J. wanted to be an acrobat and needed his
glasses. But my parents had their psychic bed-and-breakfast, I had
my schoolwork . . . my mother left me long-winded phone messages, I called once a week to check in, and that suited us just fine.

That's not to say that my relationship with my parents
was something out of *Leave It to Beaver* (which I've never actually
seen, but people always reference it when trying to say that a
family gets along just fine). My dad is, in my opinion, certifi-

ably insane, with his eye patch and the tower he built on the roof when I was eleven, in the hopes of contacting "otherworldly beings." As if it wasn't embarrassing enough that we couldn't have satellite TV because it would "interfere with the signal"—he also just can't call them *aliens*, like normal people do.

My mom was always bugging me when my aura was murky or my planets weren't aligned, as though I could really do anything about it. The scary thing is that, half the time when she was subjecting me to her "readings," she was pretty spot-on. Not that I bought for one second that it was due to any true psychic ability. I just figured, isn't that supposed to be the maternal instinct or something? She never baked cookies or sewed Halloween costumes, so it's not like I've seen evidence of that instinct anywhere else.

Ami was flying out to Nicaragua to see her extended family for the long Thanksgiving weekend. She always said that you haven't experienced Thanksgiving until you've done it with two hundred screaming, crying, laughing Nicaraguan members of the Gutierrez clan.

"Isn't Thanksgiving an American thing?" I asked.

Ami paused, as though she'd never considered that before. "I guess it is," she said. "But tell that to *mis abuelos*. Any excuse to celebrate, they're in."

I asked her if they celebrated Cinco de Mayo, then.

"We're not Mexican," she said, offended.

I gave up. While Ami haphazardly threw clothes into two of the largest suitcases I've ever seen, I carefully folded outfits for my duffel bag. Whenever I go on a trip, I have a certain combination of clothes I always take. I bring a T-shirt for every day that I'm going to be gone, plus an extra one, to give myself some options. I make sure one of the shirts could double as a slightly nicer outfit if it needed to, and I pack a single cardigan in case it's cold.

But the key, I've discovered, is the pants. Many a suitcase has bulged because of a few bulky pairs of jeans. The trick is to wear jeans and then pack one pair of other pants—no less in case you spill on that first pair, and no more so you don't over-do it. I allow myself an extra pair per week that I'm going to be gone, meaning I almost never pack more than two pairs of pants.

Unlike many female stereotypes, I am a very light packer. Not the most hygienic, maybe, but light.

"You take care of yourself this weekend, okay?" Ami said, giving me the look I'd seen a lot of lately, as though she were a mother leaving her sickly child at day care.

"I will," I said firmly, more to convince myself than Ami. "I'll give tarot readings to the tourists, go for long walks, and pick up some good books. Just watch—I'll come back so chilled out, you'll have to give me an adrenaline shot."

Ami laughed. "Well, enjoy your catatonic long weekend," she said. "But have some fun, too, you know? Go to a club, meet a guy, get his digits and then never call him. Live a little."

First of all, let's just say Lindsay Lohan is not going to be making an appearance in Sedona's nightlife anytime soon. It's not what you would call swingin'. And secondly, I've never asked a guy for his number in my *life*—except for a group project or something, when we had to make plans to meet up together and work on the PowerPoint presentation. Or Nathan's.

But I hadn't asked for that. He just gave it to me. It'd been a week since the day I ran into him, and still that index card sat at the bottom of my purse, untouched. Well . . . not *untouched*, exactly, but unused at least. I had taken it out a couple times, turning it over, trying to figure out what possible motive he could have had for giving it to me.

It reminded me of the stupid things people wrote in high school yearbooks. *Leigh, you've made algebra so much more bearable. Call me sometime!* And then, inevitably, at some point over the summer I'd get so bored watching *People's Court* on TV that I would call. And they'd be very taken aback: *Oh, Leigh . . . I'm sorry, did you need something? No? Well, I'm kind of busy right now. . . .* And I always wanted to say, Hey, I didn't want to call you any more than you wanted me to. I just got bored and for a second pretended your message actually meant something.

Was that what Nathan's number had been? A token number, dashed off to relieve some sense of courtesy or guilt? If I called, would it be a pleasant surprise or would he immediately invent some excuse to get off the phone?

Somehow I guessed the latter. So I just slid the number back in my purse and returned to ignoring it, until the next time my hand would brush against it, and I would feel compelled to take it out again, as though the numbers weren't already burned into my brain.

I didn't tell any of this to Ami. If *she'd* been the one to get Nathan's number, she would have called him by now, cheerily brushed aside that initial awkward talk, and two hours later they'd have shared their secret phobias and most embarrassing childhood moments.

Meanwhile, I hadn't even told her about running into Nathan. Ever since we'd discussed that dream, she'd waggled her eyebrows at the slightest mention of his name. She seemed really fixated on the idea that we were cosmically meant to be or something.

All I can say is, if a dream means two people are destined for each other, then why am I not with Jake Gyllenhaal by now?

Ami and I left at the same time, and I helped her load her bags into her ride to the airport. I'd offered to drive her, but she had seen some post about a carpool that she elected to take instead. It meant that she had to ride with some weird girl whose mouth always gaped open like Brendan Fraser's, but I admit that I was a little relieved. The airport was an hour away, after all, and I still hadn't seen any gas money for the time I drove her twenty miles out to the flea market. We never did find the Virgin Mary figurine she was looking for.

"You have fun, too," I said, giving her a swift hug. "And not just Hispanic Thanksgiving fun, but your own brand of doing-the-robot-to-crunk-music type of fun."

"You know it," she laughed. And then she climbed into the car, waving at me as it pulled away. As much as I was looking forward to time by myself, I would miss Ami.

Since there are only seven hundred students at my school, the parking lots aren't too large. And yet I felt as if I'd walked five miles by the time I was done walking from one end to the other. I could've sworn I'd parked in the first row. I remembered, because I'd picked up Ami from class, and we'd given a sitcomworthy high five when we saw that such a primo space was available. And yet my car was nowhere to be seen.

"Dude, where's my car?" I asked aloud, setting my duffel bag down momentarily on the pavement.

"Miss?" I turned around to see a balding man seated in a little golf cart, with the words *Parking Services* emblazoned across its side. "Are you looking for . . ." He consulted his notepad, like Gretchen wasn't totally memorable. ". . . a 1971 AMC Gremlin?"

I had a sinking feeling in my gut. "Yeah. Where is she?"

"Miss, your car was towed just twenty minutes ago," he said. "You didn't have a decal. And it was well past your third warning."

It had been my fifth, actually, not that I was counting. I guess a part of me hadn't believed that they would actually tow a car, no matter what the little note written at the bottom of each ticket said. Especially a car as cute as Gretchen.

"Look," I said, thrusting my student ID at the man who apparently had nothing better to do than tow adorable antique cars. "Obviously, I'm a student. So can I have my car back now? I'll get a decal, I promise, but I'm supposed to go home for Thanksgiving this weekend."

"Sorry, miss," he said, without even looking at my ID. It wasn't my best picture, I'll admit—for some reason I'm craned toward the camera, my neck stretched out like a giraffe's. "The cars are taken to an impound lot. You'll have to go down there to pick it up, and it'll cost you three hundred dollars."

"*Three hundred dollars?*" If I had that kind of money, I would've flown home. As it was, my parents had sent me just enough money to drive. "Do you accept creepy robotic babies as trade? I could get you one that's worth five hundred dollars."

"What?" he said, furrowing his brow until his entire bald scalp wrinkled. "No — cash or credit only. Here's the address."

He gave me a pamphlet from Parking Services, which included paragraphs about how many warnings you got before your car was towed (three), acceptable reasons to appeal a ticket ("I just haven't bought a decal" was *not* among them), and what to do if your car got towed. Apparently, because it was a holiday weekend, I had until Monday to pick it up. After that, there'd be an extra fifty dollars per day added to my bill.

"Do you get a cut of this or something?" I asked.

He shook his head. "Just buy a decal, huh?" he said, and then he drove off.

I stood there in the middle of the parking lot (which was noticeably sans Gretchen), my duffel bag at my feet and the parking pamphlet in my hand. It occurred to me that all these things about parking would have been helpful to know, like, three months ago. Then it occurred to me that I *had* known them, and for some inexplicable reason I'd chosen to ignore them. And now I was totally stuck, because there was no way that I could come up with three hundred dollars before Monday.

222

I could ask my parents to lend me the money, but they wouldn't be happy, considering the car had only cost four hundred dollars in the first place. Still, that wouldn't help me get home right now.

Flying was out, and it was too late to join a carpool, but there was one other option. It's not like I didn't know someone from my hometown who was probably going home for the holiday weekend, but was more than likely still here working on a last-minute paper.

If he just happened to be my ex-boyfriend, well, I guess I'd just have to get over it.

Standing in front of Andrew's suite, my hand poised to knock, I felt a weird sense of déjà vu. It would be easy to think of him as my boyfriend again, to forget everything that had happened and the reasons that we were apart.

Then the door swung open, and there stood one gigantic reason we weren't together anymore, wearing layered tank tops and cracking her gum.

I don't see why she bothers to layer her clothes. You'd think someone who loves sex as much as she does would wear *less*, you know, in the interest of efficiency. "Um," I said, "is Andrew here?"

She gave me an assessing look before calling over her shoulder: "Andrew!"

In the five seconds before he appeared, my heart was like a hummingbird. I thought it would beat right out of my chest.

And then I saw him, and he looked . . . exactly the same.

I don't know what I expected—it had, after all, been only a few weeks. I wondered how I looked to him. I wondered if he missed me.

"Leigh," he said flatly.

Okay, maybe not. "*This* is Leigh?" Heather said, sounding relieved.

Nice. "Andrew, can I talk to you for a second?"

"I don't mind," Heather piped up. I bet she would've minded a lot more if I had been the *other*, überfeminine version of Leigh.

I rolled my eyes, reaching to grab for Andrew's arm until I realized that I couldn't really do that anymore. Touching him was something I needed *permission* for. "Whatever," I said, snatching my hand back. "Andrew, outside? Please?"

Heather gave him a long, sloppy kiss that I know was just intended to stake her territory and make me squirm. Well, it worked, and *not* because I'm jealous. Watching her kiss him was like watching someone lick a public toilet seat. It was just gross. It didn't matter that it was Andrew, the guy I thought I'd lose my virginity to, the ex-boyfriend whom I thought I'd be with forever.

So I was jealous. Big deal.

Once Heather's lips were sufficiently covered in saliva, he stepped outside. "Listen, Leigh," he said. "I know what you're going to say, and I just don't think it's a good idea—"

I held up my hand to stop him. "Before you embarrass

yourself, I'm not here because I want to get back together with you," I said. Right now, that was actually one hundred percent true. If he didn't have an STD before, he almost definitely did now.

That was mean, but I didn't care.

"So why *are* you here?" he asked.

"I need a ride," I said. "My car—you know what? It doesn't matter. The point is that I'm supposed to go home for Thanksgiving. I know we're not really on the best of terms right now, but I hope that you can at least be civil enough to let me come with you to Sedona. I'll split gas, of course."

"I'm not going home," he said. "Sorry."

Wow, I totally had not seen that coming. "What do you mean, you're not going home? It's Thanksgiving. You have to go home."

"Well, I'm not," he said. "I have a lot of work to do, and besides, winter break is just a few weeks away. It's completely illogical to go home."

"Any chance you'd change your mind?"

"You mean any chance I'd put a thousand miles on the Beamer and get behind on my reading just so I can drive the girl who said she didn't want to see me again out to a town I could care less about?"

Okay, so that was a no. And if I was wondering if Andrew was still an asshole, I had my answer. So why did I still feel a little tug when he went back inside to Heather, closing the door behind him?

* * *

My next plan of action was to call my parents. Maybe they could wire me money, like in those Western Union commercials. Maybe my mother had foreseen this happening and was already doing so. I moved around to the parking lot in front of the suites, glancing up to make sure I couldn't be seen from Andrew's window, and dialed my parents' number.

Pick up, come on, pick up. Finally I heard my mother's voice, that familiar slight Russian accent (she's from Vermont, but says there's nothing wrong with adding a little spice), and my shoulders sagged in relief.

It was the answering machine. "You have reached Astral Body B&B," it said, "home of fifth-generation psychic 'Mama' Nolan . . ."

Normally, I got a real kick out of this message. "Mama's" first name is Susan, and I'm pretty sure my grandmother painted a lot of T-shirts and worked in the garden. She died before I was born, but I never heard anything about her being a psychic.

But today it made me want to scream, and I gave in to it, letting out a high-pitched cry as I slammed my cell phone shut. Why weren't they answering the phone when I needed them the most? What good was psychic ability if you couldn't sense that your daughter was stranded with no car? Where was that maternal instinct *now*?

Maybe it was my encounter with Andrew and Heather, or maybe it was the fact that it was now two hours after I'd planned to set out and I was still in the parking lot with

226

my duffel bag. But I just felt *desperate*, like solving this car problem was the biggest deal in the entire world.

Suddenly I remembered Nathan's number, sitting at the bottom of my purse, and before I could stop myself, I was dialing. It rang once, twice, three times as I vacillated between praying for him to pick up and wondering what I would say if he did.

Finally, the ringing stopped, and there was a brief rustle before I heard his voice. "Hello?"

I'd started to worry he was one of those people who didn't pick up calls from strange phone numbers. I hate those people. Now, I opened my mouth, tears slipping down my face again. It was just so good to hear someone's voice that wasn't a recording, an ex-boyfriend, or the girl who was sleeping with that ex-boyfriend . . . it was so good to hear *his* voice.

"Hello?" He sounded a little more impatient now, and I realized if I didn't say something soon he might hang up.

"Nathan?" I tried to keep my voice steady, but a little tremble escaped through.

I heard another rustle. "Leigh? What's wrong?"

I didn't ask how he had known it was me. Since he's seen me at my absolute lowest moments, I'm sure that my weepy, pathetic voice was a dead giveaway. "It's m—my . . ." I felt everything hit me at once—that panic when I couldn't find my car, the shock of hearing it had been towed, the way Andrew had kissed Heather. He'd never kissed me like that. It rolled like a ball of clay, getting larger as it moved faster and faster, until it couldn't be stopped. I felt like I couldn't breathe.

"What is it?" His voice was urgent. "Leigh, talk to me."

Between hiccups, I told him about my car. I explained the bald parking-Nazi, the three hundred dollars, and the robotic baby. I almost told him about Andrew and Heather, but something made me stop. It just seemed like maybe there was a threshold for pathetic, and I'd reached it.

"Where are you?" he asked.

"The parking lot," I said.

"In front of your dorm?"

"No, in front of the suites," I corrected him. "I walked over here."

Which was totally unnecessary, of course, considering that my lack of car was what got me into this situation in the first place. Nathan also now basically knew that I'd gone to see Andrew, and I had just shredded any last chance at dignity I might have clung to.

"Okay," he said. "Just hold tight. I'll be there as soon as I can."

I should have said something. *No, you don't have to do that*, or *If you have three hundred dollars to loan me, I could have my parents pay you back*. But the truth was, I really needed someone there. I needed someone else to handle this, because I just didn't feel like I could do it alone.

"Thanks," I said to Nathan, but he had already hung up.

Even with the money, I would also need a ride to the impound lot, and there was no way I was going to go back and ask Andrew. It would look like I was trying to use the "door in the face" technique to get him to hang out with me. You know, like when politicians ask you to donate a hundred dollars to their campaign, and you slam the door in their faces. Then, if they knock again asking you to donate a dollar, you just do it because it seems way better than the hundred they were asking for before.

Like I would waste any persuasive techniques on Andrew.

I sat down on a tree stump to wait for Nathan. It seemed as if an impossibly short time had passed before I saw him emerge from his car, a pair of dark sunglasses covering his eyes. Seriously, he had to have broken the sound barrier or something to get here that fast, since he obviously didn't live in the suites anymore. Or at least a couple of campus speed limits (which are set at 12 mph—what's that about? As if Gretchen's speedometer has that kind of accuracy).

"Hey, Leigh," he said, coming to stand in front of me. I expected him to be smiling, laughing at me (who gets their car *towed*, after all, especially at a school that they go to?). But he wasn't smiling, and he held out his hand. After a brief hesitation, I took it, and he pulled me up easily.

"Sorry," I said, giving a shattered little laugh. "I kind of freaked."

That had to be the world's most obvious statement, but Nathan just nodded. "It's understandable," he said. "Your car means a lot to you."

It was true that I already missed Gretchen, but that wasn't the reason I felt my eyes start to well up. "I—thanks," I said.

229

"I know it was stupid of me to call you and make you come all the way out here."

Nathan looked at me. "It wasn't stupid," he said. "I'm glad you called."

"Yeah, but there's not really a whole lot that you can do," I said. "I mean, unless you have three hundred dollars to loan me. Then we could go pick up my car and I could drive home for Thanksgiving like I'd planned."

"To Arizona? In the same car with the amazing disappearing starter that vibrates out as you drive?"

Of *course* that was something Andrew would've told Nathan. "I know," I said. "She was only four hundred dollars when we bought her, and it seems ridiculous to pay almost that much just to get her back now. But Gretchen is special to me, and anyway, the starter problem has been totally fixed—"

Nathan laughed, shaking his head. "No, that's not what I meant," he said. "I just meant, it's not exactly safe to take her on a road trip. Don't you think?"

He was right, of course. My parents hadn't been thrilled, either, particularly my father, but I convinced them that I would get a tune-up and be supercareful on the roads. In the end, my mom fell back on her classic "If it's important to you, Leigh, then it's important to us." Sometimes my parents are so cool.

"I know," I said, my shoulders slumping. "I just really wanted to go home for Thanksgiving."

"Well," he said. "You still can."

"No, I can't," I said. "I can't even afford to get my car out of the impound lot, much less airfare for a last-minute flight on a holiday weekend."

"I'll drive you," he said. "If you want."

Okay, this was crazier than the time he'd told me I could stay in his room all night and finish my paper. "Sedona is, like, seven hours away," I protested. "And it's Thanksgiving weekend. You can't possibly drive me all the way there."

Nathan shrugged, as though the prospect of a seven-hour drive was as worthy of consideration as a drive to the gas station on the corner. "Why not?"

I gaped at him like that girl in Ami's carpool. "But, you've got plans of your own."

"Not really," he said. "But I'd be okay to crash yours. I mean, if you wouldn't mind."

I thought about it. "No," I said slowly. "No, I wouldn't mind."

"It's settled, then," he said, smiling at me. "To Arizona."

"To Arizona," I repeated dazedly. And before I could really think about what I'd just agreed to, he slung my duffel bag over his shoulder and started walking toward his car. For a few moments I just stood there, as if rooted to the spot. Nathan reached his car, but instead of tossing the duffel bag in the backseat, he turned. His eyes were still covered by the sunglasses, but it looked almost as though he were asking my permission—as though he were *willing* me to follow.

So I took a deep breath, and I did.

> **MERE EXPOSURE HYPOTHESIS:**
> A theory that repeated exposure to a stimulus leads to
> enhanced liking for it

THEY say you can tell a lot about a person by the way he drives. I don't know who "they" are exactly, but I'm sure I've read that somewhere.

Or maybe I just made it up after I spent a couple of hours watching Nathan drive.

Nathan was one of those effortless drivers, his left hand resting lightly on the steering wheel, the other on top of the column shift. His Chevy Cavalier was automatic, but you could tell he was more comfortable driving a stick shift, from the way his hand lingered there, as if ready to shift into the next gear at any minute. He maintained a speed just moderately over the limit, using the pinkie finger of his left hand to flick his signal light when he needed to pass someone going a little slower. And if he ended up getting stuck behind one of those people, he didn't curse and drum his fingers on the steering wheel the way I always did. He just dropped back a little, following at speed until he had the chance to pass them.

Mostly I stared out the window, but occasionally (okay, a little more than *occasionally*) I snuck a glance at Nathan from the corner of my eye. At one point he turned his head and caught my gaze, and I quickly looked away.

But if he noticed that I had spent the last hour sneaking peeks, he didn't say anything. "Do you want to put on some music?" he asked instead. "My CD book is in the backseat."

I had to unbuckle to reach back there, but finally I grabbed his mammoth book of CDs. I also noticed his guitar, lying across the scuffed leather of the seat. "Do you take that everywhere you go?" I asked.

It must have been the way the sun was slanting harshly through the window, but Nathan's skin briefly took on a red tint. "Sometimes," was all he said.

There was more there, I could tell, but I didn't feel comfortable prying. So I just flipped through his book, trying to find a CD to listen to. I was debating between Elvis Costello and Jonathan Richman when I came across a burned CD that looked far more interesting.

"Nathan's Summer Mix," I read, sliding it out of its pocket. "It's not summer, but this should be good."

"Hey, no — " Nathan said, reaching for the CD, but it was already in the player. His hand dropped away even as the first foot-stomping, hand-clapping beat of Gwen Stefani's "Hollaback Girl" filled the car.

"What — " I started to ask, but then I just cracked up laughing. " 'Hollaback Girl'? Really?"

If Nathan had looked a little uncomfortable before, now he looked downright embarrassed. "My sister made it for me, okay?" he said.

"Whatever you say," I said, holding up my hands in a mock gesture of surrender. "I'm sure she *made* you dress up and play tea party with her, too."

Nathan grinned. "Not really. As long as she let me wear the pearls, I was pretty willing."

I smiled, marveling at how easy this was. Maybe now that I wasn't a threat to his roommate, Nathan didn't hate me anymore. Or maybe we just had a camaraderie based on us both having been screwed over. Whatever it was, I was starting to feel like, crazy as it seemed, we could even be . . . friends.

I'd take No Doubt over Gwen Stefani's solo stuff any day, but I had to admit the song was catchy, and I found myself quietly singing along to the parts I knew and fudging the parts I didn't. I'm not exactly blessed with Jessica Simpson's voice—or even *Ashlee* Simpson's, for that matter—but I'm not the worst singer in the world, either. That distinction belongs to my dad.

To my surprise, Nathan started singing along. And even more surprisingly . . . he sounded really, really *good*. His voice was low and warm, wrapping around each word and somehow making "Hollaback Girl" sound like something an old crooner could have sung.

Well, until he sang along to the whole "B-A-N-A-N-A-S" part. Even Chris Isaak couldn't make *that* sexy.

My tongue tripped over one of the most obvious lines in the chorus. *Sexy?* What was I thinking?

So okay, he had a nice voice. And possibly an even nicer chest. And although he was a little possessive about his cereal and was a math major, which has to indicate *some* kind of pathology, he seemed an overall nice guy. Nicer than I had given him credit for, anyway.

But *sexy?*

It was the dream. It had to be. I was still associating real-life Nathan with über-romantic dream Nathan, and I'm sure even the lead singer of Nickelback could appear attractive in a dream.

Well, maybe not. But I had to figure out a way to stop this line of thinking. It was not only stupid, it was . . . well, diagnosably *delusional*.

The song ended, and Nathan reached over to turn down the volume. "Do you want to stop for something to eat?" he asked. "We need to get gas, anyway."

He took the next exit and pulled into a gas station where, after considerable debate, he finally allowed me to pay for the gas. Or maybe I shouldn't say *allowed* so much as *acquiesced* after I swiped my debit card into the machine, playfully shoving him out of the way before he could even get out his wallet. To give

235

him his due, he was gracious in defeat. Meanwhile, I was oddly triumphant for someone who had just elected to spend an obscene amount of money for twelve gallons of gasoline.

While I waited for the gas to pump, I leaned against Nathan's car. "I know you said you didn't have any plans," I said. "But I'm sorry for calling you out here and ruining your Thanksgiving weekend."

He moved next to me, so close that the sleeve of his T-shirt brushed my shoulder. "You didn't ruin it," he said.

"Yeah, but . . . you were probably just going to stay back and catch up on a lot of work," I said. "And your parents must be disappointed that you're going to see someone *else's* family instead of your own."

"Actually, it's just my mom," he said, and my face immediately flooded with guilt. Of course, I had forgotten about his dad's death. "And now that my sister's in college, my mom and her boyfriend decided to take this weekend to go on a cruise they've been planning for a while."

That was the second time he'd mentioned his sister. I realized I didn't know a lot about him, not even the things that I should have known by virtue of being his roommate's girlfriend. Ex-girlfriend now. Andrew hadn't told me a whole lot, and I'd never bothered asking.

I wanted to press him more, but then the gas stopped pumping and Nathan suggested that we head to the diner next door to get some food. I had been leaning toward just grabbing some Sno-Balls in the gas station, but he insisted that no road trip was complete without a meal in some greasy local diner.

It never took much convincing to get me to go anywhere with french fries, and so just a few minutes later I was sliding into the vinyl seat of a booth, Nathan taking the seat across from me. In restaurants with booths, Andrew would always sit beside me instead of across. I know this is a very couple-y thing to do, and I'll even admit to feeling envious of other couples sitting side by side prior to my relationship with Andrew.

But in actuality, it's very uncomfortable. You spend all of dinner turning to look at the other person, and it's an even bigger issue when one of you is left-handed. Not that either of us is, but it's the principle of the thing. Andrew would also drape his arm around my shoulders and then *leave it there*. Don't get me wrong, there's a thirteen-year-old girl inside of me who thrills at the fact that a boy is actually putting his arm around her. But there's also an eighteen-year-old (soon to be nineteen) who just thinks, *hello*, it's called personal space. When the food comes, that's pretty much the cue to remove the arm.

I wondered what Nathan was like in a relationship. Did he sit beside or across? Somehow I imagined he would get the whole personal space thing—and not just because I noticed that he was left-handed.

The waitress came, and Nathan ordered a large fountain Coke and a BLT. I ordered the same thing—not because I'm one of those girls who giggles and says, "Make that two"—as though *that's* the reason a guy will want to be with you, because you order the same food that he does—but because I tend to get very jealous about people's food once it arrives. So, unless it's, like, a tuna melt, which I will never, *ever* covet, I often find that it's best just to coordinate my order with the other person, so I don't suffer from a food identity crisis later on.

"I hope I have money to pay for this," I said after the waitress left, digging through my purse.

"You got gas," he said. "I'll get this."

I ignored him, continuing my scavenger hunt. I'm not superorganized with my purse, and most of my money tends to look like it spent a few solid days wadded up in some kid's pocket while waiting to be exchanged for quarters at the arcade. I started removing receipts and pieces of paper, piling them on the table as I sifted out viable money.

Nathan watched me the way most guys react to a girl and her purse—with the awed expression of someone observing alien life-forms in their native environment. He picked up one crumpled piece of paper. "What is this?" he asked.

I only noticed what it was after he had already flattened it out and begun to read the first few items. *"Rotter Incomplete Sentences Blank,"* he read. *"Number one . . . I like to read incredibly unrealistic and badly written romance novels."*

He raised an eyebrow at me, and I blushed. Ami wasn't exactly LeBron James (or his WNBA equivalent, whoever that was), and the assignment she'd tried to toss in the garbage had been sitting in an untouched ball on our linoleum floor for about two months. I only came across it in the post-Andrew desperation to organize the room and thus, symbolically, my life. At the time, I'd felt a weird compulsion to keep it, and so I'd put the whole paper—still crumpled up—in my purse with all my other junk, figuring that one day it would come in handy.

"Hey, give that back," I said, reaching for it.

"You bought Avril's first album?" Nathan asked incredulously, bending over the paper as though he fully intended to read the whole thing.

"You listen to peppy hip-hop dance music?" I shot back, leaning over the table to snatch it from him.

I half expected him to try to get it back, but he didn't. Instead he just sat there, looking at me with eyes that were no longer smiling. "When did you fill this out?" he asked.

I didn't have to ask what he meant. "Before," I said, and then added unnecessarily, "A few months ago, the time Andrew and I later went out for Thai food."

"Ah," he said, as though he actually knew the date I was referring to, which would have been completely ridiculous. It wasn't like he'd been keeping tabs. "*That* night, aka the eight-hundred-forty-sixth time Andrew was a complete ass."

I laughed, more out of surprise than humor. "Do you mean, in his life? Because I think you might have to add another, like, two billion to that number."

"I meant with *you*," Nathan said. "But you're probably right."

So I knew that Nathan and Andrew weren't exactly bosom buddies anymore, but Nathan's words were still a little jarring.

It almost sounded like he *hadn't* hated me for not being good enough for Andrew. After months of believing that absolutely, I wondered now if, just maybe, it hadn't been . . . well, the opposite.

Not that I had imagined Nathan's less-than-thrilled attitude toward me over the past few months, but I was starting to see it in a different light. Maybe he had disliked me, not because he felt I wasn't good enough for his roommate, but because he thought I was one of those stupid girls who's with a jerk and doesn't do anything about it.

Nathan said something that I didn't catch, too immersed in my own head to follow the conversation. "What?" I asked.

"I said it surprised me that you filled that out *before* the breakup," Nathan repeated. It was the first time I had really heard someone else say it so baldly—the breakup.

"Why?" I asked. "Because it's weird that I would still have a paper from two months ago in my purse?"

Nathan laughed. "No—you could have a lost treasure map to Atlantis in there and it wouldn't be a huge shocker. It's more because of the thing about your happiest time . . . you said you couldn't remember. It just seems to me like, if you were still with Andrew, you might have remembered something with him."

I scowled. "Do you know how hard it is to come up with answers for that off the top of your head? I don't know what you're trying to imply, but I can remember *many* happy times. The stupid question is inherently unanswerable—

it asks about the *happiest* time. And who knows that?"

Nathan shrugged. "Off the top of my head? My happiest time was when I saw They Might Be Giants in concert two years ago. The show was amazing and a lot of fun, and afterward I got to meet both the Johns backstage." He raised his eyebrows at me, as if in a challenge. "Of course, there's no objective measurement to tell me if that's my absolute *happiest* time, but it's what immediately pops into my head. What about you?"

"Me?"

"Yeah," he said. "What was your happiest time?"

I'm no Pollyanna. I don't play the glad game, and I'm not going to earn any gold star for positive attitude anytime soon. But it's not like I'm a Joy Division song away from slitting my wrists, either. So surely I should be able to come up with *something*, right? What was my happiest time?

It had been fun at the awards ceremony, giggling with Ami about the ludicrousness of Li's impromptu poetry reading. But I couldn't even think of that moment without it being tainted with what had happened afterward—the stupid confetti globe, the fight with Andrew . . . the breakup.

The waitress brought our sandwiches, plunking the plates down in front of each of us and leaving without any further conversation. Nathan gave me a wry smile, as if telling me he recognized my hope for a stay of execution with the arrival of the food. But it also told me I wouldn't evade the subject that easily.

"Technically, the question is *the* happiest time," I said, "not necessarily *my* happiest time. So I would have to say . . . the happiest time is being surrounded by friends and family with good conversation."

Nathan nodded, taking a bite from one of the halves of his sandwich and effectively dropping the subject. But I knew my answer was a cop-out, and what's more, I knew that *he* knew it, too. For some reason, I felt the need to justify myself.

"Honestly, that's what came into my head," I insisted. "And you're supposed to answer as quickly as possible, without thinking about how it's going to look or what it means about your personality. So I'm under no obligation to dredge up some memory of my happiest time and parade it in front of you—not that I'm under any obligation to you in the first place."

Of course, I was. What with the whole driving-me-to-Arizona thing. But that didn't give Nathan access to my inner thoughts and desires, right? It's not like I sold my soul.

Nathan put the sandwich down. "I never said you were," he said. "I just think it's interesting that you feel you have to 'dredge' it up in the first place."

Did he have a minor in psychology or something? Because I had to admit, he was pretty good at this. A little more hard-hitting Albert Ellis than feel-good Carl Rogers, but good nonetheless.

I was still considering my response when Nathan surprised me by reaching across the table, grabbing my hand.

"Listen, forget about it," he said. "It's none of my business, anyway."

Even though that was what I had just been thinking, I shook my head. "No, it's okay," I said. "I just . . ."

I trailed off, and Nathan's eyes searched mine. And somehow, even though I hadn't fully formed that last sentence in my head and in all truth had *no* idea what I was about to say, I felt as if he understood.

"Can I ask you a question?" he asked. His hand was still covering mine.

"Yes," I said, but it came out like a whisper. My lips were dry, and so I licked them, trying again. "Yes."

"Earlier you mentioned something about robotic babies. What's that all about?"

"Oh, that," I said, choking back an awkward laugh. What had I expected him to ask me, anyway? "It's a long story. . . ."

> **GARCIA EFFECT:** A biological preparedness
> that associates illness with something ingested and pairs
> sights and sounds with physical pain

WITHIN half an hour of eating that BLT, my stomach felt like the raw meat that Rocky pounds before his fights. I pressed my hand against my middle and closed my eyes, hoping it would just go away. The last thing I wanted was to be sick all over Nathan's car.

"Hey," Nathan said, glancing at me. "Are you okay?"

"I'm fine," I said. "I just get a little carsick when I read in the car, that's all."

Although he was wearing his sunglasses, I could see his forehead crinkle. "When were you reading?" he asked.

See, this is why it's not a smart idea to try to make

something up when you're not in top form—you make stupid, amateur mistakes. Like forgetting that the key to a good lie is that it has to be at least *somewhat* based in reality. "Uh, the back of the visor," I said. "That little warning about air bag safety is really riveting."

Quickly, I snapped the visor up, hoping that he wouldn't notice that the warning was almost completely peeled away. Even though we were heading eastward, the sun was still way too bright, and I couldn't help groaning as a new ripple of nausea overtook me.

"Are you sure you're okay?" he asked. "There's a rest stop in a couple miles—do you want me to stop?"

"Please," I managed to croak. How was it fair that we ate the exact same thing, and I felt like complete crap, while Nathan seemed totally fine? Boys and their iron stomachs.

We reached the rest stop, and I jumped out without waiting for the car to come to a full and complete stop. Unfortunately, there was no way I could make it to the restroom. I barely even made it to the *bushes* before I threw up my entire lunch.

Disgusting, right? Not to mention totally embarrassing. Nathan stood a respectful distance away, leaning against his car, but I'm sure he still saw more than he wanted to. At this point, Nathan could make a slide show of my worst moments: getting dumped, crying, being the first Stiles student in history to have her car towed from the school parking lot, and now puking bacon, lettuce, *and* tomato all over a rest stop. Nice.

Finally, when I thought I couldn't possibly have anything else in me, I walked sheepishly back toward Nathan. He held out a bottle of water.

"It's warm," he said. "But I thought you could use a drink."

"Thanks," I said, taking a large gulp. "Where'd you get this?"

"I have a whole case in my trunk," he said. "For emergencies just like this, actually."

Wow. I never thought I'd meet someone as conscious of roadside hydration as I was. "Sorry about . . . everything," I said. "You must be wishing you'd never gotten involved with this mess."

"I should be the one apologizing," he said, giving me a crooked smile. "I suggested that diner, and I started the BLT trend."

"Yeah, and didn't even have the decency to suffer along with me."

Nathan laughed. "I'll go make myself throw up, if that's what you want."

"Gross," I said, wrinkling my nose. "And that's called bulimia, for your information. Or anorexia with purging subtype. You know that a lot of people don't realize that some anorexics purge, too? They just don't binge. That's the difference."

"That's what you want to study, isn't it?" Nathan asked. "Distortion of body image or something like that?"

I nodded, taking another long sip of water. My stomach was starting to settle down, but still I frowned, considering Nathan's question. "Wait," I said. "How'd you know that?"

Nathan rubbed the back of his neck. "I pay attention," he said. "Is that a crime?"

"No," I said slowly. "It's just unexpected, I guess. What else have you noticed, besides my chosen topic of study and my predilection for John Hughes movies?"

"Come on," Nathan said, with a short laugh. "It's starting to get dark. If you're feeling better, we should really get moving."

"Okay," I said, "but first, just tell me three other things you noticed about me while 'paying attention.'"

"Why?"

"I'm curious."

He cocked his head, as if thinking about it. "All right," he said. "I'll tell you three things I've noticed about you. But you have to match me, three for three."

My stomach was starting to churn again, but this time I didn't think it was because of the BLT. "Fine," I agreed.

Nathan looked considerably surer of himself now. "Let me think," he said, stroking his chin and smiling to himself. "What else did I notice about you?"

"And really obvious things don't count," I put in, wanting to prevent any kind of trickery. "Like, you can't say that you noticed I drive a Gremlin. That's cheating."

"Same goes for you, then," Nathan said. "Okay, I have my

first thing. I noticed that you get really emotional over songs."

"I do not," I protested automatically.

Nathan raised an eyebrow. "You're going to tell me that you weren't crying that time 'Wonderful Tonight' played on the radio? You remember. You, Andrew, and I were driving to campus to see that student film."

I did remember. School had just started, and Andrew and I decided to go to the premiere of one of the film department's short features. Nathan had kind of tagged along, which I found pretty annoying at the time, considering that it was supposed to be a date. Once we were at the movie, Andrew was more attentive than usual, holding my hand, even leaning over to kiss me through several parts. Now that I looked back on it, it was one of the few times in those last couple of months that he had seemed to remember that he had a girlfriend at all.

And okay, I didn't exactly recall crying over "Wonderful Tonight," but that didn't mean it didn't happen. I do tend to cry a lot at songs. I've even been known to shed a tear over Blink182's "Damnit." Something about the whole *I guess this is growing up* thing. Now, how does that make sense?

"So, Eric Clapton's a genius," I said. "What else is new?"

"Your turn," Nathan said. "Remember, you have to match me, which means it has to be in somewhat the same vein as mine."

"What does that even mean?" I asked.

"Figure it out."

It was now truly dark, and at this rate we wouldn't get to

Astral Body until well after eight. But I really didn't care. I'd called my parents and they knew I was coming late, so they wouldn't worry.

"I noticed that you take your anger out on your guitar," I said finally. "Like, when I ate a bowl of your cereal, you went in your room and started playing like you were in Metallica or something."

"Actually, it was Alice Cooper."

I rolled my eyes. "Whatever. It was a little much, considering all I did was eat a bowl of Cinnamon Toast Crunch."

"I wasn't mad about the cereal."

"So what were you mad about?" I asked.

Nathan looked at me, but with the lights on behind him, his face was cast in shadow. "Nothing," he said. There was a long silence, and then he said, "You make faces when you read, you know. I can always tell when you're reading something happy, or suspenseful, or upsetting. Your face shows everything."

"Really?" That sounded horrible. "I always thought of myself as having an excellent poker face."

"Oh, you do," Nathan assured me. "Believe me, I have no clue half the time *what* you're thinking. But whenever you read, it's all reflected right there in your face. Like that time you came over, and Andrew was busy studying, so you read *In Cold Blood*. You were grimacing and flinching through the whole book, as though it was happening personally to you."

"So, basically, I'm way too affected by music and books," I said. "Wonderful."

Nathan laughed. "I hadn't thought of it that way, but yeah . . . I guess you are."

Another car pulled in to the rest stop, and I watched a woman and two kids get out and head toward the vending machines, more as a way to stall than anything else. Even though he said he couldn't read me half the time, this conversation was still making me oddly nervous.

"Are you okay?" Nathan asked.

"Yeah," I said, turning my attention back to him. "Why wouldn't I be?"

"Just checking," he said. "You looked weird for a second there."

"Weird?"

Nathan ran his hand through his hair. "You know what I mean."

He really was better at guessing what was going on in my head than he gave himself credit for. "You run your hand through your hair when you're nervous," I said. "Or tired. Or frustrated."

"Not really," he said.

"Yeah, you do," I said. "Believe me. You reach up, and run your fingers through it, just like . . ." Before I had time to consider the absolutely idiocy of what I was about to do, I stood on tiptoe, reaching my hand up and letting my fingers slide through his hair. It was thick, and softer than I'd imagined. I cringe a little to admit that I lingered, just a little bit, when my fingers brushed the warm skin of his neck. Then I pulled away. ". . . This," I finished.

I could tell Nathan was looking at me, but I couldn't make out his expression. He was quiet, and his silence, coupled with the darkness, made me a little nervous that I'd just made a complete fool of myself. "Your turn," I said jaggedly.

"Um . . . okay," he said, uncharacteristically flustered. "You . . . smell like rain."

Whatever I expected, that hadn't been it. "Is that a good thing or a bad thing?"

"Good," he said. "Definitely good."

"You have a very nice chest," I blurted out, my face immediately getting hot. "I mean, that's something I've noticed. When you aren't wearing a shirt. Or, you know. Whenever."

Great. Now it looked like I was always checking Nathan out. Which was *totally* not the case—well, okay, not completely. But what was I expected to have done? Look away? I'm not a saint.

"I bet I don't smell like rain now," I said, giving a nervous laugh. "I probably smell gross."

Nathan leaned in, and I could feel him brush the top of my head. "You still smell like rain," he said, his voice raspier than usual.

He was standing much closer now, and I was suddenly very aware that the woman and her two kids had already driven away. It was dark, and Nathan and I were alone at a rest stop almost a hundred miles from Flagstaff. I was also very conscious of the fact that, no matter what he said, it was impossible that my breath wouldn't smell at least a little like vomit. Which was a mood killer, if there ever was one.

"We should get going," I said shakily. "I don't want my parents to have to wait up too late."

For a second Nathan just stood there, and then he leaned in toward me. Even though it was dark, I closed my eyes, half expecting a kiss. But instead he just opened my door for me. "You're right," he said. "We need to get back on the road."

I climbed into the passenger seat, and he shut the door behind me before crossing to the other side. I leaned my head back against the seat. This is what I'd wanted, wasn't it?

So why did it feel like such a letdown?

NATURALISTIC OBSERVATION: A
type of study where the researcher does not intervene,
but rather measures behavior as it naturally occurs

AFTER the incident at the rest stop, and as if by unspoken agreement, Nathan and I stuck to more casual conversation. I discovered that the "Summer Mix" included such classics as Wilson Phillips's "Impulsive" and the theme from *The Neverending Story*, which led to never-ending amusement on my part. By the end of the CD, Nathan was openly admitting that, although his sister had compiled it for him, it was based on his own guilty pleasures.

The Incomplete Sentences task, which I had originally wanted to crumple back up and just forget about, actually was revived as a source of entertainment as Nathan and I went through the items. I read aloud some of my responses—skipping over the ones where I talked about how strangely sensitive I am and the feeling of dread that I often felt, because, hey, road trips should be lighthearted. When I started thinking of this as a road trip rather than a pity drive one step up from *Driving Miss Daisy*, I have no idea, but I think it was sometime between "Hollaback Girl" and that moment at the rest stop.

"So, what do you see in romance novels, really?" Nathan asked, still watching the road.

"You can read them in one sitting," I said promptly.

"That's it?" Now he turned to face me for a brief second, one side of his mouth curving up in a smile. "I can read a cereal box in one sitting, too—doesn't mean I'd put it on any recommended reading list."

"Of course that's not *it*," I said, and laughed. "But they're like the perfectly self-contained escape, you know? In just a few hours you can enjoy sometimes-not-so-witty repartee, mostly-but-not-always sizzling sexual tension, and generally satisfying hookups. If they're good, they're great, and if they're not . . . they're better. What more could you ask for?"

"What more indeed?" The exit for our next highway came up, and Nathan expertly maneuvered the car through off-ramps and on-ramps before he finally spoke again. "So, what about *your* stories?" he asked.

At first I actually thought he meant my personal experiences of romance. In that case, I would have to say the banter was more wooden than witty, the sexual tension was more tension than sex, and the hookup was . . . well, nonexistent.

Then I realized Nathan must be referring to the part on the Incomplete Sentences where I mentioned making up stories in my head, and I felt stupid all over again. "Oh," I said, blushing a little. "They're dumb, really. Just typical girlie romantic stuff."

"I do it, too," Nathan said. "Make up stories to pass the time as I lie in bed."

"Oh, yeah? What are yours about—cats?"

The words were out of my mouth before I could stop them, and even in the darkness I could tell that the look Nathan shot me was one of confusion. At least he didn't seem to make the connection between his cat doodles—which I hadn't meant to bring up, however obliquely—and my question. I would hate to have had to admit one *more* thing I'd noticed, especially when it came from me snooping around his room.

"No . . ." he said. "Are yours?"

"No." I stared out the window, torn between my desire to know more about *his* bedtime stories and my reluctance to share my own. I've never told another soul about the stories I make up while I'm trying to fall asleep, and I would never even consider writing them down. They're just too personal.

Nathan fell silent as well, and I realized that maybe I wasn't the only one who felt that way. I wondered how many people in the world have daydreams spinning around in their heads that they would never put into words. Probably more than you would think.

We talked about other things—the mentoring program,

Nathan's music, our classes—but we always came back to the Incomplete Sentences. It seemed as if it was our way to avoid the conversation turning to other topics, like where exactly Andrew fit into all of this and why I'd practically caressed Nathan's hair. Or at least, that's how it seemed to me.

"What's your greatest fear?" I asked him, glancing back at the Incomplete Sentences.

"Probably that Sydney Belcher will cook my bunny rabbit," he said wryly. "That girl is intense."

I was glad he'd brought her up, so I didn't have to. Curiosity had been killing me ever since I saw them together at that beach party. "Yeah, what's up with that?" I asked, in what I hoped was a casual tone. "You hung out a couple times, right?"

Nathan shrugged. "She needed some math help for her thesis, or so she said. It didn't take long to figure out that she had a whole different agenda. Who asks a freshman for help with her senior thesis, anyway?"

I laughed a little too exuberantly at that, so I quickly shifted the focus back onto the psychology assignment. "No, but really. What are you scared of?"

"Losing someone close to me," he said.

For the next few moments, I listened to the sound of the highway passing underneath us and tried to think of something to say. Of course that would have been his biggest fear. I felt like such an idiot. Before I could say something about his dad, though, he brought up mine.

"So your dad wears an eye patch and your house smells

like incense," Nathan said, raising his eyebrow at me.

"It's not what you think," I said. "Well . . . I guess it kind of is. But we're not carnies or anything—my parents run a psychic bed-and-breakfast. The incense and eye patch are just two manifestations of their spirituality, or else gimmicks to sell more spirit bracelets, depending on how you look at it."

"How do *you* look at it?" Nathan asked.

I don't think anyone had ever asked me that flat out before. I was starting to think that Nathan's passenger seat should really convert into a couch in order for me to get the full experience. "I don't know," I said. "My mom doesn't predict lotto numbers or natural disasters or anything like that, but she is good at reading people. And my dad has always said he's more a filter than anything else. So, if they're passionate about it, and the tourists seem to have fun with it, why not?"

"They sound cool," Nathan said.

"They are," I said, and realized that I really, really meant it. I never gave my parents too much thought, and I guess I had kind of taken them for granted over the past few years. But for all their somewhat embarrassing quirks, they were amazing people. I was excited about introducing them to Nathan—and oddly, even more excited about introducing Nathan to them.

"What about you?" I asked casually, as though I hadn't been curious about this for the past few hours and, possibly, the past year. "What are your mom and her boyfriend like? And your sister—I'm an only child, which I always thought kind of sucks. I wish I had a sibling."

"Other than making incredibly mortifying mix CDs for me, Joanie's awesome." Nathan smiled. "But, believe me, I wished I was an only child sometimes when she would go postal because I took the last Pop-Tart, or when she'd pinch herself and say I did it to her."

I noticed he didn't immediately answer my question about the rest of his family, and I wondered if he had just forgotten or if he was being deliberately evasive. Six hours ago, I would have dropped it. Now, I just got more aggressive. "You probably got even closer because of what you both had to go through with your dad," I said.

Nathan shook his head, but it wasn't in denial. "I wondered if you knew, but I guess I shouldn't be surprised. Ever since Andrew heard about me bawling like a baby in Spanish class after my dad died, he sure does love to tell that story."

"I heard it was biology, but yeah," I said, thinking that maybe I shouldn't have brought it up but, now that it was broached, not wanting to back down. "So . . . it's true, then?"

He turned to look at me, a slant of light falling across his face. "Is it true that my father had cancer? Yeah. And is it true that I completely broke down, if that's what you'd call it, after he died? Yes. I missed my dad. I'll never stop missing him—it's like that itch you sometimes get in your ear, so deep inside you can never reach it. Someone as self-centered as Andrew could never even begin to understand it."

And then, as if he hadn't just opened himself up and poured his guts all over the car, one corner of Nathan's mouth lifted. "So," he said wryly. "You'll forgive me if I'm not thrilled to hear that Andrew's still spreading that around."

"I'm sorry," I said, the words completely inadequate. I was sorry Nathan's dad had died, but I was also really ashamed that I had never stopped to think about what Nathan must have been going through. For me, the story was just another piece in the puzzle of figuring out what made Nathan tick. To him, it was a painful and personal memory. I had no right to exploit it.

Nathan started to run a hand through his thick hair, but stopped in midmotion, as though realizing what he was doing. His hand dropped back to the gearshift. "Hey," he said. "It's not your fault."

That was a matter of opinion, but I didn't push it. We were nearing my parents' house, and I directed Nathan for the rest of the way, telling him where to go as I pointed out local landmarks. There weren't many—the C'est La Vie cafe, the public library, Madame Ruby's rival psychic shop—but he had that way of listening that made you feel as though everything you said was the most fascinating thing he'd ever heard. What had he said before? I *pay attention.*

Note to self: Learn how Nathan does this before becoming a therapist.

Finally we pulled into the Astral Body B&B, an ornate Victorian house completely out of place among the stucco buildings. My parents had had the old house torn down when I was just a baby, insisting the gingerbread-looking replacement was far more their style. They were warned they'd have termites, and we've had to tent it a couple times since then, but they never worry too much about worldly stuff like that.

I grabbed my duffel bag, leading the way up the steps as Nathan followed behind me, carrying his guitar. When we walked through the door, a little bell tinkled, and my dad came out from behind a display of Sedona postcards and calendars that tell where the planets are each day. I have, like, five of those, so I happened to know that Jupiter was currently in the part of its orbit that was closest to Earth. What that meant for the cosmos, I still didn't totally understand.

"Tuesday!" he said, opening his arms wide while I ran into them. Maybe I missed my parents more than I had thought, because it felt really, really good to be home. My mother came out, joining in the hug and the celebration. My dad asked questions about school, my mom fussed over my haircut, and I rolled my eyes at Nathan even though I was secretly enjoying myself.

I tried to see them from Nathan's perspective. My dad was very tall and distinguished-looking, really, with his white hair and his eye patch. His face creased easily into a smile, settling into lines that were so deeply etched you knew that was where his face really wanted to be. My mom looked less like a carny and more like Carnie Wilson after losing eighty pounds, with her sleek black bob and her tasteful eye makeup. Her lips were a bright red streak across her face, and when she smiled, she flashed two rows of white teeth, the front two slightly over-lapping.

Finally my mom turned to Nathan. "And you brought a new man," she said in that slightly accented voice, waggling her eyebrows at him. "He's a good-looking one."

Now I remembered why I often forgot how cool my parents were. They could also be incredibly embarrassing, especially my mother. "Nathan's not my new man," I said, giving Nathan a rueful smile that said, *Parents—what are you going to do?* "My car got towed, and he was nice enough to give me a ride."

My dad was asking about my car, but my mother had a one-track mind. "Why not? This one has a much better vibe than that other one you're with—what's his name? Adam?"

I didn't believe for one minute my mother didn't remember his name. When we'd gone to the senior prom together, she'd taken, like, a thousand pictures, for crying out loud. "Andrew, Mom," I said. "My boyfriend's name is Andrew. Nathan's actually his roommate."

Nathan shot me a look that I ignored. Ex-roommate, ex-boyfriend, whatever. I didn't feel like getting into it right now.

Apparently, neither did my mother, because she brushed off my explanation and clapped her hands together instead. "An aura photo! Yes, we will see his aura!"

"Mom," I protested. "Not tonight, okay? Nathan's been driving all day; I'm sure he's very tired. . . ."

But Nathan, the traitor, just grinned at me. "That sounds great, Mrs. Nolan," he said.

My mother made a psssh-ing sound. "Call me Mama," she said. "And this is my husband, Maple."

I know that's her psychic moniker, but I still wasn't comfortable with her telling Nathan to call her that. It made it seem like they were one step away from being in-laws or something. And Maple is a *woman's* name. I've explained that to my dad a thousand times, but he never listens. He says that it's the tree he feels most connected to, and there's just no arguing with him about nature.

"Or you can call her Susan, and he's Dave," I muttered, and she shot me a silencing look.

"Let us just set it up," she said, disappearing through a doorway hung with beads and dragging my dad with her.

As soon as they were gone, Nathan turned to me. *"Tuesday?"*

I sighed. I could have happily lived a thousand years without *that* coming out. "Leigh is my middle name," I said. "My first name is Tuesday."

I waited for some weekday-related joke, but he just nodded. "Tuesday," he repeated, and for a minute I reconsidered my choice to go by my middle name. Tuesday didn't sound so bad when he said it. "I like that. So what exactly is an aura photo?"

It wasn't like I could be embarrassed any more than I already was, so I decided to just take the plunge. "Here," I said, guiding him into the main room. "I'll show you."

My parents' style was kind of eclectic-Turkish-folksy that somehow really worked. On the scuffed hardwood floors were these gorgeously soft rugs, the couches were overstuffed and comfy, and the room was decorated in an explosion of folk art,

Eastern tapestries, and kitsch. I led Nathan to the far wall, where a picture hung slightly apart from the rest. It was one of those classic picture frames parents buy—featuring twelve little ovals surrounding a bigger oval.

"Most parents put their kid's school pictures in here," I said. "But not mine—mine put my aura photos."

It started when I was five, toothlessly smiling into the camera with a swirl of colors all around me. Over the years, sometimes the colors dimmed, indicating poorer spiritual health, and other times they were so prominent you could barely see my face. I'm not saying I buy into all of this, but my aura *was* the dimmest around third grade, which would make sense, considering the stuffed-monkey theft I had had to put up with that year.

I explained to Nathan what some of the colors meant and how to interpret the photos, although I knew my mother would go into a much longer analysis. He asked questions, but they seemed to be less about aura photos in general and more about *my* aura photos.

There was a photo album on one of the bookshelves, and Nathan sat down on the couch, flipping through it. I always thought it was superawkward that any tourist could just glance through pictures of me naked in the tub as a baby, but it was even more uncomfortable when it was someone you knew who was looking.

Nathan smiled at some of the pictures, and he asked questions about a couple, but mostly he just flipped through the album silently. He got to the end, which featured one of many prom photos. I was wearing a dark teal strapless dress, smiling up at Andrew as he slid a corsage on my wrist.

He stared down at the picture for a while before looking up at me. "You haven't told them yet."

I squirmed uncomfortably. "Not exactly," I said. "But I'm sure they suspect. It's hard to get stuff by my psychic mother and my father's eagle eye."

It was intended to be funny, but Nathan didn't laugh. He just closed the book, placing it back on the shelf between a travel book on Thailand and a Kurt Vonnegut novel.

My mother chose that moment to lean in from the doorway, her heavily painted lips smiling widely. "Come, Nathan," she said. "Everything is ready for your photo."

Without another look at me, he followed my mother through the beads. I plopped down on the couch, a tear slipping silently down my cheek. I didn't even know why I was crying, but once I started, tears flowed out of me faster than I could stop.

A woman wearing a shoulder-padded striped shirt and a pair of those awful pants that looks like a skirt came in and then immediately turned around when she saw me. I knew I was probably horrible for business, but I just didn't care.

I reached up to slide the photo album down from the shelf, opening it on my lap to the very last picture. It had been taken the spring of my senior year, when Andrew and I had still been happy—still been *together*. We were sitting on the porch swing, his arm around me, pulling me closer. I touched my fingertip to his face.

Usually my mom spends at least ten minutes analyzing the photo with the person, so I was surprised to look up and see Nathan. He had a Polaroid in his hand, and he tossed it onto the couch next to me.

"Add it to the album if you want," he said, his face expressionless. "Or don't, whatever. But I don't want it."

With that, he turned and walked out the door, and I knew from the tinkling bells that he had gone out the front door, as well. I picked up his Polaroid, puzzled.

He must have heard something he didn't like in there, but looking at his photo, I couldn't think what. His aura was very strong, especially with the color blue, which meant that he was very good at making the complicated simple. There was an orangish-brown on the left side, which indicated some past wound, but the right side was yellow, which implied future healing.

Was that it? Had my mom picked up something about his dad's death? I knew that Nathan didn't like to talk about it much, but he was clearly still grieving for his father.

Taking the photo with me, I went outside to find Nathan leaning against the wraparound porch, strumming his guitar. "Hey," I said.

"Hey."

That was as far as I had gotten in my head with the script of what I would say to him. I sat down on the porch swing, using the balls of my feet to rock gently back and forth. "Did something in there upset you?" I asked tentatively.

He sighed, setting his guitar down. "Yeah—no," he said, running an agitated hand through his hair. "I don't really want to talk about it."

"Okay."

And then, as if he hadn't just said that, he started talking. "My dad was sick for three years, you know?" he said, looking not at me but at some distant point in the sky. "*Three* years. You'd think that'd be enough time to prepare you, but it's not."

"I don't think anyone's prepared to lose their parents," I said quietly. "How can you be expected to be when you were still in high school?"

He looked at me then. "So, how long do you think it takes to let it go, then?"

I shrugged, not exactly wanting to give an expiration date. "I don't know," I said. "I don't think you ever do, completely. But I don't think that's necessarily a bad thing. It's just something you carry with you."

"Baggage, that's what people call it," Nathan said. "You're saying that losing someone means you'll always carry around that baggage?"

I don't know why, but I almost got the impression we weren't talking about his father anymore. "I guess," I said, wondering what it was he wanted from me. "But after a while it becomes a part of you, and you just . . . adapt."

Even through the dark, I could feel the intensity of his

eyes on me. "Maybe I'm expecting too much," he said softly. "Maybe it's just too soon."

I wondered what exactly he meant by that, but I never had the chance to ask. He picked up his guitar again, and he began lightly strumming. After a while, he started to hum along, and then he was singing, his voice low and rumbly in the otherwise quiet night. I closed my eyes, leaned my head back, and just listened.

When he finished, I smiled. "That was a really pretty song," I said. "Did you write it?"

He gave a little laugh. "No, Wilco did," he said. "But yeah, it's one of my favorites."

Something occurred to me, and I sat up to face him. "Earlier, I asked you if you brought the guitar everywhere," I said, "and you got kind of weird. Why? It's not like you're one of those jerks who always has a guitar but can't actually play it."

"Don't you know?"

"No."

He grinned. "Everyone knows that the whole point of learning guitar is to impress the girls. You can't just say, 'sorry, I'd love to show off, but I forgot my guitar at home,' can you?"

Now it was my turn to laugh. "I guess not."

"So now you know my secret," he said. "Did it work?"

I pretended to think about it. "Yeah, it worked."

> **STRANGE SITUATION:** A situation designed to study attachment, wherein secure attachment in a baby is measured by the degree to which the baby is upset when a caregiver leaves, and calmed down when the caregiver returns

EVENTUALLY, I know that my parents will completely redecorate my room to make it another guest room. In a bed-and-breakfast, after all, space is a pretty huge commodity. But for now, my parents had kept it exactly the same, which was kind of a relief. I don't think I could come back for my first visit after college and find my bed covered in one of those patchwork quilts my mother uses for guest rooms, or see the obligatory ten mirrors on the wall. My mother loves mirrors.

"So, this is your room," Nathan said, setting his guitar down and glancing around.

"Yup," I said. "Sorry you don't get your own room.

Usually Thanksgiving is a pretty slow time for us, but I guess we're all booked up. You're probably tired from the drive, though, so you can take the bed tonight."

He looked at me but didn't argue. "Okay, thanks," he said. "We'll switch off."

"Oh," I said, a little taken aback that it had been that easy. "No problem."

Oblivious of my inner turmoil, Nathan walked over to my vanity, the surface of which was covered in pictures of me and friends from high school (most of whom I'd already lost touch with, save the occasional Facebook message). There was also a star-shaped box I'd painted and collaged, a blown-glass paperweight, and a small statue of Buddha my parents had given me for my sixteenth birthday.

"This must have been an awesome place to grow up," he said, picking up the paperweight and looking at the colors swirled inside the clear glass.

"In some ways it was," I said. "But sometimes it was a little overwhelming. I spent a lot of time climbing out that window and sitting on the roof. I mean, I can't find the Big Dipper to save my life, but it's fun just to look at the stars, you know?"

Nathan crossed over to the window, pressing his face against the glass. My room was right above the front porch, so it was relatively easy to step onto the flat part of the roof and hang out. "Is that why you went to that stargazing?" he asked.

How *did* he know so much about me? As if I'd asked

the question aloud, Nathan turned around. "I was there," he said.

Of course. I remembered now—it had been orientation week, and one of the nightly events was stargazing with the astronomy professor. It happened to coincide with the '70s throwback roller rink party, so not many people had showed up. Nathan and I had both gone for the telescope at the same time, bumping shoulders, and he'd apologized. I'd barely looked at him—we hadn't even met yet. And now here we were, standing in my childhood bedroom.

"My dad probably has some pajamas you can borrow," I said, figuring I'd take care of that issue before it even arose. "I'll be right back."

When I returned a few minutes later, holding an old pair of cotton pajamas, the window was open and Nathan was nowhere to be seen. I set the pajamas on the bed and leaned out the window.

He was sitting on the roof, his arms linked around his knees. "You're right about the stars," he said. "I don't think you get this effect staring through a telescope, although of course that's breathtaking in its own way." He looked at me, inclining his head. "Come on, join me."

I climbed out the window, years of memories passing with me as I sat cross-legged on the roof. We sat for what felt like an eternity just like that, with no words, as though somehow they would ruin the magic of the night.

But then the question just tripped out of my lips, and

I couldn't stop it. "Do you think Andrew loved me?"

I could feel Nathan's eyes on me, but I kept my gaze trained on the sky, not wanting to see an answer in his face that contradicted the one from his lips. "I think he did," Nathan said finally. His voice sounded sad. "In his own selfish way, I think he did."

Somehow, I believed him, and his words eased some deep part of me I hadn't even recognized as hurting. "I hope so," I said. "Because he never said it first—he would only ever say 'I love you, too.' And I would hate to think that he was talking about the *band* U2 the whole time, you know?"

Nathan laughed, a low chuckle that vibrated in my bones, and like every other time I'd made him laugh, it felt like an achievement. "Hey, Nathan?"

The laugh died on his lips and in his eyes, and was replaced with a look that reminded me somehow of that night at the bonfire. "Yeah?" he said.

"I'm sorry I called you self-righteous."

He looked away then, and it was a long time before he spoke. "That's all right," he said.

The next day I decided to take Nathan to C'est La Vie for breakfast, since it was one of my absolute favorite things about Sedona and one of the few places that stayed open for at least part of Thanksgiving Day. Also, I knew that if we stayed home, my mom would just ask more questions and my dad would want to show him the various healing gems and stones we had in the front. I have a whole bunch of them mixed up with rocks I got at a science museum, and I can't tell the difference.

I hadn't slept that well the night before, which I blamed on sleeping on the floor. It couldn't have been Nathan, since it wasn't like I hadn't slept in the same room with him before. Technically I fell asleep that night I used his room to work on my paper, listening to his soft snore in the bed right behind me. So this was no different.

Except that it was, somehow, and I couldn't pinpoint why. Sure, we'd spent a lot of time together in the last twenty-four hours, and we'd had a few pretty intense conversations. But he was still *Nathan*, the math major who draws cats and had had a front row seat at some of my all-time most cringeworthy moments. So I decided that today, we were just going to have fun, without thinking about school or Andrew or anything else.

"Get pineapple cream cheese with your bagel," I suggested as we stood in line at the café. "Seriously, you won't be sorry. It sounds weird, but it's delicious."

"Why don't I just try some of yours?" he said. "I'm not much of a risk taker."

"Sure you are," I said. "You drove all the way out to Arizona to stay with a crazy, New Age family, didn't you? And you risked life and limb by having an aura photo taken. I mean, who knew what it might have revealed?"

"That's true," he said. "And I did take my life into my hands by eating that BLT. . . ."

I turned, and just at that moment, Andrew walked into the café with Heather hanging on his arm. If David Beckham had walked in, I couldn't have been more surprised. "Oh my God."

"Sorry," Nathan said. "I know that's a painful memory. And really, you deserve all the credit for eating that thing."

"No . . ." I said, but there was no time to explain. Heather was pointing in our direction, and they were heading toward us.

"What?"

"*Andrew's* here," I hissed. "With Heather."

My last thought was that I really should've washed my face that morning, and maybe put some vitamin E cream under my eyes to hide the circles. But then there was no more time to think, because Andrew and Heather came to stand right behind us in line.

"Leigh," Andrew said, inclining his head. Then, a little less politely, "Nathan? Why are you here?"

"Because I want to be," Nathan said. Although I couldn't see him, I could imagine him looking at Andrew with that cold green stare I used to think was directed at me. At least, I hoped it was directed at Andrew now, and not me.

I was going to be cool. I'd made it through our last encounter without bursting in tears or having a full-fledged freak-out, so it shouldn't be hard to make civil small talk as we waited for our bagels and mochas. "What are *you* doing here?" I asked, a shrill edge to my voice.

Whatever. Being cool is totally overrated.

"We're getting breakfast," Heather chirped, rubbing her

hand on Andrew's chest. They had been together less than a month, and already they were acting more like a couple than Andrew and I ever had. Maybe that should've opened my eyes, or made me realize something, but instead it just made me bitter.

"I meant, what are you doing putting miles on your precious BMW and getting behind in your reading?" I asked. "Oh, and coming to a town you 'could care less about.' FYI, Andrew, it's *couldn't* care less."

"Come on, Leigh," he said. "You know it would've been awkward to drive out here together. How was I to know I'd run into you?"

Nathan cleared his throat, but I ignored him. "If only my craving for pineapple cream cheese hadn't foiled your perfect plan," I said sarcastically.

"You still eat that stuff?"

He was not allowed to do that. He was not allowed to bring another girl to *my* hometown, to *my* café, and then make some comment about my cream cheese choice like we had all this history together. I mean, we did. But history was *not* going to repeat itself.

Nathan cleared his throat again, and I spun to face him. *"What?"*

"Can I take your order?" a hassled-looking teenager asked from behind the counter, and Nathan raised his eyebrow at me.

"Um, just a bagel with pineapple cream cheese and a medium mocha," I said. "And he'll have . . ."

"I already ordered," Nathan said.

"Perfect," I muttered, digging through my purse, but Nathan shook his head and put a ten-dollar bill on the counter.

The clerk opened the register and started counting out change, dropping it into Nathan's outstretched hand.

"So, I see your ride situation worked out," Andrew said from behind me.

"Couldn't have been better," I said. "Good thing *some* people aren't so hung up on themselves that they can't be bothered to help anyone else. When I called Nathan, he was more than happy to drive me to Arizona."

"How convenient."

"Leigh, can I talk to you?" Nathan said, tugging on my arm. Reluctantly, I followed, leaving Heather and the clerk wearing twin expressions of *What the hell is her problem?* Andrew looked unruffled, as usual. But then, he *knew* what my problem was.

"What are you doing?" Nathan asked once we were alone, on the other side of the café.

"What?" I asked. "Okay, of course I'm going to pay you *back* for breakfast. I was just distracted, that's all."

"That's not what I meant," he said quietly. "I mean, what are you doing, letting him get to you like this?"

I let out my breath in one long puff. I knew I was handling this all wrong, that I should be calm and distant, like the past year never happened. But it had. Andrew had kissed me and told me he loved me (kind of) and held my hand.

Andrew brought me soft foods when I had my wisdom teeth taken out, for crying out loud. And then he dumped me, because suddenly I wasn't willing to shift our relationship to the next gear, when I hadn't known until the week before that he'd even *noticed* what gear it was in.

"I know," I said, rubbing my forehead. "I just can't believe he would tell me he wasn't coming home when he was. I can't believe he—" I broke off, before I said something I'd regret. "Anyway. You must know how I'm feeling. You dated Heather, after all."

"*One* date," he said. "And this isn't about Heather. I couldn't care less about Heather."

I smiled—faintly, but at least it was a smile. "You used it correctly."

"Of course," he said. "After all, if you *could* care less about something, it means that you care about it at least a little bit. Right?"

"Right."

"Well, right now, I couldn't care less about Andrew or Heather," he said. "You know what I do care about?"

"What?" I looked up at him, realizing how crazy it was that he looked so familiar now. If he came to a stargazing session, there was no way that I'd forget. And I wouldn't avoid him, either.

He grinned. "Breakfast."

I let out my breath. "Typical," I said, smiling. "Well, while you're eating your boring plain bagel with regular cream cheese, just don't come crying to me for my pineapple. You had your chance."

We headed back toward the counter to pick up our bagels, passing Andrew and Heather as we did so. I thought about saying something else, but at the last minute I just asked for our bagels to go. It was dumb, I know, but I couldn't help thinking that the problem was that I *could* care less about Andrew. And there was only so much pretending I could do otherwise.

WISH FULFILLMENT: In Freud's dream analysis, this occurs in the latent dream and represents the sleeper's hidden desires.

THANKSGIVING dinner at my house was always interesting. For one thing, there was no turkey, or any meat at all, for that matter. This year we were having the traditional twice-baked squash and rice and mushroom stuffing with yeast gravy, but we were also having Tofurky-hummus sandwiches on pita bread that my mother was cutting into turkey shapes with a cookie cutter. Or at least, they were supposed to be turkey shapes. They came out looking more like Rorschach blobs. I helped her carry the spread to the table, where my dad, Nathan, and a family of three waited.

The family looked pretty put off by the sandwiches, but

I say that's what you get for spending Thanksgiving at a psychic bed-and-breakfast in Sedona. They should have been glad they were getting anything, since it was almost four o'clock in the afternoon and *way* past the time for breakfast. The ten-year-old boy—I'd heard the father yelling at him to put down *Sextrology*, a book my mother had left lying out on the coffee table, so I knew his name was Kyle—dug right in. But the parents looked a little more skeptical.

I figured, if you can be open-minded about a woman with one of the worst Russian accents I've ever heard reading your fortune from *tea leaves*, a couple of hummus sandwiches shouldn't faze you. But that's just me.

"These are delicious," Nathan said. "Thank you."

My mother beamed. "Mama's recipe," she said.

Nathan took another bite and winked at me, confirming my suspicion that he was just being polite. I hid a grin behind my own sandwich.

"You have a beautiful daughter," Kyle's mother said, and one of those looks passed between them that mothers share sometimes, where it's like, *Isn't the miracle of life wonderful?*

"Tuesday is our joy," my mom said.

My father piped up through a mouthful of potatoes, "She's in college, studying psychology."

I heard an actual note of pride in his voice, and I felt a little touched in spite of myself. Maybe it was just because I'd been so emotional lately, or maybe it was just that I'd always assumed my parents were a little disappointed in my choice of study.

"Beautiful *and* smart," Kyle's mother said, smiling at me before turning her smile to Nathan. "And with such a nice boy!"

Okay, this was getting obnoxious. "I'm not *with* him," I said.

My mother waved her fork, a bit of cranberry sauce slipping from it back to her plate. "It's only a matter of time," she said. "Tuesday just got out of a relationship with another boy, one with a bad aura. This one is much better."

My fork clattered to my plate, my eyes swinging to Nathan. He'd told—after laughing with me on the roof, after the moment of understanding I'd thought we shared at C'est La Vie—he'd been talking behind my back. To my mother. And he didn't even have the decency to look guilty. I felt betrayal rise up in my throat.

"You're an asshole," I said, tossing my napkin on the table.

The chair scraped on the wood floor as I stood abruptly, everyone at the table looking at me with an expression of speechless horror. I could tell Kyle's mom was adding *psycho* to her list of my attributes, and even ten-year-old Kyle, who had giggled over *Sextrology*, was looking at me like I was a freak. Nathan's fork was suspended in midair, his face a mixture of confusion and concern that only further fueled my anger.

I spun on my heel and left, slamming the front door behind me with a force that made the bells jangle wildly. I knew I was acting like a bit of a jerk myself, but I didn't care. Why would Nathan do that? Did he think he was doing me a *favor*, telling my parents about Andrew, when I wasn't even sure I wanted them to know yet?

I felt restless and upset, but once out of the house, I just plopped down on the front steps, running out of steam. I heard the front door open behind me, and I wasn't surprised when Nathan sat down next to me. If I expected an apology from him, though, it didn't appear that one was forthcoming.

"Why was it so important that your parents not know?" he asked.

He didn't even deny what he'd done, which I guess was noble in its own way, but it just made me madder. "Because," I muttered.

"Because *why*?" he said, sounding a little angry himself now. "Because you two are going to get back together, and you don't want to have to admit that you broke up in the first place?"

Tears pricked at the back of my eyes, but I couldn't bring myself to say anything. How could he be so cruel?

He sighed, a heavy exhale of frustration. "I didn't tell your mother anything," he said. "Give her a little credit. She's a perceptive woman."

"Why, because she's *psychic*?" I sneered.

"No, not because she's psychic," Nathan shot back. "Because she's got *eyes*. You wear your breakup like a Girl Scout badge. At first I tried to tiptoe around it, knowing that it was still pretty fresh and you must be hurting. And even when we ran into Andrew today and you're obviously not over him, I figured you just needed time. But Jesus, Leigh, you can be so *blind*."

I was crying full force now, but what else was new? It seemed like I was always crying. Deep down, I knew that what Nathan was saying had some merit, that I had chosen to cling to my sadness rather than face the truth. But that didn't make it any nicer to hear.

"You always hated me," I whispered. "And who can blame you? I'm a stupid emotional wreck." Never was that truer than at this very moment.

"Andrew's the stupid one," Nathan said, his voice bitter. "And surely you must know I never hated you. Far from it."

I gave an undignified sniffle. "But you were always so . . . *disapproving*."

Nathan laughed with little real humor. "Maybe that's because I was," he said. "I disapproved of the way Andrew treated you. And I *really* disapproved of the way I felt about you. You were my roommate's high school sweetheart, and even now, when you're crying over *him*, I just . . ."

I felt like I was standing on the precipice, and my decision to jump or not was the most important one I could make in my life. "What?" I whispered.

He looked at me, and his eyes were very, very serious. "I just want to kiss you," he said.

"*Me?*"

"Yeah, you," he said, giving me a wry smile. "I gave you my number half expecting you would never call, and so when you did . . . why do you think I was so gung ho about driving all the way out here? I wanted to spend time with you."

I stared at him, wide-eyed. Nathan wanted to spend time with me? He wanted to *kiss* me? Of its own accord, my gaze dropped to his lips. I wondered what it would be like if he actually kissed me—would it be like my dream?

"Okay," I said.

His brow furrowed. "Okay what?"

I licked my lips. "Kiss me," I said.

His eyes searched mine. "Are you serious?"

I edged closer to him on the step, hesitating only slightly before putting my hand on his arm. We were only partially protected by shade, and his skin beneath my hand was warm from the sun. "I thought you said you wanted to," I said.

Nathan glanced down at my hand, and I wondered if I'd been too bold. But then he spoke, and I could tell from the husky edge to his voice that he wasn't totally unaffected. "Believe me," he said, "I want to. But I can't just kiss you if it doesn't mean something."

I didn't know what it would mean. All I knew was that I wanted this, too, and had for a while, whether I'd wanted to admit it or not. Since that moment in the diner where he took my hand, and I felt that *spark* between us. Maybe even since that dream I'd had, I don't know . . . maybe even longer.

Instead of answering him in words, I leaned forward, my lips brushing against his, lingering only for a moment before I pulled back.

He'd closed his eyes, and when he opened them again they were a dark green, almost black. I could see the war within them, but then his hands came up to cup my face, and I felt a wave of triumph as he pulled me closer, slanting his mouth over mine.

It was just like my dream, except we were on my parents' porch instead of a beach, I was wearing an old tank top and jeans instead of a gauzy skirt, and we were sitting instead of standing.

Oh, and it felt ten times better.

It should have felt weird, kissing Nathan like this after all that had happened. But it didn't. It felt the way it had in the dream, really *right* somehow. That fluttery feeling was there, in my stomach, as Nathan's hands cradled my face, drying the wet tracks of my now-forgotten tears. But whereas in the dream I was mostly passive, now I actively wanted more. I buried my hands in his thick hair, deepening the kiss.

While we were in the middle of proving the sextrology of a Pisces and a Cancer being a passionate match, Kyle threw open the front door. I pulled away so fast I almost fell over backward, and it was only Nathan's hand tightening on my waist that held me steady. Somehow in the last few minutes, without my realizing it, his hand had found its way underneath the hem of my shirt, singeing the bare skin where my waist curved into my hip.

"Ew." Kyle made a face only a ten-year-old who'd had his cootie shot could make. "Get a room!" He spun and disappeared through the door, clearly not getting the cleverness of his own joke, seeing as we *were* at a bed-and-breakfast.

I felt like a coach on the sidelines of a football game after his players have dumped a vat of ice-cold Gatorade on him. It must have shown on my face, because Nathan dropped his hand.

"You're having second thoughts," he said flatly.

His hair was a little tousled, his lips soft from the kiss, and I couldn't bear to look at him. "Yes—no," I said. I took a deep breath. "I guess I am."

"It's Andrew, isn't it?" There was a resignation in his voice that twisted me inside a little, but I couldn't deny it.

"I'm just worried he's my Tyrone, you know?" Of course he didn't, and I rushed to explain. "Like Rebekah from mentoring that I was telling you about. The second guy was better at the physical stuff, and let me tell you, you're a *really* good kisser. Better than Andrew, I'll even give you that. But in the end, all she really wanted was Tyrone, and sleeping with his best friend did nothing but ruin that."

I knew I could have handled that a lot more gracefully. It made it sound like what I was really hoping for was to get back with Andrew. Which, despite what Nathan might have thought, was totally *not* the case. I might have been blind before, but I wasn't now. I knew that Andrew was an ass, and as much as a part of me really missed him, another part of me kind of . . . didn't.

But in some ways, that was exactly what scared me. I

mean, I had dated Andrew for *over a year* and I was only just beginning to realize how very wrong for me he was. I had only known Nathan for a couple days, and already it felt like he really *understood* me in a way no one else ever had. But was that even possible? And what could I know about it, if my judgment had been so off before?

"So, tell me, Leigh," he said, and there was a quiet edge in his voice that made me glance at him. "Will you ever be able to look at me and see . . . *me*, Nathan, not just as Andrew's roommate?"

The thing was, I already did. It was scary how quickly I was seeing everything in a different light, and I felt a desperate need to cling to something that, however sad, was at least *safe*. This thing with Nathan—whatever it may be—was just happening way too fast. How could I even know what I wanted, when it seemed to change with every passing second?

My gaze never left Nathan's, and I could almost see the change in the green depths of his eyes before the words left my mouth, as though he had already known. "No," I said. "No, I don't think I'll ever . . ."

The unspoken words hung between us, charging the air with their silence. For a moment I thought about taking it back, throwing my arms around him and admitting it was a lie.

I opened my mouth, but I just couldn't do it. "I'm sorry," I said instead, and the words had never been more inadequate.

Nathan gave a short laugh, and it was so devoid of any joy that I wanted to cry all over again. Why couldn't we go back to the way things had been last night, when we sat on the roof and talked under the stars? Why couldn't everything just be easier?

"I would understand if you wanted to leave tonight," I said, my voice small. "I'll ask my parents to reimburse you for gas money, and I can just catch a flight back to school."

Nathan didn't say yes, but he didn't say no. He just looked down at his hands, his profile hard in the slanting light of the setting sun. "There was a moment, though," he said finally, a slight question in his voice, and I knew what he meant.

"There was a moment," I agreed quietly, and my heart ached to tell him how many.

But instead we just sat there on the steps in complete silence, watching the sun disappear behind the horizon.

SYMPTOM SUBSTITUTION: An uncon-
scious process by which a repressed impulse is manifested
in another symptom, like depression or anxiety

I SHOULD'VE known Nathan would still drive me back to
California. He just wasn't the kind of guy who would leave me
there, and it's not like he wasn't driving back, anyway. We spent
the rest of Thanksgiving avoiding each other, and then we
drove back the next morning, each of us claiming a sudden
need to catch up on schoolwork.

Of course, I had to hit my parents up for a little gas
money for the drive back, because there was no way I was going
to make Nathan pay for it all, given the circumstances. Even if
he was my boyfriend, it'd be a little weak not to offer to pitch
in, when the whole trip had been for my benefit in the first

place. And, obviously, he wasn't my boyfriend. I doubted he was even my friend anymore.

Most of the drive, he had the music turned up really loud, so the only time we got to talk was when we stopped for gas. "I've got it," I said, jumping out at the station.

He didn't argue. "I'm going inside for drinks," he said. "You want anything?"

Yeah, for things to go back to the way they were before, when we were talking and laughing and having fun. Sometimes I just wanted to tell him . . . what? There was nothing left to say. "No," I said. "I'm fine."

What I really needed to do was put my personal problems on the back burner and throw myself into school-work, I decided. I had been a Kristy Salazar for way too long—it was time that I focused on my classes and that final project for Intro Psych.

I would not think about Nathan. What was the point? I'd already rejected him. It seemed like it was time to think about something else, *anything* else, other than my sorry love life.

When we got back to school, one of my first moves as Leigh, the new and improved student, was to contact Linda at the mentoring program about my doing a project involving body image. For someone I had written off as an empty shell, she was surprisingly helpful. She told me I should develop a brief body image workshop and use pre- and post-tests to assess the girls' body image and self-confidence. We determined that I would prepare the workshop and, after jumping through all the necessary hoops, I could conduct the study next semester. It couldn't get done in time for my final paper, but it'd make a pretty awesome independent study project.

A week had passed since Thanksgiving break, and there weren't supposed to be any more mentoring sessions until after Christmas. So it was a bit of an understatement to say that I was surprised when I opened the door of my dorm room and found Rebekah standing on the other side, cradling the robotic spawn of Satan in her arms. I mean, I had pointed out my dorm to her when we took that tour, but whoever thought she would actually come *here*?

"Rebekah," I said. "What are you doing here?"

"I ran away," she said. "Can I come in?"

I wasn't prelaw, but I was pretty sure that harboring a runaway was some kind of crime. "Um . . ." I said.

She rolled her eyes. "So call my mom and tell her I'm here. She don't care."

I let her come in, but I didn't waste any time picking up the phone and dialing the number she gave me. It wasn't like I was so far removed from my adolescence that I didn't remember how lame it was when someone called your parents, but I was also an adult in the eyes of the law. If I could barely survive in college, how would I handle prison?

"Hi, Mrs.—" I began, before realizing I didn't know Rebekah's last name. Great. She picks me to be her sanctuary, and I don't even know her last name. "Um, is this Rebekah's mom?"

Once she confirmed that she was, I explained who I was and Rebekah's sudden appearance on my doorstep. Her mother's response: "She botherin' you? No? Then why you botherin' me?"

So Rebekah's comment wasn't just teenage angst but rather, you know, the truth. "Well, sorry to bother you, ma'am," I said, "but in case you need to reach me, my cell phone number is—"

I was left with a dial tone ringing in my ear. "Wow," I said.

"I know," Rebekah said. "She can be a bitch."

"Is that why you're here?" I asked, clearing a space on my bed for us to sit down. Ami and my quasi attempts at cleaning toward the beginning of the semester had spiraled downward into an out-and-out collection of mess. There were piles of clothes all over the floor, books and papers stacked on every surface (I *had* been trying to organize my first-semester notes, hence the covered bed), and free bathroom products littering the bathroom. At orientation, there were baskets and bins filled with free toiletries for the taking. Of course, Ami and I took armfuls of stuff and then went back for more—not that we needed any of it. But, hello, they were *free*.

"I was supposed to give the baby back," she said. "But I don't want to."

"*Why?*" I asked before I could stop myself. "Seriously, that thing is like Rosemary's Baby. Plus, I'm pretty sure Linda would be mad if you didn't return a five-hundred-dollar infant."

"I know," she mumbled. Then she said something else, something I didn't catch.

"What?"

"I don't want to be a bad person," she said, louder this time.

I was going to crack some joke, about how I was pretty sure that kidnapping a fake baby wouldn't put her on Santa's good list this year. But then she looked up, and I saw that her eyes had a sheen to them. For once, she didn't look scornful or sarcastic or cynical. She just looked kind of sad.

"How could giving back the baby make you a bad person?" I asked. "You're *supposed* to give it back. I think it's Molly's turn with the little devil now."

"I wanted to give up my other baby," she said. "Doesn't that make me a bad person? It doesn't make me *good*."

"It just makes you young, and scared," I said. "Even your body knew that. That's why you had that miscarriage—because you just weren't ready to have a baby. One day, you will be, and you'll make a great mom—in, like, ten years, because, as dumb as Linda can be, I totally agree with her about waiting to have a child. But for now, you're just a kid. And that's how it's supposed to be."

"I guess," she said.

"It is," I assured her. "Believe me, it's hard enough being a kid without having to raise one while you're at it."

"Yeah."

"So you're going to give the baby back, right?" I asked. "No offense, but Tyrone, Jr., kind of creeps me out."

"True," she said. "He is an *ugly* baby."

"At least if he vacuumed or made toasted breakfast sandwiches, he'd be useful," I said, "but as it is, he's all the bad parts of being a baby and none of the cute parts. Must have gotten it from his dad, Tyrone, Sr., huh?"

"Tyrone who?" she said, and just when I opened my mouth to answer, she laughed. "Jus' playin'. I know who Tyrone is. But he's old news, ya know what I'm sayin'?"

I really didn't. "But I thought . . . he was your soul mate," I said.

Rebekah shrugged exaggeratedly. "There's more fish in the sea, ya know? I can't be cryin' about Tyrone forever."

I really hadn't expected such nonchalance, and it threw me a little. But why should I have been surprised? She was, after all, fifteen. I realized how stupid I had been ever to use her situation as a parable for my own. Was it possible to analyze something to the point where you could no longer see it?

"Yeah," I said, trying to find some common ground. "I've decided I'm done with guys. I'm just going to focus on school for now. That's really what's more important, anyway."

Rebekah shook her head, and I rushed to defend myself. "What? It is. Right now I'm in a position to make decisions that could affect the rest of my life. What I choose to study could affect where I go to grad school in four years. What grad school I choose will affect where I live, what contacts I make, what I study . . . the job I eventually get. This is big stuff. You should be thinking about it, too, you know."

"I get good grades," Rebekah said.

"I'm sure you do," I said, although honestly, up until that point I probably would've guessed the opposite if anyone had asked. Not because Rebekah didn't seem smart—she did, sometimes too smart for her own good. But she didn't seem as if she'd care much about school.

"And I'm bettin' you get good grades, too, huh?" She set robo-Tyrone down on the bed, peering closer to my bookshelf to read the titles there. Somehow I doubted that she'd see my romance novels as evidence of a high GPA.

"Well—" I started to explain that Stiles didn't actually give grades. Which is cool, because you can screw up and still pass, but also totally sucks, because every tiny detail of your suckage is laid out in clear language for everyone (read: grad schools) to see.

"You do," Rebekah said impatiently. "You think too much. You're school-smart, but real dumb."

It was unclear if she meant that I was "real world" dumb or had just failed to use the correct adverb to modify the word. Either way, it was hardly flattering. "What?"

"You're not a victim," Rebekah said, "but you act like you are. In my book, that equals dumb."

"That's not true," I protested.

"You act like your player boyfriend really messed you up," Rebekah said, ticking off the points on her fingers. "You can't tell that black-haired skank how you feel. You 'choose' school, but only 'cause you ain't got any other options. How's that for dumb?"

I was speechless. "Andrew dumped *me*," I said. "How am I not the victim in that scenario? I didn't even see it coming."

"Exactly. 'Cause you're dumb."

You're dumb, I wanted to say. It was childish, I know, but I couldn't help it. You can't ride a public school bus for ten years and not have an instinct to lash out when a kid calls you names.

I was still formulating my comeback when Rebekah spoke again. "You know what, though?"

"What?" I asked wearily.

"You're nice," Rebekah said. "And fun to talk to. I figure you could be smart, too, if you really tried."

"Thanks," I said wryly, although inside I felt warmth spreading through me. "You're fun, too. Even if you are a smart-ass."

"Better than a dumbass," Rebekah pointed out.

"True," I said. And then I heard it—the disturbing cry of an electronic baby. Tyrone, Jr., was crying like he'd never stop, and Rebekah picked him up, patting his hard plastic back.

"I just fed him," she said. "I think he needs to be soothed."

And then the image of her comforting a fake baby was too much, and I just started laughing. Rebekah started laughing, too, and that's how Ami walked in on us—Rebekah and me laughing so hard that tears were squeezing out of our eyes, and Tyrone, Jr., still screaming his scary head off.

COUNTERCONDITIONING: Relaxation responses are reinforced to an anxiety-invoking stimulus, until eventually the stimulus no longer invokes fear.

BEFORE I drove Rebekah home, Ami and I decided to take her to the Toad's Monocle for something to drink. I told Rebekah she *had* to try the Bee's Knees, while Ami pushed the strawberry lemonade. Rebekah ended up getting a hot chocolate, even though it was still eighty degrees outside.

"So," Ami said when we sat down. "Have you talked to Nathan at all?"

I gave her a look, and her gaze darted to Rebekah. "Sorry," she said. "Are we not talking about that?"

"Who's Nathan?" Rebekah said, hanging the book bag with Tyrone over the back of her chair. Every time I think that

I'm done being grateful that he's not a real baby, Rebekah gives me another reason.

"It's no big deal," I said. "He's my ex-boyfriend's roommate. Ex-roommate."

"That's a lot of exes," Rebekah said.

"Yeah," I said, giving a halfhearted laugh. I still hadn't told Ami the whole story, and I wasn't sure that I wanted to do so right here with Rebekah and her "baby" in tow.

Despite my best efforts, I hadn't been able to stop thinking about Nathan. A few days ago he'd sent out an e-mail to the campus forum about selling a futon, and I pored over every word as though it were a love letter. And let me tell you, "comfortable and versatile, if slightly banged up," even if it was the way I'd been feeling lately, didn't give a girl a lot to go on.

At one point I even went into the math building, which *must* mean that I had it bad, because that is one weird place. It's very sterile, with cold, tiled floors and glass-paneled doors, although I did notice that its bathrooms were way nicer than the psychology building's. I wandered through the halls, feeling a little stupid but still nervously anticipating that Nathan would be just getting out of a class and we'd run into each other. I had even rehearsed a couple stories—in one I was seeking help on statistics from a professor, and in another I was meeting a friend.

Neither of those excuses came close to being believable. Clearly I was losing my touch.

Then I actually saw him—just a glimpse through the

door of the computer lab. He had his iPod headphones in and was engrossed in something on the computer screen, and he didn't see me. He looked serious and unapproachable, and I hesitated for a moment, wondering if I should drop in and say a casual hello. But in the end, I just kept on walking.

"Leigh?" Ami said, bringing me back to the present. "Did something happen with Nathan?" Her inky black eyes were more concerned than ever. I could see she was genuinely worried about me, and she deserved the truth.

"I think—" I started to say, but I never had the chance to finish that sentence. Instead I saw a look of horror on Ami's face, and I turned around.

Andrew had just walked into the café, and he was heading right for us. I rose as he approached, as though we were in some period piece and our genders were reversed. And even when he was standing right in front of me, it was somehow hard to register that Andrew was *there*. It was even harder to believe that, apparently, he was there to talk to *me*.

"Hi, Leigh," he said. He glanced down at Ami, giving her a perfunctory nod. "Ami."

"Jerkface," she said, her polite tone and nod matching his.

"*This* is the boyfriend?" Rebekah asked.

Andrew ignored both of them. "Can I talk to you?" he asked me.

I couldn't seem to find my tongue, and Ami leaped to respond. "Why would she want to talk to *you*? I suggest you crawl back under that rock you slithered from and leave us alone."

"Wow, that was badass," Rebekah said to Ami, impressed.

"It's okay," I told both of them. "We should really talk."

I tried to give them a smile that let them know that, even if I wasn't accepting their assistance, I still totally appreciated it. But Ami huffily picked up her drink, shooting one last poisonous glare in Andrew's direction. "Fine," she said. "Come on, Rebekah. But we'll just be over there if you need us." She gave Andrew another sneering once-over to make him aware of the likelihood that I would.

They left, and Andrew pulled out my chair and gestured for me to take a seat. He'd never done that kind of thing when we were actually together, and I was struck by the irony of his doing it now.

"What do you want, Andrew?" I asked, taking my seat and getting to the point. It came out more harshly than I had expected. Not that that was a bad thing.

I guess he didn't want to waste any time, either. "In a nutshell?" he said. "You."

Another irony—those four words would've completely melted me just a little while before, when I was standing outside his door begging him for a ride. They would've even given me serious pause if I'd heard them that day in C'est La Vie. Now? Nothing.

A corner of my mouth lifted, and Andrew saw it and took encouragement, reaching over to grasp my hand. "The worst thing I ever did was break up with you," he said earnestly, "and getting with Heather was a huge mistake. I can't believe I was so *blind*."

That was exactly what Nathan had called me, but I felt like I had never seen more clearly. Andrew was all charm and no substance—and that was particularly unfortunate, because, frankly, he wasn't that charming. I had no doubts that if we did get back together, it would quickly revert to what it had always been—Andrew's selfish need to get his own way.

"No, Andrew," I said, reclaiming my hand. "*I* was the one who was blind. But it's different now."

"No, it's not," he said. "I know that it seemed like things changed once we got to college, but I still really care about you. It'll be just like it was in high school—you and me, together."

"Andrew, *I've* changed. As Gwen Stefani would say, I 'ain't no Hollaback girl.'"

His eyebrows drew together. "What does that even mean?"

I had actually only just figured it out myself, so I was kind of excited to explain it to him. Weird, given the circumstances. "Like in cheerleading, a 'hollaback girl' is one who just repeats back whatever the head cheerleader shouts. It means I'm not going to be the girl who just goes along with whatever you say."

Andrew shook his head. "You want to punish me, fine. I understand that—hell, I respect it, even. If I were in your shoes, I'd want to get some of my own back. But are you listening to me? I'm saying I'm *sorry* and I want you back. Don't throw that away because you're too proud."

"I'm not throwing it away," I said, "because I don't want it in the first place."

Andrew finally looked at me then, *really* looked at me, and he let out a low sigh. "You're with someone else, right?" he said. "That's the only explanation."

"Actually no, I'm not," I said, but he wasn't listening.

"Let me guess—Nathan," he said with a bitter laugh. "It has to be Nathan. Christ, he told me day *one* that he liked you. But don't forget *our* history, Leigh. We were great together."

Apparently I wasn't the only one who needed a history lesson. But right now I wasn't interested in Andrew's brand of revisionism. "Wait. Nathan did what?"

Andrew snorted. "Come on, Leigh. Like it wasn't disgustingly obvious he had a huge thing for you."

If I thought I was following this conversation, I had just completely lost it. "What?"

"You met during orientation," he said, "and Nathan had a crush on you."

"The stargazing," I remembered dazedly.

"Yeah, whatever," Andrew said impatiently. "He came back to the room that night and kept talking about this girl he'd seen at the stargazing. He was shy, and so I told him if he pointed you out, I'd try to finagle a meeting."

I swear, Andrew's the only person in the world who could use a word like *finagle* with a straight face. "But he was talking about me," I said.

Andrew shrugged. "When we figured it out, we had a good laugh about it," he said defensively. "But of course you were my girlfriend. So that was that."

Maybe Andrew and I had had something in common,

after all. Maybe we both were afraid of change—both in our relationship and in ourselves. But I was through with it.

Even though I hadn't been superfriendly to him, Nathan had come running the second I needed him. Andrew had lied about going home just to avoid giving me a ride. Nathan had known me for a semester, and still knew why I was so upset to win second place in a contest. Andrew barely understood why I'd entered it in the first place.

The few times I'd hung out at Andrew's dorm, Nathan had been the one I'd watched from out of the corner of my eye the whole time. Nathan was the one who made my skin tingle whenever he entered the room. In my dream, it was Nathan. It had always been Nathan.

"Andrew," I said, my voice quiet but firm, "we're not going to get back together."

He was silent for a few moments, looking at me. Finally I saw something like resignation in the set of his shoulders. Still, he couldn't resist a parting shot. "You'll regret this. You know you still love me."

I thought I did. But then again, I'd assumed love was safe, like ordering the same thing at a restaurant every single time. I didn't realize that it could be a greasy roadside sandwich and vomiting, followed by a conversation that made time slow down and my heart speed up. "Good-bye, Andrew."

He left then, leaving me staring wordlessly in the spot where he'd stood. Ami and Rebekah hurried back so fast that I knew they'd been listening, and Ami waited until the café door shut before leaning in.

"What was that about?" she asked.

I remembered what I had been about to say before Andrew showed up. Now I spoke the words aloud that had been echoing in my brain, teasing the tip of my tongue.

"I think I'm in love with Nathan," I said.

Ami acted like I should immediately go to the middle of the quad and publicly declare my love or something, but of course, we had to drop off Rebekah first.

Rebekah's house was definitely run-down, with chipped paint and grass growing too long around the mailbox. But it was still nicer than I expected. Clearly she didn't get along with her mother, but I wondered what her life at home was like otherwise.

Obviously, when we got to the door, she didn't want me to come in. But she did turn around before she disappeared inside. "Leigh?" she said.

"Yeah?" I had to squint into the sun a little bit, and it was hard to see her among the shadows of the porch.

"Are you gonna do the mentoring thing next year? I mean, when school starts back up after break?"

"Yeah, definitely," I said, and Rebekah smiled. "I mean, I kind of have to. I'm going to do this project next semester, about body image and adolescent girls."

Rebekah nodded. "Cool," she said. "Anyways, thanks for hangin' out today. And buying that drink from the weird toad place."

"It was no problem," I said. "And hey—"

Rebekah already had one foot in her house, which was dark inside. But she waited, still clutching Tyrone, Jr., under one arm.

"You've got my number," I said. "And you know where I live. So no matter what happens with the whole mentoring thing, you can always reach me if you just want to talk, or hang out again. Okay?"

She didn't say anything else before she closed the door behind her, but I saw her grinning.

So, the quad was a *little* much, even for me, but I definitely wanted to contact Nathan to tell him how I felt. Ami and I made plans the entire drive home, and by the time we got back to our dorm, Ami had it all figured out.

"Okay," she said. "So you kind of rejected him. Big deal. He liked you the moment that he *saw* you, even though it was dark and bugs were eating you both alive. That's not the sort of thing that just goes away in a week, right?"

Ami's words gave me a little hope, but I still had my doubts. "I don't know," I said. "I changed my mind about Andrew pretty fast."

"Totally different," she dismissed. "Andrew was a complete douche."

I didn't know exactly how feminine hygiene products acted, but I was pretty sure I hadn't acted much better with Nathan. If I were him, *I* wouldn't trust me.

"I don't even know where he lives," I protested. I mean, I knew Nathan still lived on campus. But I couldn't exactly go banging on the doors of every single dorm room in the school.

If this were a movie, Nathan would have had a spot that he had just happened to reveal to me was where he went when he "needed to think." That information, seemingly superfluous at the time, would later come in really handy in a situation just like this. I would go to the spot by the ocean, or under a tree, or in this one out-of-the-way coffee shop, and he would be there.

I knew Nathan hung out in the math computer lab, but that was really too clinical to be conducive to the kinds of things I wanted to say to him. Or do to him, if things went well. God, I hoped they went well.

"So, *call* him," Ami said, rolling her eyes. "As if you haven't worn that little calculus flash card to parchment by now."

Which was hardly fair, considering I'd memorized the number a long time ago.

Still, I felt a frisson of excitement as I picked up the phone and punched in the numbers, my hand shaking slightly. Ami disappeared into the bathroom, and since she had just peed, like, twenty minutes ago, I knew that she was just trying to give me privacy.

It rang for a while, and I mentally started to compose a breezy message that would convey my desire to talk without seeming desperate. But then the ringing stopped, and I heard a voice on the other end. "Hello?"

It was a girl's voice. In all of my worrying, I hadn't *really* believed that Nathan would have found someone else by now. In the absolute worst scenario I'd pictured, he was completely over me and wouldn't give me a second chance. But another girl?

"Hello?" the girl's voice said again, and she sounded so . . . *nice*. If I were a better person I might have even been happy for Nathan. But then, that's probably why he's with her and not with me. Because I'm *not* a nice person. In fact, I wanted to gouge her eyes out.

You know, if that were even possible over the phone. And not so gross.

I thought about hanging up, but I had an image of the two of them laughing over the weird crank call. What happened if he saw the number and recognized that it was me? I didn't see why Nathan would have my dorm room number, but I didn't want to take any chances and have him call me back.

I cleared my throat. "Uh . . ." An ignominious beginning, to be sure, but at least I was talking. I floundered around for something else to say before hitting on an inspiration. "I'm calling about a futon for sale?"

She cheerfully extolled the virtues of the futon, mentioning its cheap price and comfort, and I wondered if she were living there. She couldn't possibly be, but once the thought popped into my head, I couldn't shake it. Why else would she be answering his phone and selling his furniture?

She offered to give me directions if I wanted to "take a

look at it" for myself, but information that would have been thrilling two minutes before now just fell flat. Maybe she was a roommate, I thought. There were some relatively cheap apartments by the campus, but it made more sense to share with someone, right? And why not a friendly girl who sounded blond and fun and like she had never played mind games with a boy in her life?

But her next words shattered my last hope. "Nate and I will be out to dinner until nine or so, but if you want to call back maybe tomorrow, I'm sure he could tell you more," she said. "And of course, if you want to drop by, just call first, and it should be no problem for you to look at it."

They were going to dinner? Roommates could eat out together, right? I mean, Ami and I went out to eat sometimes . . . even if it was at Taco Bell and not at an actual restaurant. But somehow, the way she dropped that nickname—*Nate*—I just didn't think so.

"Okay," I said, as though my heart weren't breaking, "Thanks a lot."

I hung up, and when Ami emerged from the bathroom, I just gave her a watery smile and shook my head.

"Ah, Leigh," she said, squeezing my shoulder. She didn't say anything else, because, really, what was there to say?

I had had my chance, sitting back there on those steps in Arizona. And I could blame it on Andrew or on the timing or even on ten-year-old Kyle, but the truth was . . . I *wasn't* a victim. I'd made this mess myself. And now it was too late to fix it.

FICTIONAL FINALISM: A concept in
Alfred Adler's theory of personality, it is the notion
that an individual is motivated more by his or her expec-
tations of the future, based on a subjective or fictional
estimate of life's values, than by past experiences.

THE Stiles Academic Showcase helped (somewhat) take my
mind off Nathan. So what if I were destined to live out the
rest of my pathetic life crocheting booties for other people's
kids and taping extreme makeover shows while at least six cats
swirled around my legs? At least I would have my career.
Right?

I wondered if you could lead such an unfulfilling life and
be a successful therapist. Viktor Frankl believed that mental
illness and maladjustment stemmed from a life of meaning-
lessness. But my life wouldn't be *meaningless* . . . just loveless,
maybe.

It always seemed strange to me that Vik could have been such a great therapist. I mean, he survived the Nazi concentration camps. If that were me, and I had to listen to people bitch and moan about their troubles, I don't know that I could stand it. I'd be, like, oh, yeah? Try losing your entire family because some dude with a weird moustache was a crappy artist.

I'm sure that's what he would tell me if I were his client. After all, who am I to complain? I have my family and friends. I have my health. Then there are all those things that I secretly believe I have but am worried it would sound cocky to say I have: relative attractiveness (thank you, haircut), intelligence (more book smarts than common sense, but what are you going to do?), and confidence (some, anyway). When I'm given Likert scale questions about myself on a scale of one to five, five being the best and one being the worst, I usually bubble in a four or five on just about every one.

If you averaged out scores on each aspect of my life right now, I would guess the mean would be around three or so. But that's also because the mean is affected by extreme scores, like my love life, which would be getting a one at this point. If you took the median, which is not affected by outliers, I'd proba-bly have a four overall. And that's not so bad.

Ami was still sleeping, and I plopped down on her bed, unapologetically waking her up. She half mumbled, half spat something in Spanish that I'm sure was not *tengo una fiesta in mis pantalones* (I have a party in my pants), one of the only phrases

I really remember from high school Spanish. Hers sounded a little less fun loving.

"Are you going to the showcase?" I said.

"Leave me alone," she groaned.

Some weaker-willed people might have considered that a sufficient answer. I didn't. "Come on," I said. "You really should go. Everyone's going to be presenting their crappy undergraduate research, and there might even be some drippy kids from high schools there to check it out. It's the last big event before winter break."

"I don't care."

I poked her in the side. "You can network," I said, a wheedling note to my voice. "You love to network. There might be people from grad schools there."

Ami's mom had passed her real estate exam when Ami was in middle school, and now she's a pretty successful real estate agent. Maybe it's just because I really dig the ecological model of psychology, but I think that has a lot to do with the way Ami is. She's constantly spinning things, selling herself. I admire it because, in some ways, it's just another way of making stuff up on the spot, the way I like to do.

Ami opened one blurry eye before shutting it again. "Forget it, Leigh," she said. "I'm not going to grad school, anyway."

"Why not?" I asked, alarmed. I mean, I know I rebelled against everyone trying to shove it down my throat *now*, but that didn't change the fact that I knew I wanted to go to grad school in the future. It was only the first semester, but Ami's evaluations weren't fantastic, and her activities, outside of a handful of art tutorials, were almost nil. But I thought that was just the beautiful, sickening thing about art programs. None of that really mattered.

Ami grudgingly removed the pillow from on top of her head, shoving it underneath her as she propped herself up on one elbow. "Formal education is, like, the death knell of an artist," she declared with slurred haughtiness. "I want to be on the streets, making art for the people. And you just don't do that with a degree from Parsons."

I knew better than to argue with Ami. "Okay," I said. "Well, I'll grab some brochures for you in case you change your mind." Which she would. In a week she would be listing the copious benefits of grad school and whining that she had missed the showcase. But Ami's opinions, while often transitory, were impossible to budge while she held them. So I just didn't bother.

When I got to the showcase, the student center was filled with . . . well, students. There were also booths set up all around the room, with mainly seniors and juniors and a handful of underclassmen standing around posters displaying their research.

I saw the psychology section and headed toward it, more out of morbid curiosity than anything else. Not surprisingly, the only two people manning the booth were Sydney and her new sidekick, Ellen, the most psychotic pair to study psychology in the history of Stiles.

"The kind of networking you do today will be your greatest asset in your academic career," Sydney was telling Ellen. "As we all know, personal impressions are *very* important, so it's crucial that you nail the interview. There are over two hundred other people applying for the same spot, so you can't just rely on perfect test scores or letters of recommendation. I mean—"

Sydney broke off, obviously noticing me for the first time. God forbid she give my ungrateful ass any of the same advice. "Hello, Leigh," she said.

"Hey, Sydney," I said. "Ellen."

I waited for Sydney to start her presentation of her thesis project, which looked like the most boring topic *ever*. She tried to jazz it up by titling her poster "What's the Buzz About Bees?" and putting a cheesy cartoon bumblebee border around it, but it didn't change the fact that it was a serious snoozefest. Now it just looked like a second-grade science fair snoozefest.

But apparently I wasn't even good enough for that. "Did you ever pick a topic for your final project?" she asked. "You were supposed to meet with me about that, you know. I'm your TA."

"I know," I said. "But I just talked with Harland. I'm doing a meta-analysis of a bunch of studies using the International Eating Disorder Database."

Sydney snorted. "Well, good luck."

"Thanks," I said, as though she'd meant it.

Her eyes narrowed. "I heard about you and Andrew," she

said. "I'm so sorry. I was really looking forward to me and Nathan being able to double with you two, but I guess that's not going to happen now."

All this time I had been so worried about what others were thinking about me, it never really occurred to me that other people might be scared, too. I couldn't believe there had ever been a time when I'd legitimately worried that Nathan would actually go for someone like *Sydney*. He was way too smart not to see through her crap, and too good a person to respect someone so petty and mean.

Until a week ago, he had also been too interested in *me* for Sydney to have a chance.

I could have played that card, ignoring the fact that in reality, I had blown my chance with Nathan. It almost would have been worth it to see the look on Sydney's face. But instead I just gave Sydney a beatific smile.

"That is truly a shame," I said. "But hey, *great* poster. I love the border."

I spun on my heel and walked away, but as I did I saw Ellen out of the corner of my eye. She'd looked up at Sydney's poster and actually blanched.

I was halfway to the British and American literature table when Ellen caught up with me. "Leigh," she said. "I just wanted to say . . . your project sounds really cool. With the database and everything. And I'm really sorry to hear about Andrew."

It was weird, but she actually sounded sincere. Stranger

still—two weeks ago the very mention of Andrew's name would have sent me into an emotional tailspin, but now I felt only a vague sentimentality. It was funny how quickly things could change.

"It was a long time coming," I found myself admitting. "We're better off this way."

Ellen's hands fluttered in jerky gestures of sympathy, and I realized that most of what I had seen as bitchiness was really just social awkwardness. "That's just like me and my fiancé," she said. "We broke up a few days ago."

"Congratulations," I said, a small smile touching my lips. Instead of getting offended or upset, Ellen just laughed.

"It's weird not being in a relationship, you know?"

Did I ever. But if there was one thing I had learned this past week, it was that fear of being alone was not a sufficient reason to have a relationship. With Andrew, I had taken the word *commitment* to a whole different level. It was as if I'd gotten in line at the supermarket, and the person in front of me was sifting laboriously through every coupon in the Sunday supplement before writing a check for the total. I knew I should probably bail out and try another line, but it felt as if I had no other choice than to stick it out.

With Nathan, it had been the opposite. I was in the right lane, but when it came time to check out, I just couldn't go through with it.

Ellen's gaze skittered to mine uncertainly. "Listen, I know that we're in the same field of research," she said. "And I could really use a second coder for these commercials. Do you think you'd want to help me out? I could help you find articles for your project, or I could buy you coffee or something."

"Um . . ." I totally appreciated that Ellen was trying to extend the olive branch. But, with Ellen, who knew if she were going to turn around and try to gouge your eye out with it? God forbid I might not code her commercials exactly right.

"I'll make it Dunkin' Donuts," she said. "You like their coffee, right? I always see you walk into class with one."

Then again, that was a pretty convincing olive branch. "Sure," I said. "You have yourself a deal."

Once I'd made my rounds of each department's area at the showcase, I decided to hit up the admissions representatives from grad school. I know—it was a good three years before I would even have to worry about that.

But maybe it wasn't such a bad idea to get a head start. I had my eyes on the UCLA booth when I bumped into someone.

"Oh, sorry," I said, and then I looked up.

My heart slammed into my chest. "Nathan?" I said, although of course I knew it was him. He looked exactly the same—that tousled dark hair, those steady green eyes. But there was something slightly different about him, too. Those few days I had spent with him had made him seem so familiar, but looking at him now I realized I had no idea what was going through his head.

"Hey, Leigh," he said, and even though it wasn't really

cold in the room, I felt goose bumps rise on my arms at the rumble of his voice.

"Hey," I answered lamely. It was situations like this when I kind of wished my mother had been a real estate agent, too. Because if there were ever a time when I really needed to sell myself, it was now, and all I could think was, *You break it, you bought it.*

That might work for a crystal unicorn, but I didn't think it worked for hearts.

"How's—" I asked just as Nathan started to speak, and we both stopped. I gave an awkward laugh that came uncomfortably close to a titter. "You first," I said.

He cleared his throat. "How's Gretchen?"

That was it? He wanted to know about my car? Granted, the last time he had seen me, my car was doing time in an impound lot. But still, I was fairly sure that most professions of undying love didn't start off with a question about a girl's car.

Gretchen had come back from the impound lot intact but a little sadder, somehow. Her specialty license plate proudly declared her an antique, but she really just seemed old, and I was conscious of the fact that she was getting on in years.

"She runs," I said with a shrug. "I never did repay you for that breakfast. . . ."

Nathan dismissed the debt with a wave of his hand, looking uncomfortable at the very mention of it. "Don't worry about it," he said.

We stood there silently for a few moments, and I was painfully conscious of how the old Nathan would have filled that silence. He would have made some joke about pineapple cream cheese, or asked for an update on the robotic babies. He would have found something to tease me about. He would have asked me which school I was there for.

But this wasn't the Nathan I remembered from Arizona, and I really had no one to blame but myself. Because I'd lied about how I felt, this was polite Nathan, who had a new girl-friend who answered his phone and made his futon arrangements for him. This was Nathan, who, although his politeness prevented him from saying it, probably hated my guts.

"Did you ever sell that futon?" I asked casually.

"Yeah," he said, and then his eyebrows drew together. "Did you call about it?"

Crap. "What?" I asked, stalling.

"Joanie said a girl called and stayed on the phone a little while, asking about the futon. I figured it had to be someone who knew me, since I didn't put my number in the e-mail. But it was you, wasn't it?"

Never in my life had I felt so mortified and so elated at the same time. Joanie, Nathan's *sister*, had answered the phone! She must have been visiting him. It explained everything—the nickname, the comfort with which she'd answered the phone, the dinner plans. I mentally apologized for wanting to gouge her eyes out, however hypothetically.

I thought about denying it but figured there was no point.

"How'd you guess?" I asked, giving him a rueful smile.

"I didn't," he said quietly. "I hoped."

Something inside me took flight at those two words. *I hoped.* Maybe there was a chance he didn't hate me, after all. And maybe, just *maybe*, there was still a chance that I could make things right.

People were milling about around us, but neither Nathan nor I noticed as his eyes searched mine. "So why did you call?" he asked.

There were a thousand questions in that question, and I thought carefully about how to answer them all. The old Leigh would have shot something off about needing a futon, but I didn't feel like hiding anymore.

"I met Andrew at the café the other day," I began, and it was as though a shutter had come down over Nathan's eyes.

Immediately I knew I had made a terrible, terrible mistake, and I rushed to explain. "He came in, actually," I said. "And I was there with Ami and Rebekah, and we were hanging out. I was really in the mood for one of those Bee's Knees, you know, the one with the honey?" I shook my head, as though physically shaking off the need to babble. "Anyway, *he* found *me*, and started talking about how he wanted me back—"

Nathan held up his hand. "It's okay, Leigh," he said. "I get it. I'm glad everything worked out for you."

I felt like I was swimming in molasses, trying to get somewhere but just unable to do it. "No, but—" Someone rushing to one of the tables bumped my shoulder, and I rocked a little. Maybe if we could go somewhere quiet, somewhere where we could *talk*, I could finally tell Nathan how I really felt. "This is kind of hard to talk about here," I said. "Do you want to go get some coffee? Or maybe a BLT? I won't puke on you, I promise."

I shot him my most appealing smile, hoping that the inside joke would get him to smile, or at least to give me another chance. But his face remained completely impassive.

"Listen, I have to go," he said. "I've got work to do and a bunch of stuff to unpack." He looked at me, and I think I could probably devote my final Intro Psych project to analyzing that one look. "Take care of yourself, Leigh."

And just like that, he was gone. I wanted to shout his name, tell him to come back. I wanted to run after him and explain everything, whether he wanted to listen or not. But instead I just stared at his retreating back until he disappeared through the double doors.

Maybe karma does exist.

Really, I wanted to go back to the room, cry my eyes out to Ami, and immerse myself in every heartbroken female stereotype of soap operas and pints of Ben & Jerry's. Instead I wandered listlessly around the academic showcase, picking up brochures and free pens with all the energy of the undead— and not like the fast-moving zombies of modern movies, either, but rather the persistent sloths of the original George Romero films.

I ran into Joanna by the UCLA booth, and not that she was the last person I wanted to see (because there was a list about a mile long of *those* people), but I just didn't feel up to talking to anyone right now. I thought about just spinning around and heading in the other direction, but she'd already seen me and waved.

"Hey, Leigh," she said. "What's up?"

And it all came spilling out. The way my relationship with Andrew had ended. The way I'd blown it with Nathan. The way he looked at me now, like I was a semi-interesting painting in a museum, but not one that he'd bother to buy the postcard for.

"Wow," she said when I'd finished. "You know, usually when I ask that, I just get a token 'not much.' But no, this is way better. I really respect your honesty."

That was a laugh.

"Why don't you try the applied mathematics table?" she asked.

"Thanks," I said. "But seriously, I doubt that *math* is going to help me right now. I'm not even that good at it! I only like statistics because you can use it to find answers about other stuff, instead of just numbers for numbers' sake."

Joanna laughed. "No," she said. "I meant, why don't you try asking someone at the applied mathematics table if they know where Nathan lives?"

Okay, as if I could feel any stupider than I felt before. "Oh. Do you think they'd know? I mean, just because they're math majors doesn't mean they know anything about Nathan."

Joanna gave me a leveling look. "You think we're the only major that's superinsular and clique-ish and gossips about everyone else in it? Believe me, if Nathan bought a new brand of toothpaste, those math nerds probably already know about it."

"You're totally right," I said. "Oh my God, Joanna, you're a genius."

Joanna acknowledged that with a little shrug of her shoulders. "Come on," she said. "I'll walk with you over to the table."

Okay, the first thing I have to say about math majors is that they have *really* impressive theses. Like, they make my whole idea about body image seem like I need to buy some Elmer's glue and go back to kindergarten. The guy who was presenting at the showcase had a very professional-looking board with a superlong title about correlative effects of binomials and logarithms or whatever. It made no sense to me, but that just made it more impressive.

"Um . . . hi," I said, once Joanna gave me a little shove. "Does anyone here know Nathan Maguire?"

"I'm his TA in Regression Analysis," the thesis student said.

"He's in my calc class," another student piped up.

"Does anyone here know . . . where he lives?"

And it was that easy. Two minutes later, I'd found out that he lived in C-Dorm (weird), didn't take notes in class (he was probably too busy doodling cats) yet seemed to know all the answers, and that he lived in dorm room 341. I wrote it on my hand so I wouldn't forget it.

I'd definitely looked better, and he had pretty much dismissed me less than half an hour earlier, but when everything falls into place, you don't tend to think about what the logical or sensible thing to do is. You carpe diem, which I'm pretty sure is Latin for *seize the address*.

Or, as Rebekah might say, you just stop being dumb, grow a pair, and go after the guy.

> **PEAK EXPERIENCE:** A profound and deeply moving experience in a person's life that has an important and lasting effect on the individual

FIRST I'd ventured by the math table, and now I was hanging around the sketchiest dorm on campus. I wondered if he kept his desk in the closet. I wondered what he thought of the communal bathrooms.

This was definitely love.

I was breathless when I arrived at his door. At least I thought (*hoped*) it was his—the tarnished brass number read 341, just like the slightly smeared number on my hand. Before I could think myself out of it, I gave the door three sharp knocks.

At first I thought maybe he wasn't home, and I felt a huge

wave of disappointment wash over me. But then I heard sounds from inside, and my anxiety came rushing back. I reached up and grabbed the elastic band from my hair, running my hands through it and letting it fall around my face. A little vanity might not help, but it wouldn't hurt, either.

The door opened just a crack, and a sliver of Nathan appeared. I gave him a tentative smile.

He shut the door in my face.

I stood there, stunned. Okay, so I had jerked him around a little bit. Basically, I'd been a *jerk*. But I didn't realize until that moment just how much I had been counting on Nathan at least hearing me out. He was too polite not to. Wasn't he?

I was staring at the brass number on the door, debating about whether to knock again, when the door opened. Nathan was partially hidden behind it, but he was holding it open, waiting expectantly for me to come in.

It was then I noticed the kitten. Cradled in Nathan's hand was more a tiny ball of orange fur than a cat, and I couldn't take my eyes off it as Nathan closed the door behind me. Somehow it was easier than looking at him.

"You got a cat," I said, Captain Obvious. That must have been the reason behind the shut door. He'd been making sure the kitten didn't run out. We weren't really supposed to have pets in the dorms, but Stiles kind of looked the other way. As long as it wasn't a ferret, that is (those were persona non grata at Stiles, ever since the college had had to pay a two-thousand-dollar bill to clean a room postferret).

"Yeah, well." He kneeled down, and the kitten leaped from his hand and scurried under the desk in a flurry of orange fluff. Nathan's desk was not in his closet, as I'd assumed. Instead, it was under his bed, which was now lofted. "I always wanted one."

"What's its name?" I asked. It was always awkward, I felt, calling an animal "it" when you weren't sure. Some people, the same ones who buy little sweaters for their dogs, really take offense at it.

Nathan didn't strike me as being in a rush to purchase a kitty sweater anytime soon. I wondered if he had ever doodled a cat in a sweater. I bet he had.

"Euclid," he said, a corner of his mouth lifting. "Dorky, I know."

No argument there, but it was also incredibly endearing. My throat felt tight. "It's a good name," I said. "I mean, I couldn't get away with naming my cat after the father of geometry. But that's just because I failed it in high school."

"Twice. I know." He looked up. Until that moment, we'd both been watching the desk, as if waiting for Euclid to come out. Or, in my case, *praying* that he would. As long as I could focus on the cat, I could ignore the rapid beating of my heart.

Now there was no ignoring it. It was like a tribal drum. I wondered if Nathan could hear it. I wondered if you could overdose on emotion.

"You must be asking yourself why I'm here," I said,

leaning awkwardly against his dresser. The only way for us to sit down together would be to climb up on the bed, and there was no way to suggest that without being *really* awkward.

"It crossed my mind." He didn't make a move to sit, either, even though there was a standard-issue Stiles desk chair right next to him. It was as if he didn't expect me to stay long. Or didn't want me to.

A little of my bravery vanished with the sight of that wooden chair. I glanced around the room. "So this is where you live?" I asked, my voice a horrible imitation of casual.

"For now," he said.

It was even smaller than legend had described it, and it already seemed stamped by *Nathan*, and for that reason alone it was the most inviting, intimidating room I'd ever been in. I realized Nathan hadn't been lying earlier when he said he was going to unpack boxes—several open ones were scattered around the living room, and dirt streaked his plain white T-shirt.

"So you're just going to live alone?"

"I might get an apartment next year," he said. "I have some money my dad left me, and I tutor a few times a week to earn some extra cash."

"Oh." Another thing I hadn't known.

"Leigh?"

I looked up. "Yes?" My voice was breathy, expectant.

"I really have a lot to do."

The last of my bravery deflated like a balloon the day after a birthday party. Had I really thought he was going to be happy to see me? He would rather unpack boxes than spend five minutes in my presence.

"Right," I said, pinning a smile on my face.

"Right," he repeated, more to himself than to me.

He didn't need to walk me to the door, since it was about eight inches from where he was standing. So instead he just leaned against it, his hand on the knob, and he and I were so close I could feel my entire body hum. I wished I were the kind of person who could just move in for a kiss. In many ways, it would have been so much easier than trying to find the words. But that just wasn't me.

His eyes were a dark forest green as he looked down at me, as if compelling me to . . . what? Kiss him? Leave? I couldn't tell.

Say something, say something. I cleared my throat.

"I came here to tell you . . ." I thought about my next words carefully. Finally I glanced up at him, my gaze holding his. "Remember that Incomplete Sentences paper?"

He smiled—slightly, but it was a smile. I took hope from it. "I remember."

"I didn't know my happiest time, because it hadn't happened yet," I said. "It was when I was with you."

His face was still. "Leigh . . ."

But I wasn't going to be stopped, not now. The words had to be said, and I knew if I heard what he was about to say, I might never say them.

"I wanted you to know that," I said. "Whatever else

happens . . . that night, sitting with you under the stars . . . those moments on the porch steps . . . I was really, really happy."

He closed his eyes. "Leigh, *don't*," he said.

I remembered another time he'd said that. He'd been guiding my hands away from the broken glass of the confetti globe, protecting me from the shards of Andrew's and my relationship. Then his voice had been soft, tender even. Now it was just ragged.

It should have shut me up. It should have given me the message: *He doesn't want to hear it. He couldn't care less.* But something in his voice told me he could *definitely* care less—a lot less, and it spurred me on. "No, you need to know this," I said forcefully. "It kind of freaked me out how much you seemed to understand about me, even before Arizona. It made me want to protect myself, even if it meant that I wasn't completely honest with you. But now, I have to be."

I took a deep breath. I'd always been a wader. It was time I did a cannonball. "These are things you should know about me: sometimes when I shave my legs, I miss the strip on the back of my calf. I cry when the beginning credits of *My Girl* roll, because I know how it's going to end. I did *not* have sex with Andrew. I don't think I really wanted to."

Something in Nathan's eyes flickered then, but still he was silent.

"And I lied when I told you I could never think of you as anything but Andrew's roommate. Nathan, I can't *stop* thinking about you. I've tried, but I can't."

"So then, how can I trust you now?" Nathan asked. His tone was light, but his face was guarded.

Now would be an ideal time for that kiss, my brain whispered, but I couldn't take the coward's way out.

"Because," I said simply, "I'm in love with you."

At first he just stood there, looking down at me. As many times as I tried to tell myself that what was important was being honest, and not necessarily the way he reacted, I could feel the first tendrils of devastation curl around my heart. It felt cold and shriveled in my chest. But still I wouldn't wish the words back.

Finally he smiled. "You have no idea," he said, "how much I've thought about you saying that." And then he did what I hadn't had the nerve to do. He pushed his hands in my hair, and kissed me.

I would've been fine with making out for the rest of the day, but eventually he pulled back. His hands cradled my face, and his green eyes were serious on mine. "I love you, too," he said. He gave me a crooked smile. "And as genius as Bono is, I don't mean the band. I knew I wanted to be with you the first moment I saw you, looking up at the stars."

He leaned in for another kiss, and for a moment I felt some of my old fears and insecurities creep back. What if Nathan discovered that the reality of me didn't live up to his ideal? Could we last through four years of college? What if we didn't get in to the same grad school? Would our relationship survive?

But then his mouth covered mine, and every feeling evaporated from my body except for that tingly flutter in my stomach that sent goose bumps all over my body. To hell with it. I wrapped my arms around Nathan's neck and kissed him back.

"Nathan," I breathed. I wanted to tell him how good this felt. I wanted to tell him how happy he made me. I wanted to tell him that this was no transitory thing, that I could finally see a future. And it was him.

"I know," he said. "Me, too."